Dear Beneficiary

Dear Beneficiary

Janet Kelly

Cutting
Edge
Press

A Cutting Edge Press Paperback Original

Published in 2015 by Cutting Edge Press

www.cuttingedgepress.co.uk

ISBN: 978-1908122-87-2
E-PUB ISBN: 978-1-908122-88-9

Dedicated to
Rebecca and Rachel. My Feisty Roses.

CHAPTER ONE

There's definitely something to be said for having a thirty-eight-year-old black lover. Particularly when you've recently turned sixty.

Although no one, particularly me, could have imagined the impact such a relationship could have on my otherwise ordered outlook. Meeting him took me to places otherwise unconsidered, on more than one occasion.

'Not there, Darius,' I once told him, during a physically experimental moment, and thankfully he renegotiated his entry point. As it was eleven-thirty in the morning, I thought I was being adventurous enough.

After our relationship ended I busied myself with new opportunities in a life I was finding increasingly challenging. Not so much because of its solitude, but by the way it seemed to be changing on every level. I took up knitting and found it pointless. I reorganised my books into alphabetical order according to their authors and planted an azalea bush, which subsequently died a quick death. It didn't help.

I'd spent a long time being diligently married to Colin. There was no doubt he was highly respectable and always, always dutiful – but somewhat dull. It's difficult to admit but I don't miss him much, a fact that's highlighted even more now I have someone to compare him with. I suppose I loved my husband in the way you might love anything you've been stuck with for forty years, a bit like an old sideboard, but not in any great soulmate type of way. Ever since I've been on my own, which I have for more than three years, I've come to realise that my active life does not have to be over just because I'm widowed.

I often thought about Darius but recognised, in my most stoic moments, that our relationship had to end. Apart from the fact he needed to return to Nigeria for family reasons, we couldn't be seen together (the neighbours would start their own Surrey Defence League in protest!) and him being the same age as my children would create endless arguments about age-appropriate behaviour; all rather silly, really.

I couldn't help but wonder if I might ever see him again, if fate would ever allow me such a luxury. As it was unlikely, I figured I would have to look for something else to do. I searched around for a 'hobby or interest', as women's magazines advise, to occupy my mind – and was thrown into despair at the opportunities for women of a certain age. If you don't like making cupcakes and have an aversion to anyone who discusses the merits of being post-menopausal, there is little on offer. I did notice, however, that the world opens up if you have a computer.

So when my grandson, Tom – at eighteen, the eldest of my daughter Bobbie's three boys – arrived one soggy Saturday afternoon in the persistent hope of stodgy food and a financial hand-out, I decided to ask him if he could help me get to grips with technology.

Tom is something of a geek; a large but obliging lad, clearly not used to exercise or nutritional considerations. Bobbie tried feeding the family with vegetables, fish and fruit but being surrounded by testosterone-fuelled males with a constant and unholy desire for white fats and carbohydrates she knew she was on a hiding to nothing. Rather than fight for a sensible diet she filled the freezer with pizzas and left them to their own devices. Despite the lack of tone and muscle, Tom made up for any physical shortcomings with great quantities of intelligence and logic. He was also a very kind boy, caring to his grandmother and fond of small furry animals.

'Tom,' I'd asked as he sat in my kitchen over a Diet Coke and slice of home-made banana cake. 'You understand the interweb, don't you?'

He smoothed his hand over his mop of black, curly and slightly grubby looking hair, looking quizzically at me as if he'd never really understood who I was.

'Do you mean the internet, Nan?'

I sighed in exasperation. He was being obtuse and slightly pedantic. He knew what I meant but liked to haul me up on semantics. He was like his grandfather in that way.

'Yes, of course, that internet thing. I want to go on it so can you help me?'

Tom wasn't one to miss an opportunity. He spoke with his mouth full of cake, excited by the prospect of his certainly solvent, if not well-off, relative being encouraged to buy the latest technology on a whim. He was no doubt hoping I'd go off it a few months later, to his benefit. I could see him making a mental note to seek out the most advanced, and expensive, computer he could find.

'What do you want it for? Poker or porn?' he'd chuckled, without any concept of how close his suggestions might be to my recent activities with the shiny Darius or the fact I was secretly hoping it might give me a lead to his whereabouts.

I was embarrassed, which was unusual for me. I pushed away a strand of wiry grey hair, prodding it back into the neat bun that had reappeared since the disappearance of my lover. It had been my trademark feature for more years than a donkey would be able to give time to, so people had become suspicious of the new look I'd adopted for Darius's benefit.

'Thomas Butcher, you are being inappropriate.' I told him. 'I want to get modern and that seems to be the way I have to go. Like it or not.'

I paused and went to refill the kettle at the Butler sink. It was in place not for its fashionable status but because I'd liked its practicality. It was robust, solid and could hold far more than its stainless steel counterparts. In many ways it reminded me of Darius and his sturdy countenance. If I compared my men to sinks, Colin was more like the one in the cloakroom: small, white and not entirely essential.

'Plus the bridge club have started sending emails instead of letters, so I've missed a number of meetings from not having an email address,' I told him, in a bid to banish the reverie of my memories. Tom looked fondly at me.

'Do they know you aren't online?' he said.

'I've told them,' I replied, and Tom gave me a look. I hoped it wasn't suggesting what I'd thought it might be; that they hadn't wanted me to get the information they were sending out to all their members.

'But they won't have any excuse if I get an email number, will they?'

I'd never contemplated entering a world that involved communicating via a screen. It all seemed too arbitrary and cold. But my life was chilly and more complicated than I'd hoped it might be at sixty. Something was lacking, and on occasions I even wondered if I should've joined the Church – if only for somewhere to go on a Sunday, the bleakest day of the week to be alone.

My mind thought of the future and in the end I decided I could have another thirty years of dealing with a changing world. A computer was something I had to have, if only to broaden my shrinking horizons and keep a possible connection to Darius. When he'd left, he'd given me his business card with all his contact details. A phone call seemed too direct, whereas one of those email things might be a polite way of getting in touch, a bit like sending a Christmas card with the annual 'we must get together' message that no one acts on.

Mind you, I do so hate those types of round-robin reports of family achievement. One of my school friends had children of such literary and musical genius they apparently outwitted all their teachers at the local primary school within a week of starting. I couldn't help but smirk when I heard that Jocelyn, the boy, had been expelled from his very expensive public school for cheating in his Religious Studies exam. He was caught when he removed his trousers halfway through, to refer to notes he'd written all over his thighs in ball-point pen. His mother had annually promised that we would all know of her son in time, and that prediction was certainly achieved. He received a conditional discharge for the offence of gross indecency (teenagers being prone to inadvertent and unwitting erections) and could never get the faint remnants of the quote 'You shall not live, because you have spoken a lie in the name of the Lord' to entirely wash away.

'Just tell me what I need to buy,' I said to Tom, who was visibly flushed – no doubt thinking of the access I'd have to technology that was currently out of his budgetary reach.

I read his thoughts and told him money was no object, knowing that would give him freedom to buy the best email system available. That'll teach the bridge club!

When Tom arrived with my new equipment I was impatient to get going with it all. He was thrilled to inform me the package came with something called a Blueberry. Or was it Blackberry? Either way it would take phone calls, emails, text messages, and by all accounts run my life if I let it.

I'd like to say I was impressed but I hadn't a notion of what my grandson was telling me as he took it out of the box and showed me all the functions. I was more interested in the computer, as it looked large enough to be able to do what I needed and offered a promise of connection to Darius. My dreams had been filled with his presence, and on many occasions I would wake up expecting to see him next to me. The disappointment was like winning the lottery and finding out you'd lost the ticket.

'So how do I get online then, Tom?' I asked as I squashed myself next to my grandson, while he peered intently at the screen of the new desktop PC. 'Can I write an email to the bridge club yet?'

'Just be patient, Nan,' muttered Tom. 'I'm setting you up now.'

Tom bought the sparkling new computer, now the subject of his unswerving attention, from a specialist store in Tottenham Court Road. The addition to my household was funded entirely from Colin's legacy of a healthy government-funded pension, enforced parsimony and sensible saving. He probably would have preferred to spend his hard-earned cash on golf membership, an unsuitably fast car and women possibly slightly looser than myself (he would've died of shock at my antics with Darius, but being dead already he was thankfully spared the level of looseness I was prepared to go to, given the right encouragement). I suspect the constant need or expectation of sensible behaviour left us both always slightly wanting on the level of spontaneity, but certainly very safe in terms of his economic viability. The latter being a non-negotiable characteristic in a husband, as far as I'm concerned.

Once the PC was strategically placed on the spare room table, next to the electronic piano and below a dusty looking shelf full of folders marked 'justice's manuals' – a legacy from my days on the magistrates' bench – it was all I could do to contain my excitement.

This was much to Tom's irritation, as he really wanted me to leave him with the kit for a few hours so he could test out the graphics card and speed of connection to his game challengers, one of whom he was sure he could beat into oblivion with the assistance of the state-of-the-art connectivity this system was capable of offering.

'What's my email address?' I pushed. 'Can I email Marjory?'

Marjory is my sister and she lives in Manchester. We haven't spoken or written in years, after an unsavoury incident involving a used condom. Jonjo, Bobbie and Titch had been staying there with their cousins, and none of them would admit to anything. I knew it would be nothing to do with my children as they would know better and I told Marjory so. She was quite rude, actually, and wouldn't accept that her kids don't know how to behave. Anyway, there's no loss there but possibly the remote nature of an email might offer the chance to circumnavigate stubborn pride and years of embittered family feuding.

'Do you know her email address, then?' asked Tom.

Not to be thrown by tricky technological questions I took a wild guess. Spinning around from the PC I said that of course I did.

'It's Marjory Fuller, *at* something.' I felt a bit silly at that point, as it dawned on me there was probably more to this internet lark than I'd first thought, but I wasn't going to be deterred. I'd every intention of mastering new methods of communication. However, a few diversionary tactics don't go amiss when caught out not knowing one's stuff. I also recalled Darius's business card and the various contact details but didn't think it wise to present it at this point.

'Right. Time for a cup of tea and one of my best cakes,' I said, making a hasty exit out of the room on a mission to the kitchen. On the way down the stairs I stopped to look at my reflection in the mirror on the landing and thought I could see some distinct ageing.

I wondered what Darius would see. A slight sagginess to the otherwise rounded and highly placed cheekbones, a few extra lines around the mouth and crow's feet? Or laughter lines, as my mother would call them; even though laughing wasn't a natural activity for anyone in our family.

No I thought. *The light isn't good and you had a bracing but windy walk to the library which is enough to make anyone look a little haggard.*

I hoped Marjory hadn't fared any better on the physical front, particularly as she always had a tendency for overindulgence and laziness. She wouldn't bother with the 'cleanse, tone and moisturise' routine like I have, and has always had little resistance to pies, chocolate and second helpings.

I heard Tom hitting the keys on the computer keyboard with a dexterity known only to the latest generation. Not touch-typing, just a complete knowledge of where to go and what to do. I turned back to look at him and wondered how he could have such certainty about something at such a young age. It only seemed like a few weeks ago I was teaching him how to spell his own name, and that took some time.

He plodded down the stairs after a few minutes, his jeans far too long and stained at the bottom where he had trodden them into a variety of puddles and pavements over the last winter. He was no slave to fashion. Even his hoodies came from British Home Stores.

He gave me a hug before he walked into the kitchen. My eyes followed him, stopping momentarily to note the hall which, I thought, was looking a little austere with its lime green walls and wooden floor. From the back Tom looked like one of those stuffed bears you see in the fairground; all snuggly and round, with hunched shoulders and a general slackness, which in Tom's case was developed from spending his formative years hunched over computers.

I'd never had any problem developing a relationship with Tom. Where others in the family would see me as some silly old woman, he was always affectionate and warm. He says he finds me funny, and when describing me to his friend at school called me 'cool', which wasn't a word I expected to be assigned to me. I smiled, thinking what his description would be for an old lady lost in romantic notions about a man who couldn't possibly be mistaken for her son on account of his colour.

'You be careful now you're online,' he said, warning me of the possible dangers of what he referred to as 'surfing'.

I made him laugh by not knowing what he was talking about and he suggested it was quite understandable I was a bit out of touch at my age, a comment I thought to be a little unnecessary.

'How much trouble can I get into from my own spare bedroom?' I said, as I closed the front door behind him.

CHAPTER TWO

It didn't matter how long I stared at the computer screen, it didn't feel familiar. I'd been trying to work it all out for three days, one of which was mainly spent finding the 'on' button.

There seemed to be some emails, little headings in a list, promising intrigue and communication, but even though I'd managed it the day before, I couldn't remember how to open them. I couldn't quite master the art of mouse control either, so even when I could get the pointer anywhere near a message the little arrow would move tantalisingly close to where I needed it to be and then run away to hide in the corner of my screen, shaking like a frightened mouse might.

After prodding at the keyboard a few times I decided I needed help, although it galled me to admit it. I looked on the wall for the Post-it note with Tom's mobile phone number scrawled in his spidery writing and found it stuck behind the desk. I couldn't reach it with my fingers, a ruler or the metal bit from underneath my bra. I tried to move the desk but Colin had thoughtfully screwed it to the wall after it had collapsed under the weight of his briefcase.

It might have been sturdier had he read the instructions and worked out why he had eleven screws and a metal bracket left over after self-assembly. Thankfully I remembered I'd written Tom's number in my address book.

Standing on my swivel chair, a legacy of my husband's decision to work two days a week from home, I reached up to the tattered book on a shelf above my desk. It contained many addresses, most of which I never used because the contacts were dead, superfluous or downright dull. I wobbled furiously and had to hold on to the curtains for balance, pulling the last three hooks out as I did so, scattering a flurry of bits of paper to the floor.

'Bugger,' I said out loud, smoothing down my skirt even though there was no one to see my under garments.

I put my feet back into my comfortable shoes and, ignoring the mess I'd made, searched through the pages as I made my way down the stairs, somewhat gingerly as I could feel I'd pulled an otherwise unknown muscle somewhere near my upper thigh area. By the time I got to the hall I had to pause to rub the inside of my leg as it was throbbing from overexertion.

The last time it had felt that used was after Darius had decided to try the 'erotic V' position from the Kama Sutra using the kitchen table, which I insisted was far too low for the purpose. The position demands certain acrobatic capabilities, and it soon became clear my yoga expertise wasn't sufficient for the task, which involved me sitting on the table edge while Darius stood in front, bending his legs so he was in the best 'entering' position.

He had to bend a fair way down to accommodate the activity but persevered, despite obvious signs of strain. After I put my arms around his neck, then pulled first the right, then the left leg up onto his shoulders he was struggling. The next instruction was to lean back while he directed his thrust by holding on to my bum. However, even his rugby-player thighs couldn't take our combined weight and we ended up in a heap on the floor with my legs somewhere near my ears – and not in a good way.

I picked up the phone and started to dial the number recorded under 'T' for Tom.

'It's Nanny,' I said, once he'd finally answered. 'I need you to come over and help me with that computer thing. It doesn't appear to be working.'

Tom was used to my calls. I often rang him two or three times a day and usually required him to undertake some kind of very minor technological task – like tell me how to work my DVD player or, more recently, how to get onto that Google thing. I needed mostly to look up the Hockley bridge club. Not necessarily to ensure any further invitations, but more out of a desire to ensure that irritating control freak, Mavis, put me on the email list. I wasn't going to let a woman with a stomach bigger than her bust exclude me from the club without a fight.

Shortly after Colin's death, Mavis, one of the founding members, had invited me to join the club, in a spirit of support and community piety. She was the wife of one of Colin's colleagues and we'd met regularly at dinner parties over the years. We'd socialised only as couples, as Mavis didn't really have the kind of personality I enjoyed. In fact I thought she was rather bossy, far too overweight and much too interested in the various symptoms of ageing to be the sort of companion I would choose.

She asked me once if I'd been overwhelmed by my husband's demise as she couldn't imagine life without her balding bore of a husband. She didn't call him a balding bore, as she thinks he's so attractive every single woman wants to steal him away from her, but that's what he is to most of us. Other than Mrs Hunt from Osprey Drive who, since her divorce, has been trying to coax him into private bridge lessons under the pretext of not being able to absorb the rules while playing at the club because of issues with her hearing aid.

Anyway, I may have appeared overwhelmed for a few months but I soon got back into the swing of things and had the bridge club in a far better order than she'd ever managed. Mavis didn't approve, though. She got mightily huffy about my organisation of the sandwich supplies and objected to the extra expenditure on proper butter rather than spread. I'd held back on the suggestion of ciabatta and dipping oil for the Saturday meetings for fear of bringing on a panic attack, of which Mavis has many.

I like to tackle the provision of sandwiches with a degree of order, whereas Mavis found my common-sense approach intimidating. She didn't actually use that word, as she had burst into tears last time we had a discussion about the catering, muttering something about not being able to cope any more.

Maybe that's why I don't get the emails. I could just see Mavis telling the committee that all communication would be electronic, despite knowing I didn't have a computer and clearly thinking that if I didn't like it I could lump it.

Well, what they didn't know is lumping it wasn't an option. Not one to be beaten, I accepted that there was no choice but to enter into the world of technology and get myself online. Otherwise I could be missing out on a big, wide world.

CHAPTER THREE

Unlike some people, who really don't know how to get things done properly, Tom is always very helpful and gets me sorted out quickly. I get the impression he laughs at the fact I don't understand computers but then why would I? I was brought up with a pen and paper and the ability to make conversation rather than have mute discussions via an inappropriately small and inanimate piece of technology.

I do spoil him a bit. I know he comes to me for cash, cake and somewhere to go when his mother insists on making him wash, wash up or speak nicely to some passing stranger.

Tom arrived at my house within twenty minutes of my call requesting further help. He'd flipped the letterbox so it made a loud banging noise. He never used the doorbell because he didn't like the tune. We were supposed to be able to choose one of many, including a Christmas version: 'Ding Dong Merrily on High' but Colin could never work out how to do that. We ended up with some tinny tune not dissimilar to those heard in shopping centre lifts, and it didn't help that ours also seemed to activate a few other bells in the immediate neighbourhood.

I answered the door, still rubbing my thigh from my earlier tumble from the twisty-turny chair that I always knew I didn't like.

'Yo,' he'd said, glancing at me from underneath the peak of his Chelsea Football Club cap. He didn't support them but had found it on a bus.

'I need you to help me sort out my messages. I can't get to them so don't know what they say,' I told him.

Tom had already started upstairs and so I followed him, giving my thigh another good rub on the way up. I was heading for a bruise, I could feel it.

He was soon settled in front of the computer, telling me he was glad of the excuse to leave home as Bobbie was about to launch into one of her tirades about the state of his room.

'She's been getting on my case,' he explained, adding that his mother also claimed to be concerned about her discovery of a strange smell and three packets of cigarette papers.

I questioned it myself but Tom said he occasionally liked to have a herbal cigarette, and there was no point trying to explain to his mother that had he been at university instead of taking some time out he'd be smoking all day long with no one to tell him it was wrong. He told me he was beginning to regret choosing to take a gap year just so he could stay at home.

The idea was that he'd get a suitable work placement to help further his understanding of IT for when he took up his offer to study at Cambridge, but the economy collapsed just in time to render his enthusiasm pointless. Four hundred job applications later – which started off with him applying for desirable posts and ended up with him trying for anything to earn a minimum wage, or even no wage if the experience was suitable – and he'd more or less given up. He earned a bit here and there from some occasional gardening and maybe the odd bit of computer sorting for relatives but was otherwise unoccupied, facing at least another eight months before he could escape to what he described as 'the boundless comforts of student life'. If living on beans in a room similar to that found in prisons is deemed as comfort it shows what a rotten time he thought he was having.

Looking at the screen once he got settled into the offending swivel chair, Tom opened up the mailbox and told me that there was nothing of any concern. I just needed to learn how to open the messages. I wrote on the back of my telephone bill the instructions Tom gave me and was relieved my technological incompetence hadn't caused any major problems.

On Tom's last visit he'd installed what he called a 'spam' filter and closed down my first email address, after I'd tried to look up venues for swing dancing. Somehow I'd managed to get on a 'swingers' site' with the result some of the incoming messages I'd been able to read were not only unsolicited, but graphic and increasingly prolific. And there is no point being a swinger if you've no one to swing with.

Tom opened and filed all the new messages that had come in.

'You can throw these ones away, Nan,' he said, referring to a few that were obviously meant for someone else.

'Why are these people asking me if I want a bigger erection? Did they never do biology at school?'

Tom stopped me answering a number of messages claiming that if I did I would just get more. I couldn't quite understand why that would happen. If I told them I wasn't interested in knowing how to stay hard all night or buy pills for lasting pleasure then surely they would leave me alone?

Apparently not. Tom said people who use the internet can be a bit dodgy.

'Please be careful,' he said. 'If you keep giving your personal details you will get into even more trouble and I might not always be able to get you out of it.'

He was referring to the fact I'd inadvertently joined a social networking group for gay nuns and, on the same day, volunteered for an extreme medical trial in Northern Cyprus. I was just looking for ways of filling time by looking for some freelance secretarial work. So why that Scottish-based Muslim organisation dedicated to seeking out terrorist opportunities in Alaska decided I was the one for them was beyond me.

'Not everyone on the internet is who they say they are,' he warned.

He tried to circumscribe my world, but his paranoia about safety seemed to be excessive. How much trouble can a computer cause, for goodness' sake?

On his last visit he had set me up on Friends Reunited and Facebook. He uploaded my 'profile', along with some of my most flattering pictures. I put some effort into it and soon managed to find a couple of people I knew from the past including vague acquaintances from part-time jobs I'd held down during the later years of my children's adolescence. None had replied.

Tom was working on sorting out things called 'files', which he explained were just like the metal filing cabinets I still had in the home office but were 'virtual', when I decided it was probably best to go downstairs and get some cake. The kitchen was definitely my area of expertise. He may know a thing or two about 'megabytes' and 'rams' (see, I was listening, even if I did think he was referring to a goat with a heavy overbite) but I know about catering.

I took him back the gift of buttered fruit loaf and, as I placed it on the computer desk, peered over his shoulder at the screen, now showing three messages. He'd told me I could see the new ones because they were in bold. Plus the fact I hadn't already seen them would be a giveaway, but I allowed him to patronise me a tad. Two of them were for pharmacy products and one from Friends Reunited.

'You've had a message from someone called Bob Bryant,' said Tom.

My cheeks went warm. I hadn't heard that name for years and it seemed impossible a message could come from the past through a system so very much part of the future.

'Oh goodness, I went to school with him when I was living in Banbury,' I said. 'He was something of the school heart-throb.'

'And how old would he have been at the time?' said Tom, grinning.

I worked it out and felt silly.

'Six-and-a-half. He had a lot of charisma.'

Tom nodded to himself and ate his fruit loaf, virtually in one mouthful. He read the message and it occurred to me the world of technology made everyone overly wary. There was no doubting that Bob was being very friendly and was keen to meet up.

'There,' I said. 'You may think people aren't as they seem, but Bob is definitely Bob,' I commented after reading the full message, twice.

''ow do you know?' Tom asked while looking at Bob's profile

picture – which I had to admit made him look like a cross between Ken Dodd and a Martian rather than heart-throb material.

'Because he mentions his birthmark – look,' I said, pointing Tom to this detail in the message. 'And I know exactly where it is!' I said, triumphant that I held knowledge about which Tom had no idea.

'And where would that be, then? On his bum?' he laughed.

'No, Tom,' I told him. 'It's on the end of his penis.'

I saw that Tom looked a bit perplexed at this comment and so went on to explain: 'He showed it to me when we went into the big holly bush one play time. It was quite large from what I can remember.'

I stalled for a bit at the memory of primary school and all those very first experiences and promises of a world of revelations. Then I noticed Tom looked slightly embarrassed.

'The birthmark, I mean. Not his penis,' I qualified.

As I spoke I thought to myself how strange that Bob's was the first penis I'd seen – my father and brothers never displayed theirs – and the last belonged to Darius. What a difference a few decades make. My stomach warmed and again I felt a little lonely.

'So are you going to meet him, then?' Tom said.

'Oh no, dear. Look what he says here – he was a postman until he was fifty-five. We would have nothing in common,' I told him. 'He is just someone to write to, that's all.'

Tom got up to leave.

'Well I suppose it beats watching *Countdown* or reseeding your lawn,' he said, making a move to go downstairs.

Retrieving his coat from the banisters he shuffled off out into the street, pulling his cap down over his face and hunching up against the rain that had just started to drizzle ineffectually against a bright grey day.

As I closed the door behind him, having waved goodbye, I heard the distinctive ping which I knew to be a new email. The excitement is addictive, and to be honest, even the occasional weird message from a sex worker in Russia can be more interesting than the terminal drivel on daytime television. I leapt up the stairs with a bound, realising in doing so that my groin injury finally seemed to be on the mend.

I searched around for my reading glasses for a few minutes before remembering placing them on my head sometime earlier. I retrieved them with a sense of relief. The sense of anticipation was quite thrilling as I read the contents of the new message:

DEAR BENEFICIARY, the message started.

> Your friend in charge of the Bank of Nigeria Financial team is in the utmost respectful delight to inform your good person that you have $3,000,000 to collect from their account in good thanks for your kind investment and expectations. Legal problems with the owners in the country prevent rightful return and for your assistance the fund can be shared between you and the choice of your medical teams to bring about good fortune to your friends and their family. We need your immediate information to ensure speedy resolution of this matter and to avoid fraud. Forward your bank details most immediately to arrange distribution of our cash to you as our beneficiary in law.

My heart missed a beat. In fact, it missed several beats. I hoped it wasn't a reaction to my new blood pressure medication.

This was a message from Nigeria. It had to have something to do with Darius, as it mentioned the medical problems he was facing with his mother. *Oh my goodness.* I'd given up hope of ever setting eyes on him again. Even on the odd occasion when I'd given in to some 'auto-eroticism', purely for the purposes of a good night's sleep, I hasten to add, I only ever thought of him in abstract ways. I'd tried to eradicate the feeling his memory induced because it made me sad, as I never allowed myself the thought we would be reunited.

I wanted to cry.

CHAPTER FOUR

When I saw the advert for the Advanced Driving course I never thought it would lead me to Darius. I thought it would be nothing more than a new activity and a way to save money on the insurance I was now paying for my very own car. After Colin's death I was solely responsible for all elements of my life, including the purchase of a vehicle – the first I could genuinely call my own since I passed my test some thirty-five years ago.

Colin always did the driving, even when he broke his toe tripping over one of Titch's Lego buildings of the Park Royal Asda Superstore. Colin hadn't allowed me to get anywhere near the family car after I managed to attach it to a builder's skip I was passing, and carried on driving. He'd been appalled at the fact I kept trying to drive despite having come to a halt, resulting in the offside front panel shearing clean off.

'Didn't you think to stop at any point?' he'd shouted at me. I reasoned no one had been hurt and it was an accident (even though I was upset at how the builder had spoken to me, once he'd seen his skip was firmly attached to my Rover estate's wing mirror). Colin had just walked away from me, shaking his head, and called up the insurance company. He'd found it painfully embarrassing explaining to the assessor what had happened, not least because the representative from Direct Line had been unable to stop himself from laughing for longer than a few seconds at a time.

So I signed up for the course with enthusiasm, at first hoping the afterlife provided viewing opportunities so Colin could see what I was up to. I changed my mind fairly soon after the first class.

Darius was dressed in a dark blue suit that seemed too tight across his massive chest, the whites of his eyes sparkling against his beautiful dark brown colouring. The tall, dark man was very well turned out, wearing expertly polished, lace-up leather shoes as dark as his skin. He also wore a crisp white shirt and a pale blue tie with little motifs of what looked like elephants. He fascinated me, and I was compelled to sit next to him. He was like a magnet, full of excitement and possibility. Not only that, he knew how to iron a shirt.

The classes were held at the school all my children had attended, just two miles away from home. The physical journey of going back into the hall where I'd witnessed numerous renditions of traditional Christmas carols, musical concerts involving Jonjo's enthusiastic but painful violin solos, various children's prize-givings and parents' evenings was difficult. I felt like an amateur athlete who, having run a full marathon was being told they have to go back to mile 15 and do the last 11.2 miles again.

I overcame any initial desire to run away when I spotted Darius. I wondered how I might get to know him. I couldn't help but look at his thigh muscles, which were huge. I didn't for a minute think he'd got his clothes from Burton's, as his appearance suggested something far more sophisticated, and I doubted very much they would do his size.

I'd looked over and tried to catch his attention by smiling every time I thought he might look my way. He sat on the edge of his seat, using his substantial legs to keep his balance as he looked at a leaflet on 'Parking for the Elderly'. His hands were huge, as were his feet. I could see the bare skin of his ankles above his dark grey socks and wondered what he might look like naked. The thought of it made me blush.

The group leader handed round some forms, asking us to fill them in and, while doing so, to introduce ourselves to each other. At last I'd found my chance to make conversation.

'Hello there. I'm Cynthia,' I'd said, extending my right hand to meet his. Darius took his time responding, which had me worried for a bit, but then he stood straight up, took my hand and pulled it to him before kissing me lightly on both sides of my face.

'Osezua, or Ozzy for short,' he said.

I thought I was going to faint.

I didn't like his real name and couldn't pronounce the zed without crinkling up my lips, so I changed it to Darius. He didn't seem to mind. He was really a very obliging partner in so many ways, even if some of the positions I encountered played havoc with my weak wrists.

Yes, I've a few failings I can put down to age. I forget where I've put my glasses and the names of my grandchildren – but doesn't everyone?

But the excitement, the connection, the sheer physicality of what I had with my young lover brought me benefits, as well as some welcome challenges. He introduced me to things that would have made Colin's hair curl, if he'd had any.

I would often think how easily Darius accommodated my needs and how often I felt myself thinking about him for no reason. He was so very *stimulating*.

'That's better,' I remembered telling Darius after he'd adopted a more sensible approach following my complaints about my sacro-iliac joint not being as flexible as it might be. He'd reverted to what I think is called the missionary position, although goodness knows why. I didn't think missionaries had sex, and if so does being on one's back make it more godly?

I couldn't help but think back to our time together as a colourful display against an otherwise bleak background of mundanity. It was an oasis from which I could drink pure pleasure in an otherwise dry and dusty life, one I only realised was dull in hindsight.

So when the email from Nigeria came through, I couldn't believe he'd been thinking of me all that time. I read it again and knew this was a message that had something to do with my former lover – and that he wanted assistance in obtaining a large sum of money, some of which would be made available to me.

He'd previously explained that his family had needed his help and that the authorities were difficult to deal with. He also told me Nigeria was full of legal and administrative corruption. We'd discussed the poverty of his country and the greedy destruction of its leaders on many occasions, so this is what it was all about. Bringing the matter to my attention means he will be able to get the funds for his family's medical treatment and I will also benefit by getting a commission for helping him out. A perfect solution.

Of course I will help him, I thought. *If it is just a matter of using my bank account to liberate what is his, then I will offer him what I can.*

It was only natural to start thinking of the financial rewards. I'd be able to help the family. Maybe pay off the children's mortgages and help send the grandchildren to university. Colin's legacy wasn't enough for that by any stretch, so this could be a real godsend. Better than winning the lottery, although the thought of seeing Darius again would be reward enough.

I fished around in my desk drawer to find my cheque book and entered the details of my account carefully into a blank email message, to ensure no mistakes. I wrote a quick reply, taking care not to make any assumptions.

My Dear Darius

    It is so lovely to hear from you. I did often wonder why you never contacted me after our last meeting but I understand this is because you had many pressing matters to attend to, about which I'm very sorry to hear. Please find within this message my bank details. You are free to use these at your will to sort out your problems and I look forward to seeing you. Hearing from you has reminded me how much I miss our talks and your company.

I signed off and pressed the 'send' button, albeit with some difficulty as that mouse thing still had a mind of its own, and clapped my hands to my chest in glee. I spent the next few hours planning, on paper, what I could do with my share of the funds.

I'd worked out that three million dollars was around two million pounds; a significant amount even for someone who had already benefitted quite considerably from their husband's sensible insurance planning.

Of course I'd help out the family, but that would still leave a significant sum to enhance what life I have left to me, which considering how I fare against others my age should be a reasonable one.

'An adventure,' I said to myself, while imagining how the bridge club folk would react to my good fortune.

'Yes, I'm going to have a bloody good adventure,' I muttered, before going back to my notebook and pen to continue to hypothetically divide my share of these unexpected funds between duty and my now expanding future.

CHAPTER FIVE

I was trying to pull on a pair of tights when I heard the phone ringing. I'd been to the local baths for my regular forty lengths morning swim and was still damp from the shower. However hard I tried to put them on they would twist and turn to the point where I looked like I'd been in a bad accident as a child.

My descent down the stairs to the hall was reminiscent of a Norman Wisdom film and it was only the banisters that saved me from crashing to the floor. I do sometimes think it could take weeks to be found if I ever ended up incapacitated for any reason. Maybe that's why so many old women only wear trousers.

Breathless, I picked up the receiver.

'Hello, Cynthia Hartworth.'

'Is that Mrs Hartworth?' said the voice at the other end.

'I think you'll find I just said it was,' I replied. *Don't these people ever listen?*

'It's your bank here,' said the woman. 'I just need to take you through security to ensure it's you I'm speaking to.'

'Of course it's me you're speaking to,' I told the silly woman. I was hot and bothered and the tights were getting to me. I wanted her to hurry up.

'I know, but we need to be sure. Could you give me your date of birth?'

I sighed at that question. I was always told it was rude to ask a woman's age but answered anyway.

'Yes, it's April 12th, 1952,' I said.

'And can you confirm the first line of your address and postcode?'

'You should know all this, shouldn't you? Why do you need me to tell you? – I've been banking with NatWest for over forty years,' I replied.

The voice on the other end sounded bored. Maybe they were used to such commentary, having to ask such ridiculous questions every day and thereby making themselves appear to be somewhat backward.

'We just need to check your details with you, as anyone could answer your phone and it's bank policy to go through security questions only you will know.'

I tried to hold the phone under my chin while wriggling the right leg of my tights into the correct position. The toe of the ten-denier raw mink nylons had been twisting around my ankle, to the point where the crotch was nearer my knees than the pant area.

'Oh for goodness' sake, what do you want anyway?'

I knew I was being rude but couldn't help myself. I'd other things to think about, not least the fact I'd now pierced the offending tights with my right thumb and I'd only bought them the day before.

The voice continued: 'We have some concerns about your account. A considerable amount of money's been transferred and we need to verify if that's what you intended.'

My thoughts were brought to attention. I'd largely put Darius's email to the back of my mind. It had been a few days since I'd replied and I had guessed it would take some time to sort out the legal problems mentioned, so I hadn't thought the cash would be transferred so quickly. My pulse quickened. Maybe this meant my reunion with him could be sooner than I'd hoped.

'Oh my goodness, has the money come through? I expect you want to give me advice on how to spend it!' I quipped, quite childishly in hindsight, but the thrill of knowing things were starting to move had put me in an unusually frivolous mood.

I jumped up and down on the spot, not so much out of excitement but because it gave me the right kind of purchase on the top of my tights to fight my way into them properly.

'Actually it's the other way round, Mrs Hartworth. Your account has been completely cleared of all funds – over ten thousand pounds, which, I should say, is rather a lot to have in a current account.'

I stood still for a moment. I did recall the email saying there were complications of some kind. Maybe that's what it was all about. There was undoubtedly a reasonable explanation.

'Are you sure? I think you must be mistaking me for another Hartworth. My address is 15 Sycamore Close, Epsfield. The nice part.'

'Those are the details we have, Mrs Hartworth, we don't have anyone else of your name at this branch. We believe you have been the victim of a scam and our manager would like to see you. Could you come in to the branch this afternoon?'

I'm not over-keen on seeing bank managers. Often they try and sell life insurance or pensions, neither of which I need. Colin always dealt with that side of things and took advice often when playing golf with Mr Gamble (I always thought that a strange name for a bank manager) and was no doubt persuaded that sound investment also required vast premiums, of which, I suspect, Mr Gamble took a healthy percentage. It was certainly enough to pay for membership of Epsfield Golf Club.

I shouldn't criticise his methods as it's because of his tenacious attention to Colin's worth after death that I've been doing as well as I have for money.

So, not feeling in the slightest perturbed about what had happened, as this would all be part of the overall plan leading to the receipt of a large amount of money, I booked an appointment with Mr Gamble that afternoon.

The car was in the drive and I knew I'd have to take it into town for the appointment. It didn't ever occur to me to get buses or any type of public transport if I could avoid it. I always end up sitting with someone who has body odour, or is so fat they take up more seat than they have paid for. Or with a child eating something sticky.

I was still cautious about driving on my own, but knew I'd have to drive to the bank so I could put them in their place. I couldn't wait to see their faces when they realised I would be coming into so much money!

It occurred to me I might need some proof and I took the opportunity to write another email to Darius, so he could confirm the situation. I'd been itching to get back in contact but knew that to appear too keen wasn't an attractive trait. I'd learned enough about men to know that they like to do the chasing, although maybe he'd been playing it just a bit too cool by leaving me in the dark for months. However, I'd an urgent need to clear up the bank matter to get them off my back, so the reasons for making contact again were significant enough to override the rules of courtship.

I'd two hours before leaving for town and wanted to keep myself busy to avoid all thought of road rage, traffic jams and the eternal issue of reverse parking. I couldn't find the card with his address, so hit 'reply' to respond to the original mail.

Dear Darius.

I know it has only been a few days since you wrote asking for my help regarding the issue with your funds, and so I'm not expecting to hear from you just yet. However my bank has informed me that all my money has been taken from my current account. I expect you needed it to pay for lawyers and such to organise the transfer but perhaps you could confirm so I can get the little Hitlers off my case. They are so small-minded they really just don't understand anything outside the boundaries of Surrey life! I'm very excited to hear from you and look forward to your response.

I placed an 'x' at the bottom of the mail and wondered what letter I could put to signify more than a kiss.

CHAPTER SIX

The drive into town was problematic. Firstly, I'd lost my car keys. I scoured the house and three handbags before finally finding them inside the sugar jar. I couldn't remember opening the jar, let alone placing the keys in it, but then Bobbie had said she does similar things all the time so I didn't worry about it. It's all part of having a busy and full life and I dismissed the thought of dementia quickly. But then it did occur to me that most thoughts get quickly dismissed with dementia . . .

Once in the car I discovered the petrol gauge was lower than I'd hoped. I seem to have some kind of pathologic hatred of getting fuel. Colin said I would run the car on fumes rather than go and fill up, but then he was used to it with all the driving he did for work. And being a man helps.

As if my fears were completely founded, it was only the quick wit of the petrol station manager that stopped me filling up with diesel. He ran over to the car and whipped the pump from my hands, spilling what was in the pipe over my shoes.

'That could've cost you a bomb. Not to mention the inconvenience of sorting it out. It completely stuffs your engine, putting diesel in a petrol car,' he said. Like I'm supposed to know that, I thought, as I wondered if the smell of diesel would remain as pungent as it did at that moment.

'Well, how silly having the pumps next to each other,' I said, after the hoody-eyed manager droned on at me about the complexities of having an engine drained while he filled up my car with unleaded.

'Well I won't need to, will I, so no harm done – apart from my shoes, of course.'

I was quite annoyed by his patronising attitude and also getting late for the appointment so I shoved forty pounds in cash in the manager's hand and, without waiting for the two pounds change, sped out of the garage, only to narrowly avoid running down a mother and her two small children as they crossed the road at traffic lights.

The woman gave me the sanctimonious look that only mothers can give when you've accidentally done something that might harm their precious child. The same sort of look that goes with people who have stickers stating: 'Baby on board'. It's like you would drive down the road looking specifically for the youngest people to have an accident with! I poked my tongue out at her and drove on, mounting the pavement to get out of her path while she shouted something unpleasant.

I arrived at the bank eventually, having endured many hoots and hollers from a variety of other drivers, all seemingly in a great hurry to get about their business. *They'll have heart attacks carrying on like that*, I thought. *Better to arrive late than dead on time.*

It was quite annoying to find all the parking places had been taken. If they knew I was coming in you would think they'd have left a space. I got there with three minutes to spare. I left the Corsa on a double yellow line right outside the bank. After all, I wasn't going to be very long and it was only three o'clock in the afternoon.

A short, blonde girl, who looked just about old enough to put her feet on the floor when she went to the toilet, showed me into the manager's office. Mr Gamble, a bearded man with a look of tiredness running through everything he wore, looked up at me over the top of his thick-rimmed tortoiseshell glasses. He looked out of the window at a commotion going on outside his window before he spoke.

'Cynthia. How are you?'

I got the impression he didn't really care about the answer but gave the usual 'Very well, thank you' response without actually thinking about what I was saying. I was keener to get on to the issue of why it was his business to get involved with my dealings with Darius.

'I think you should know that I'm entirely happy about the funds transfer your assistant rang me about and see no reason for this meeting,' I said.

'But it has gone to a Western Union account where the recipient cannot be traced, Cynthia. This is most irregular,' said the manager, who was probably only in his fifties but looked like he had been waiting for retirement since his first promotion.

'I've a good friend in Nigeria who is sorting everything out. He knows what he is doing, and once the complicated legal matters have been resolved I'll be receiving considerable compensation for my assistance,' I said.

'These people in Nigeria are con men. They take your money and you never see it again. They spam people all over the world with emails, and some, like your good self, fall for it.'

'Mr Gamble,' I said pointedly as I stood up, wondering why my tights still weren't straight. 'Not only do I have a spam filter, but you need to know that my friend in Nigeria is also my lover. He'll look after my interests, of that I'm sure.'

Mr Gamble had started to twitch and his right eye was closing involuntarily. I seemed to have shut him up with my declaration. He opened and shut his mouth twice before shaking his head side to side and agreeing with me that what I did with my money was my business. I suspect he thought that being a woman who'd relied on my husband's money I should be more circumspect with my spending, in Colin's memory.

Ha, I thought. *My current financial freedom, Mr Bank Manager, is entirely that, and earned after forty years of guilt-ridden spending, even on an extravagant piece of meat for Saturday night dinner. So what I do now, financial or otherwise, is my call. So there.*

I told him I didn't want to listen to his concerns and that I knew what I was doing. I could tell he thought he'd have to eat his words if he carried on and wisely allowed me to leave.

What I did agree by way of compromise was to open a new account and transfer some savings over to cover my bills. I suppose he had a point as all my money had been taken from my current account, so there wouldn't be anything left for my direct debits. I should have told Darius to leave me with something.

I insisted the existing account be kept open for the receipt of funds, as there was no way of knowing when they would be sent over, or by whom.

On the way out, Mr Gamble tried to tell me to be careful with my money and suggested investing in one or more of the different types of schemes the bank could offer. Well, I wasn't falling for that old flannel and told him so.

'I'm very happy with the way I handle my money, thank you. However as I shall be receiving rather a large sum in the near future I may well discuss other options when the time is right. Good day, Mr Gamble, and please do not concern yourself about me,' I told him.

He shuffled back to his desk as I left the bank through the front doors and walked straight into a police officer keen to find the owner of a Vauxhall Corsa that he said had completely blocked the bus lane and created a traffic jam of not insignificant proportions.

'I had an important appointment,' I explained in my defence, but he didn't appear to be listening. 'There was nowhere else to park. I was meeting the manager. '

The police officer was still distracted. He was dealing with some verbal abuse from a bus driver and all the other drivers behind him.

'They've all been stuck here while you mince around at the bank not caring what happens once you have dumped your car wherever you feel like it,' he said.

There was more hooting and the officer had to raise his voice to be heard. Meanwhile my tights were playing havoc with my thigh injury, which seemed to return when I least expected it to. I twisted them round again by pulling them up through the waistband of my skirt and ended up hopping around trying to get them back into place.

'I don't care if you were meeting the Queen of England, madam. You've parked illegally and without any concern for other road users.'

He looked at me while I continued to address the issues with my hosiery, clearly designed for people with corkscrew legs.

'Could you please listen to me while I'm speaking to you,' the furry-faced policeman said. Shaving wasn't an activity he had to give much thought to. 'Stop dancing around and get your car moved.'

I couldn't stand it any longer so removed my sensible court shoes and hauled the offending tights down my legs and over my feet, throwing them to the side of the road in disgust.

The policeman's face was a picture. His cheeks went rosy pink and his mouth was moving up and down like a goldfish in a dirty bowl. I tried not to laugh as he started the usual cautionary procedures for an arrest.

'I'm very sorry, I'm menopausal,' I said to him, although the information went over his head. Normally that statement stopped men in their tracks, but he seemed quite determined to make me pay for my crime.

'You will need to report to the police station within seven days, bringing your driving licence and insurance details,' he said, placing a piece of paper firmly in my hand. I could read the words 'offence' and 'charges' on it, so stuffed it in my bag to read later. The thought of appearing at the local magistrates' court filled me with a horror beyond having to contemplate a conviction, criminal or otherwise.

'I'd get yourself a solicitor if I were you,' he added, as he stomped off to deal with the queue of bus passengers and a driver refusing to budge.

There were quite a lot of people shouting when I got back into my Corsa and they seemed to be looking at me. This road rage business is getting out of hand.

I looked into my driver's mirror and saw my lipstick had faded and my hair had started to fall out of its bun, so I went about putting my appearance right. The hooting got louder so I stood my ground. If my lipstick needed doing, they would just have to wait.

Might as well be hung for a sheep as a lamb.

After sorting my hair I drove off into the High Street and noticed the policeman was running towards me with his phone stuck to his ear. He waved his arms about as I continued down the road but I ignored him. I'd had enough for one day and he seemed to be in a particularly bad mood.

Once I got home I parked the car in the drive before letting myself into the house. The light was beginning to get hazy as the nights were getting longer, and colder. It would be marvellous to disappear somewhere hot for a couple of months. Which of course I'd be able to do once the money came through.

I looked out my car documents and was pleased to note my driving licence was clean and my insurance papers were where I remembered filing them. I made a mental note to take them to the station on my way to the bakery in the morning.

The computer was still on from when I'd sent the earlier email to Darius, and I went to check on it before running a bath. It'd been a long and stressful day and, apart from the fact I felt like relaxing in hot water, I still smelled of diesel and was keen to wash it off. The familiar quickening in the pit of my stomach recurred as I saw I'd received another new email.

Dearest Beneficiary,

The Federal Government of Nigeria through provisions in Section 419 of the Criminal Code came up with punitive measures to deter and punish offenders. This is to officially announce that some Syndicates were apprehended in Lagos, Nigeria a few days ago and after several interrogations and tortures of people of your contact your details were among those mentioned.

After proper investigations and research at Western Union Money Transfer and Money Gram office Nigeria, this proves that you have sent money to our country without safeguard.

In this regard a meeting was held between the Board of Directors of the Economic and Financial Crimes Commission (EFCC) and as a consequence of our investigations it was agreed that we have deposit your fund at Western Union Money Transfer agent location EMS Post Office, Lagos, Nigeria. We have submitted your details to them so that your fund can be transferred to you on arrival.

Contact William White Email:williams90@superposta.com
Assistant Investigation Officer,
The Economic and Financial Crimes Commission (EFCC), 15A Awolowo Road, Ikoyi, Lagos, Nigeria

I read the email a few more times, not really understanding it. But one thing did stick in my mind . . . Darius had been tortured for trying to get the money he was owed. My insides contracted and my heart rippled with concern. *My lovely man mustn't be in any danger.* It was one thing to know he was far away in another land, happy and healthy. To know he was suffering, alone, was my own personal torture.

I would have to do something. But what, I wasn't sure.

CHAPTER SEVEN

It had been some time since the last occasion Darius turned up at my house, as expected, a little over two months after we'd met. We'd seen each other regularly in that time and had developed a routine of him visiting me at home at the weekends and one or two evenings in the week.

It was early on a Sunday morning and he was clutching a large bunch of lilies. I hadn't the heart to tell him I was allergic to them, and explained my sneezing fits as the start of a cold.

He'd been quiet and, for the first time since we'd got together, hadn't made any physical move towards me other than a soft kiss to my right cheek. I might have been disturbed by this had I not been busying myself with the act of stifling my reaction to the flowers.

'Cynthia. I have to go home to my country,' he'd said quietly. He had stared intently at the floor, avoiding looking at me.

'What do you mean, go home?' I'd enquired. 'Why and for how long?'

Darius stood up and held me at the waist, towering over my five foot two frame. I swear I could see a tear in the corner of his left eye.

'I had a call last night and my family is in trouble. They need me – I must go and help them.'

He said he couldn't tell me the exact details because he didn't know very much more. He'd had a call from his father, who asked him to go home. Darius's mother had been ill for some time but she'd taken a turn for the worse and his father was having difficulty getting the authorities to provide the right treatment.

'My father is an old man, Cynthia, and is frightened. I'm the only son he has and he relies on me to get the treatment my mother needs. It's difficult in Nigeria as we don't have anything like your

NHS. It may be it will just take a few words in the right place to get everything sorted out.'

Darius's company had booked the flight from Heathrow. He'd already packed and was ready for the car that would pick him up first thing in the morning. I begged to know why he couldn't deal with everything from England. We have phones, emails and texts – even bloody letters!

'Surely your company can help out back in Nigeria? Do you really need to go?' I asked, throwing my arms around his chest and clutching onto him as a drowning man might a bit of driftwood.

He explained that Nigerians work better face-to-face and that his father always felt vulnerable when he was away. His mother suffered from a degenerative illness and it wasn't just about her care. Sometimes his father just needed to know there was someone else around to help.

'My sisters are married and have moved away. They have their own families to look after. In my father's eyes I need to help and of course I will.'

Darius was being kind and considerate so I tried to stop my selfish pleadings, acknowledging that his family needed him, possibly more than I did.

He kissed me gently and said he'd really miss me, that being in England had been a far better experience because of my kindness and hospitality. I'd hoped he'd say because of his love for me, which he couldn't live without, but he didn't. He did look sad enough for me to believe he wasn't running away, that he did have feelings for me and he'd no choice but to go home. He handed me his business card and told me he'd be there for me if I ever needed him. I needed him then, so that wasn't true.

I tried to tell myself I wasn't too distressed by the end of our relationship. It had only lasted a couple of months, nine weeks in fact. Hardly a lifetime. In some ways I'd been glad it was over as I had started to fall in love with him and that would never do. Although Darius had been a delightful distraction it was difficult explaining the time I spent with him. My family often questioned why I wasn't available for Sunday lunches, mid-week babysitting duties and the occasional Saturday shopping spree. Whereas previously I'd been amenable to spending time with family, weekends had become precious. I wasn't prepared to trade my trysts with Darius for the banality of Lakeside consumerism under any circumstances.

I knew I was denying feelings that had grown quickly and unexpectedly for a man I could never have dreamed I would want to be with. I've heard you can't choose who you love, and I'm certain he wouldn't have come out top in an identity parade of potential partners. Not dressed, anyway.

When I closed the door behind him tears welled up and the strength in my legs gave way. Grief took over, more so than after hearing of Colin's passing. A quick but brutal heart attack had taken him without warning. He'd always passed his medicals with flying colours and, being a moderate man with no excessive hobbies or habits, was expected to live a long and healthy life. Colin didn't get stressed, either, so couldn't be seen as a typical 'heart attack waiting to happen'. Other than occasional palpitations brought on by the council tax demand or the refuse collectors leaving potato peelings on the drive, he was easy-going and pragmatic. It certainly wasn't the way I expected him to go.

I'd missed the practical things and the constant daily companionship, but never felt his loss as I did the departure of this delicious and highly unsuitable young man. He'd injected something far more than his enormous manhood into my very being. Darius had got to my heart and I felt bereft.

I looked at the business card he left me and was tempted to call the number, but I knew I wouldn't be able to work all those noughts and crosses you have to put in when calling abroad. Thoughts of when we'd been together flooded back. If I'd known it was going to be the last time I'd be touching him, feeling him, I would have focused more, rather than lapsing into the occasional thought about whether I should get a new duvet cover.

Knowing wallowing would be fruitless, I decided on a practical approach to dealing with the end of the affair. Every rising emotion would be stamped on. Every memory I would erase – either with a few stiff drinks or diversionary tactics. I would definitely take bridge more seriously and join the Ladies Lunch and Pleasant Outings committee at the golf club.

None of these things had worked particularly well. My heart was in pieces and my ability to conduct myself on a daily basis was almost impossible. Just going to the local shops for a paper involved huge amounts of energy I could barely muster. I watched other people getting on with their lives. They all seemed to be in happy couples, blissfully unaware that the woman walking towards them wanted to throw down her bags and scream at the world for being so unfair. Often I'd go home and just cry, soothing myself with flashbacks to the blissful, passionate coupling that had filled my soul with every single thing that had ever been missing. Is this what I'd been missing out on all my life? Only to taste it and lose it within a few short weeks?

I would read poetry, hoping for solace in knowing that I wasn't the only one to feel this exquisitely exhausting and overwhelming pain. Alfred Lord Tennyson had no idea of what a woman could feel when he wrote 'Better to have loved and lost, than never to have loved at all.'

There were times I wished I'd never met Darius at all.

CHAPTER EIGHT

I'm not sure how I got to be sixty without really noticing. I'm not particularly worried about it, just taken by surprise. People tell me I don't look my age. I put that down to keeping a slim, neat figure and moisturising every day, although I have good genes – inherited from my mother's side of the family. She looked a bit like Vivien Leigh, and some say I do too. I certainly don't look as old as Mrs Goodwin over the road, who hasn't retained any youthful looks. I think she was born old, welcoming a future full of uni-slippers and Steradent. I'm rather pleased to retain a youthful appearance which happily includes pert breasts, which considering the four children I've had are something of a testament to the benefits of swimming.

Marriage to Colin had its positive points. I have a comfortable home, and since his death I've learned a few things about DIY and rarely cried. Except the time I set fire to myself after trying to change a socket in the kitchen. It taught me the value of calling a professional when electricity and water are involved in the same place at the same time.

I had routines. Colin liked them and they gave my life structure. Mr Hartworth, as he was known within the diplomatic service, was particularly good at routines.

Too good, I'd say. Compared to Darius, who likes the element of surprise, I might even go so far as to say that Colin was so predictable his mental health could be called into question.

I still have a fair amount of the good wine he laid down for special occasions but have demolished many of the other systems we had in place when domestic life ran very smoothly. It was just habit. Years of corporate socialising with Colin's 'very important' colleagues demanded it. I didn't question it at the time but I often wonder why I put up with so many boring bastards, each with very elevated ideas of their worth in society. I suppose I was just doing the right thing – in their opinion rather than mine, but I hadn't thought I was entitled to one.

I didn't need much entertaining. Even my TV still sits in the same small and unobtrusive corner, resting beneath an old G Plan cabinet of indeterminate years, bought by Colin without any discussion with me. It's covered with numerous gilt-framed pictures of my children: Jonathan, or Jonjo as I like to call him (much to his wife's disgust); Patrick, who I call Paddy in deference to my Irish ancestry; Roberta, or Bobbie; and Titch. Well, Kathryn is her real name but she was always very small and the youngest, so the name stuck. I also have nine grandchildren of varying ages with such a variety of names I wonder who thought of them all. It is hard work remembering which one is which. After the first, Tom, they seem to meld into variations on a theme. I get their names wrong sometimes. Still, it causes much amusement at family gatherings – which I stopped going to soon after the funeral.

Don't get me wrong, I adore my family and they seem to like me up to a point, but I do find large parties, with lots of people, tense and irritating. My children think I'm ancient and my grandchildren think I'm deaf. One way or another they patronise me, usually in very loud voices, and I seem to be able to say things to my children that upset them, while everything I say to the youngsters seems to be funny and I'm not sure why.

I didn't want to waste whatever time I have left to me, so I would often leave get-togethers early and then I'd have to wait some days before calling Bobbie in the hope that any resulting angst had gone. I did feel guilty about my waning interest in maternal responsibilities but I'd done my time looking after that lot and it was time to live a little.

Once I'd extricated myself from most maternal duties I enjoyed taking on new activities even if they may have been what was expected of a widow of a certain age.

My upbringing did equip me to some extent to follow the

patterns of traditional married life, but with no one to 'keep me in line' I decided there was no harm in letting loose a little, even if I did have to do it in private. Without the need to be a role model as a mother or wife, I was free to have a clandestine affair with a shiny black management consultant I'd met on an Advanced Driving course. And why not?

Darius intrigued me with his deep, dark voice that night at the riving class, as he told me he'd been in the UK for just over three months, on secondment from a Nigerian IT company. He added he was working on a special project, something to do with investigating fraud within a large financial corporation. Hotel life was dull, and although he'd been offered the chance of rented accommodation instead, he'd thought it pointless as that would mean he'd have to cook for himself – at least in a hotel everything was provided.

'So why are you doing this course?' Darius had asked when we first spoke, looking at me as if he was actually interested rather than being polite. The blood coursed through my veins and trampolined on the ventricles of my heart while my stomach flipped up to meet it. I explained that since being on my own I was a nervous driver and wanted to improve my skills. I hoped I hadn't been too subtle about being single.

'And what about you?' I'd asked, trying to keep my voice from shaking. I was mesmerised as he explained he'd been bored with what Surrey had to offer in terms of a night life and opted for continued education as a means to pass the time he was committed to working in the country. He'd said he'd been contracted to work in the UK for up to a year.

'I do a lot of driving in my work and wanted to make it more interesting,' he'd said, adding that his hotel was only a short walk from the school and he wanted to take part in something local.

'It's a chance to get to know people,' added Darius. I sincerely hoped he wanted to get to know me.

The class went by in a blur. My heart raced and my stomach churned faster than a cheese-maker. I vaguely recognised the feeling, which must have dated back to my early teens when I fell for the gorgeous Kevin Smith who lived three doors up from us and owned his own drop-handled racing bike. I adored Kevin, who was two years older than me. Being fifteen he didn't want to be seen with a thirteen-year-old girl, the sister of one of his school mates, but I would follow him everywhere. I think I must have annoyed him because one day he called me over to his group of friends as they were standing outside the fish and chip shop one Thursday evening when I was on my way to Girl Guides.

He leaned forward and I thought he was going to kiss me but he didn't, he just asked me to buy him some chips. I used the money my mum had just given me for my weekly subs to do so.

After queuing nearly twelve minutes to buy them I came to hand them over and he laughed in my face before racing off on his bike, his mates in tow. I tried to catch up with him and nearly caught the back of his shirt as it flapped behind him, but he just pedalled faster, shouting 'Go away, little girl' as he did. I was heartbroken but still loved him, as one always loves the one who gets away.

As for Darius, I couldn't see him behaving so badly. I was smitten. At first I didn't anticipate he would have any interest in me on a physical level. I was old enough to be his mother, for goodness' sake – despite retaining excellent bone structure and good skin.

I hung on to the hope that he'd see in me what the lady at the Boots make-up counter could see. A few weeks after Colin's death I'd treated myself to a new foundation and, having nothing else to do, took up the offer of a free makeover.

'You have amazing skin, you know,' she'd said as she dabbed on various colours and consistencies onto my face. 'A lot of women in their forties start to lose structure but you look fab,' she added, pulling my eyelid down and scribbling black gunk along the edge. I thought I was going to end up looking like a panda after a long night.

'I'm nearly sixty, actually,' I said, feeling very flattered but trying not to show it.

The make-up woman screeched so loudly a few passing customers looked at her disapprovingly. I'd have done the same in different circumstances.

'Well, I never would have believed it!' she said. 'You're gorgeous. I hope I look as sexy as you at your age.'

She hasn't been the only person to tell me something similar. I've been likened to film stars, mistaken for my daughters' sister (much to their annoyance) and refused entry to an over-fifties Christmas luncheon on the basis I didn't qualify. So I reckoned physically I could be in with a chance of finding some romantic interests in my later years.

But being an open-minded and intellectually broad kind of person, I'd been keen to develop our friendship on a deeper level, and offer my skills as a home cook and social entertainer to a man clearly deprived of such comforts. Darius was attentive, and the way I caught him looking at my legs suggested his interest was more than platonic. I'm not a natural flirt, but on the many times our eyes made contact he'd hold my gaze for just slightly longer than I felt comfortable. I'd seen that look before and had a good idea what it meant.

On the way down the school drive back to the car park on that fateful night, I suggested Darius might like to visit me one evening for a light supper and maybe to listen to some music. Throughout the evening he had intimated he'd very much like some company and was keen to explore more of what British culture had to offer.

It wasn't long before our shared isolation became a source of mutual attraction, at which point I allowed him to provide an uncharacteristic injection of carnal pleasure. It had happened naturally and without any guile on my part. Yes, I'd worn stockings and my sexiest little black dress. I'd gone to the hairdresser's for the first time in six months to have my grey hair, usually tied in a tight bun, delicately coloured and dried into a soft and loose arrangement. I even shaved my legs! I hadn't done that for years, as the hairs I had left were mostly unnoticeable, having diminished in their strength over the years. It formed part of the process of getting ready to meet a man and I was amazed how quickly those feelings came back to me after decades of dormancy. I felt young again, only with far more knowledge and a total commitment to making the most of what might be on offer.

CHAPTER NINE

When Darius arrived at my house the first time, he smelled divine. It was a heady mixture of cleanliness and a crisp cologne, encased in fresh air from where he'd walked in from the chilly night breeze. I put the rush of blood to my head down to the small glass of Martini I'd drunk to calm my nerves before his arrival. No one had ever regarded me as a passionate woman on any level, and it certainly wasn't a trait I saw in myself, so I was surprised, but happy, to feel so giddy.

After a meal of chicken breasts wrapped in ham with a small salad, dressed with a mixture of sesame oil and balsamic vinegar, we sat together on the settee to watch a classical concert on BBC 4.

I remembered how gentle he was in his approach, and how considerate, even though he liked to take me by surprise. Like the time I was focusing on keeping my balance in the 'doggy' position and he whipped me round onto my back like a chop in a frying pan. As much as I'd hoped, I'd never believed he'd find me attractive. I had been prepared for a platonic relationship but when he made it clear he had other ideas I was willing his touch, his closeness, and welcoming the nerve-jangling excitement I'd been deprived of.

He'd always pick up on my signals quickly. Maybe the dress was a bit too short? He responded by kissing my lips gently, kneeling down in front of me and making me feel incredibly small against his vast build. His sheer size was overwhelming in many ways, so his position was ideal. I watched as his lips, larger than I'd ever seen and pink inside the darkest chocolate coloured frame, met mine. Something deep in the pit of my belly stirred and I started to wonder if I'd cooked the chicken properly.

When his hands moved up my body from my hips to just under

my breasts, I caught my breath and kissed him back. His thumbs barely moved to touch the end of my nipples, and I jumped. Not with shock, but spontaneous reaction to the effect he was having on my body.

'Let's go upstairs,' I'd whispered to him, barely able to contain the thought of the possibilities to come. I imagined his naked body sliding against mine, engulfing me with its hugeness and overpowering me with desire, rendering me useless against his demands and heady with pleasure.

He said nothing, but followed me to my room which still had the hallmarks of marriage; two dressing gowns on the hook behind the door, two sets of wardrobes and bedside tables complete with lamps for each person. Three years on and I still couldn't quite convert from being part of a couple to being single. By keeping his belongings it was like Colin had just gone away on business and would soon be back. That was easier than coping with the eternal aloneness of widowhood.

I slipped my clothes off quickly. I'd become suddenly shy about the suspenders, fearing he would think me too forward, so I jumped under the duvet and hid my body beneath the covers. Only the top half of my head was on show – my eyes had to be clear so I could watch this massive man take off first his pale pink shirt and then his jeans, socks and underwear.

He'd already removed his shoes at the front door on my request.

I've never seen boxer shorts so close up before. Colin always wore white Y-fronts with rather too much space at the front. More importantly at that moment I'd never seen a penis like it. Not only much larger than Colin's, my only other lover, but so erect it looked like it was going to burst. I noticed its strong upwards angle and considerable girth, and was surprised to see the end of it was pink. Like his lips, a surprising contrast to the blackness of the rest of his skin.

Darius slid smoothly into the bed beside me and then disappeared below the covers. The soft roundness of his lips moved gently down my stomach until they met the area most demanding his attention. His hands were clasped around the top of my legs, his thumbs pressing at the soft, overly sensitive skin at the top of my inner thighs. I wasn't sure whether moving around was sexually acceptable, but I'd no choice as the extreme pleasure I felt was coursing through my body, nudging every nerve-ending awake. Every time I lifted my hips from the bed he'd use his strong mouth to push me back, raising the stakes with every lick and nip.

He was a tease, letting me believe he was going to stop, that it was all over and my release would have to wait. I'd be disappointed and then he'd start again, daring me to think my time, and I, might come.

'You're very beautiful, Cynthia,' I could hear him mumble under the duvet cover. I thought to tell him not to speak with his mouth full, but didn't want to distract him. I was hoping he was on the final run, the Beecher's Brook of our physical journey – the one offering the most excitement, danger and ultimate satisfaction, if ridden properly.

He went to work again, faster and with more determination. He put his cupped hands under my buttocks and worked furiously at me until my blood pulsed and my head filled with nothingness, just a swirl of electric anticipation.

The explosion of physicality was like nothing I'd known before. It was then I thought I'd probably had an orgasm; my first involving someone else.

Once he had taken me, gently at first but with increasing energy, for the third time, I felt incredibly sore in the genital region. It had been some years since I'd been 'bothered' by Colin and certainly not in such a forthright fashion. In fact I could only ever really remember thinking that sex seemed to cause so many problems considering how dull it could be.

But now I could see what the fuss was about, I looked forward to every occasion with Darius. We did things I didn't know you could do with another person, and also had a few close shaves, like on my birthday when the entire family decided to let themselves in to the house to cook me a surprise lunch, thinking I was playing golf.

Darius only just fitted into the wardrobe and it was unfortunate he had to stay there quite so long.

He said he'd never met anyone quite like me, which I took as a compliment. He added that apart from being good company, he also liked my cooking. So our relationship wasn't just about sex.

At first I found his attention difficult to believe. Then he told me I reminded him of a teacher he used to have – the mother of one of his school friends. The family were from north London, and while the father was working for an oil company in Lagos, she'd give English lessons to local children.

'I was thirteen,' he told me. 'I thought she was a goddess. Once I saw her changing to use our swimming pool and I couldn't take my eyes off her. She wore this grey pencil skirt with a slit up the back and I'd look at it, wondering where it would lead. When I saw her remove it I was in heaven,' he'd said.

He also told me he'd had a number of girlfriends but found them wanting, each in different ways. They were either set on marriage and children or would withdraw emotionally in a passive-aggressive bid to manipulate him into following their lead.

'You are like that teacher. You're the mistress of unspoken communication and never apologise for who you are,' he said, hugging me close. 'You don't need to be rescued or make cute "womanly" mistakes to make me bend to stereotypes. All I know is I don't have to be with you long for something magical to happen.'

My lips made a wavy line for a smile. I'd never been spoken to so gently, so warmly and with so much feeling. Perhaps true love does exist, despite age, class and culture?

I explained the story of Mrs Robinson from *The Graduate* and we watched it one rainy Sunday afternoon, sitting on the sofa. He told me he completely understood the young Benjamin's fascination with Anne Bancroft's character, adding that she wasn't nearly as sexy as me. He then proceeded to take my clothes off with his teeth, carefully peeling away the barrier between our bare flesh before he slowly caressed my body with his soft hands, building up my anticipation before he took me on the Persian rug, bartered for with much effort on a family holiday to Turkey.

The following week I'd made chocolate cupcakes (I found out he had something of a sweet tooth) and he'd brought the soundtrack of *The Graduate* with him. He made me dance to 'Mrs Robinson', singing the words until he got to 'Jesus loves you more than you will know', substituting his own name for Jesus, and we both laughed at the line 'put it in your pantry with your cupcakes' – it was then I knew our relationship meant more to him than just scratching at a physical itch.

Having said that he spent a good deal of time investigating nooks and crannies I didn't know existed. As for the multiple orgasm – I'd spent forty years thinking it was a fantasy.

It was a good arrangement.

CHAPTER TEN

I've often found it quite difficult to get out of the driveway without hitting one or the other side posts. I'm sure they are too close together, as they make the angle difficult when reversing.

Colin used to say I never looked properly and drove like a 'typical woman'. Well, in my opinion that is hardly a matter for derision as a 'typical woman' would read a map, ask directions if they were lost and let people through when they have accidentally got into the wrong lane, all qualities that make superior drivers if you ask me.

I can't be that bad. I did start an Advanced Driving course, after all. Even if I was a bit distracted throughout the one and only occasion I attended and didn't really believe anything that dreadful woman said about using speed on bends. Anyway, my car has more dents in it than a teenager's stock car, as well as a shaky front bumper from the incident with the next door neighbour's raised bed. If only I hadn't decided to go on a late night trip to the supermarket for Maltesers.

I'd gone in search of chocolate because I always get a taste for it after drinking sherry. I'd only had a couple. Oh yes, and the Spanish brandy, but it isn't really brandy so doesn't count. There was so little to look at on the television and my book had started to bore me, so the distraction of illicit and pointless calories had a certain allure. Nothing was capable of distracting me from the gap Darius had left in my newly awakened life – and my growing concern for him. I hadn't heard any more about his predicament and was at a loss about how I could act without knowing exactly where he was or what I might be able to do to help.

It was only a little accident but seemed to befuddle all those who eventually became involved. There was an awful lot of pushing and shoving by a lot of people (men) who finally decided they couldn't use sheer will and fading testosterone to get the car to move. A neighbour called the AA to get it lifted up and off the brickwork. The damage was probably more to my ego than anybody's property, although many people (apart from the people next door, whose cyclamens were crushed beyond recognition) were very much amused for many months.

On hearing about the incident, Jonjo castigated me for the potential consequences of being caught drinking and driving, particularly in my position as a local magistrate. It all reminded me slightly of the incident with the skip, at which point I thought how judgemental my son had become.

'It is hardly a great example to society, is it?' he'd said – rather pompously, I thought.

'There's you happily taking away the licences of any hapless driver who happens to tot up twelve points for daring to drive at a decent speed on motorways so they can go about their business, and you're endangering all and sundry just for the sake of a bag of sweets!'

The tune of 'Mrs Robinson' sprang into my head and the line 'most of all you've got to hide it from your kids' seemed highly relevant, as if written just for me.

What he didn't know was that I was no longer allowed to sit on the bench after telling one of the unemployed defendants he should jolly well get a job and stop relying on the benefits system to pay his court fines. I'd been feeling particularly alone that day and had been reminiscing about my time with Darius and whether my messages had got through to him. The thought of never seeing him again had put me in a particularly bad mood.

That and the conversation I'd had only a few days previously with the young policewoman at Epsfield station after my parking incident put an end to my interest in the legal system. After dutifully reporting as requested, I was told the officer who'd arrested me had lost all his paperwork in an altercation with some angry bus passengers and had since been signed off sick with stress.

Anyway, apparently one isn't allowed to express disgust at laziness and theft – or suggest to young parents they should think about contraception if they can't afford their children. I wasn't exactly asked to leave the magistracy but was told I might need 'retraining' so decided to resign. I didn't fancy being patronised by a left-wing legal executive on the merits of social inclusion or how to work effectively with the morally challenged.

'I'm retired now so it hardly matters,' I'd said, sounding petulant even to myself. 'So who cares what I do in my own time?'

Jonjo looked at me as if I was some kind of stranger who had walked into the family home uninvited, and then wondered if his childhood had been a dream and he had really grown up somewhere else. He looked at me quizzically.

'You didn't tell me you had retired. When did that happen?'

'I didn't know myself until a few weeks ago,' I said. 'I'm getting a bit old for it all now anyway, and there is far too much training. It takes up so much time.'

I wanted to change the subject. I sensed Jonjo thought I was going off the rails by small degrees and his reaction to my resignation suggested he was secretly rather pleased I was no longer a magistrate. We once had an argument about sentencing for drug dealing and my thoughts that in some very rare cases it should lead to capital punishment. Jonjo was horrified and said the thought of someone like me judging those who possessed cannabis for personal use filled him with horror. My own view is he was trying to cover up for his own seedy behaviour with that woman he went out with from the Hinchey Green council estate. The state of the skin around her fingernails was enough to tell you she was up to no good. At the time of his various public and usually drunken antics with the mother of four, who knew the father of none, he said he was escaping the narrow constraints of his uptight upbringing and that he took pleasure from marginal disregard for the law.

What he doesn't know is that Colin was the driving force of disapproval for the majority of our time as parents, and while Jonjo might have lived in fear of facing my wrath, it was his father who would have issued the harshest responses to his behaviour – had he known the full facts at the time. I couldn't be bothered to argue any further, having decided many years ago that motherhood as a career choice was highly undervalued and mostly a task for which the sacrifices and effort are generally only appreciated posthumously.

Jonjo piped up: 'Oh, that's a shame. I know you rather enjoyed it. But I suppose they have their rules.'

'Mostly it was boring,' I told him. 'And I've better things to do these days.' *Like remembering my sexual antics with a black man over twenty years my junior*, I thought, wickedly.

I swear Jonjo raised his eyebrows at me but I let it go. I suppose he might have been thinking that I didn't really have better things to do but then he didn't know what I got up to in my own time. *Thank goodness.* I flushed as I thought of what Darius could do with my time (and various bits of my anatomy).

'Well, maybe it's turned out for the best, then. But I still don't think you should go out driving when you have been drinking. You could kill someone,' he'd said.

I was feeling sorry for myself and didn't want to listen to him. I wanted to do something that didn't involve being told off by my children. I'd been waiting very patiently for a number of weeks and, in the absence of any idea what to do about my lover I needed something to take my mind off him, if only temporarily. I had finally decided it was time to go to the bridge club and find out why, since I was in possession of a sound and very viable email address, I hadn't received any communication from them.

I parked in the last spot in the church car park, for which I was thankful as the church seemed very busy; even for days when a funeral is taking place. Checking my jacket and smoothing my hair, I marched in what I considered to be a determined fashion to the hall's entrance. I pushed the doors open firmly and in doing so they smashed against a small table holding leaflets for local community activities, knocking half of them to the floor. I tutted in frustration at the mess, as I'd mentioned this problem many times to the committee. I ignored the flurry of papers. Why should

I pick them up when they were so obviously in a stupid position in the first place?

When I arrived, the doors to the church hall were closed but unlocked. It was usual for the group to wait until everyone had arrived, after which they would secure the entrance against any passing murderers looking specifically for bridge club members. Most were convinced that the day they left the door open, their downfall would be guaranteed.

I wasn't quite of the same opinion. I told them they were paranoid and they should have sufficient confidence in their own abilities to talk themselves out of a violent death. I certainly wasn't going to spend my life worrying about what could happen. It seems that whatever I've been planning falls foul of fate anyway.

When I got into the hall I saw a few old faces. I mean old, too; used up, exhausted and lacking in the sparkle that makes youth what it is. Like a white shirt that's been laundered so many times it never really ever looks white again, regardless of the number of bleach washes.

Only a few of them retained any evidence of previous excitements, illicit knowledge, private reveries of days gone past; and these flashes came in the occasional surge of energy that could only be seen by looking directly through their eyes and into the core of their diminished souls.

'Hello, everybody. Sorry I haven't been for such a long time but I haven't been getting your emails.'

I looked accusingly at Mavis, with the sort of stare I reserved for this and any other confrontational occasion.

'I'm sorry, Cynthia,' said Mavis, who kept her eyes focused away and towards the door. 'I didn't think you had email. I just assumed that someone would let you know what was going on.'

'Well, they haven't. So I'll inform you of the address and I hope you'll be sending me details of all events in future,' I said, somewhat haughtily.

I sat firmly on the only available chair in the hall and wondered if this is what my life had come to. I missed having Darius and the anticipation of a thrill, however short-lived. I wondered if that was what it was like to give up a drug and started to feel for the people I'd seen in court. They were driven to do things to repeat the buzz that made them feel alive, special and above the mundanity of everyone else's tired and tiring existences.

Tears were rising alongside an acid indigestion brought about by repressed emotion so I busied myself with my bag and coat. It was as Mavis was giving out pens I decided to make my stand.

'So, can I be assured you will now be sending me emails? I'm fully on the interweb and have my own address and hard driver. So no excuses, eh?' I expelled a forced laugh to make sure she knew that while I was quite happy to be jovial at this stage, things could get difficult.

'No excuses, Cynthia, no excuses,' replied Mavis, looking a bit despondent. I should have noticed she hadn't asked for the actual address.

The games began and I lost. It was my partner's fault. That silly Cecil D'Eath, who refused to acknowledge how his name was pronounced.

'It's Death, as in the act of being dead,' I told him once but he insisted I'd got it wrong.

To make out it's some kind of French derivative was downright pretentious. If you hate your name that much, even if you have grown into it by dint of the inevitability of ageing, change it. No one cares anyway, but they do care if you make a twerp of yourself.

Throughout the afternoon all I could think of was sex. Having been deprived of it in any meaningful way for most of my adult life, until the recent enlightenment with Darius, I was hankering after a good old seeing to. Shocked by the change in my own desires, I wondered if it was Darius who'd opened up my horizons, and a fair few other things, or the onset of late middle age? After all, sixty is the new forty, or so I'm led to believe when reading *Cosmopolitan* magazine at the hairdresser's.

I don't see anything wrong with stretching the boundaries of propriety after a lifetime of compliance. Everyone over fifty should think about throwing away the rules now and then, particularly if you have played by them for so long. I no longer cared a jot what sandwiches were available or whether everyone got their chosen filling. Let them eat bloody cake.

At the end of the bridge session, I left the hall hurriedly and was a little surprised to find my car had been moved and a rude note left about parking in the spot reserved for the hearse. A large yellow parking ticket was stuck to the windscreen, right in front of the driver's seat. I pulled at it but it wouldn't budge so had to drive with my head out the window for the entire journey home.

I raced back as quickly as possible not only because of the ticket but in case anyone wanted to mention the last hand, the one that led to a spectacular downfall. At the time I'd been looking at the ace of clubs and reminiscing about Darius and his expert tongue.

It was about time I got in touch with him – in person.

CHAPTER ELEVEN

'Will the last passengers for flight NA345 to Lagos please go to gate number 105,' a voice boomed over the tannoy at Heathrow airport.

I'd been in the toilet, throwing up what appeared to be the remains of my macaroni cheese from the night before. I was surprised to note the strange addition of carrots, which I couldn't remember having eaten, but other than that felt a lot better. I don't like being sick and haven't been for years, so can only put it down to nerves. At least at my age I knew it wasn't pregnancy.

It could've been the bottle of wine I'd drunk by myself before going to bed. I'd been looking around for something to take my mind off the flight and found one of the good burgundies Colin had laid down for an occasion he never came to see. He was a bit like that – keeping everything for 'best', but then nothing was ever good enough to qualify. I decided just the simple fact a good bottle was available to me, and I was able to open it with a waiter's friend, unaided, was good enough reason to celebrate.

There was no doubt the decision to go and find Darius was getting a bit nerve-racking. I knew I couldn't ignore his plight when I received his email. I just booked the journey and made a decision not to worry about the consequences. I didn't have time to reconsider, until it was too late.

I took a quick look in the mirror and had to adjust my hair as it had fallen out of place while I was in the unfortunate position required for vomiting.

You don't look too bad under the circumstances, I thought, as I applied a fresh layer of the 'Delicate Rose' lipstick I've been wearing for the last decade. The woman at the beauty counter said it matched my English rose complexion. And that if I bought three I qualified for a free make-up bag, which I've never used.

'Would the final passengers for flight NA345 to Lagos please go to gate 105 for boarding. This is the last call for this flight, which will close in two minutes,' the anonymous voice warned.

They can call as much as they like, they can't go without me, and as I was still feeling a little shaky I didn't want to rush about. Numerous trips with Colin have taught me if the baggage is on board, the passenger has to be too or they will delay the plane. He used to delight in sauntering his way to the plane, particularly if they'd had to call for him by name. I suppose it made him feel important.

Normally, on my own, I'd have been a good ten minutes early and waiting at the front of the queue to get settled in the plane first, as I always hated the looks of contempt from seated passengers while we made our way to the last available seats. However, I didn't want any more stress or the embarrassment of having to find another toilet quickly so I stayed near the one I knew about for as long as possible.

I swung my travelling bag over my right shoulder. It was brown leather and probably very expensive as Colin had bought it on one of his trips to New York. He gave it to me on his return rather than wait for a birthday or Christmas which did make me wonder what he was feeling guilty about. Probably looking at an air hostess on the way home, or accidentally tuning in to the hotel's porn channel. He wasn't the type you could imagine doing anything to warrant claims of cheating, on any level. He'd even refuse to put kisses on birthday or leaving cards for female colleagues in case it was construed as sexual harassment.

I strolled towards the gate. The queue had dwindled and there were just a few people left to check in. As I got to the desk a large, black woman dressed in a myriad of colours pushed in front of me. She was wearing a swathe of thin cloth wrapped loosely in various directions, which I thought looked strangely stylish. Normally I'd have said something at the woman's rudeness but I was fascinated by the clothing. I could never work out how anyone could wear all that material without looking like they were going about their business in a set of sheets.

'I love your dress,' I said to the woman, who was at least a foot taller and probably five stone heavier than me. 'Did you make it yourself?'

As I was waiting for an answer, hopefully a polite one in the interests of making conversation, the woman turned to me and sucked her teeth, ignoring my question and gliding forward as if she had rollerblades concealed under the voluminous folds of her outfit. She made it clear she wasn't interested in any discussion.

'Please yourself,' I muttered under my breath, as I opened up my passport and tickets for inspection. I wasn't sure where I'd be sitting on the plane, although I'd asked for a window seat.

I was amazed at the lack of interest the Nigerian Airway's representative had shown in my ticket or passport. I tried to make small talk, but to no avail, as she wouldn't make eye contact. I hadn't seen anyone look so bored since Titch was asked to play a tree in a school production of *A Midsummer Night's Dream.* Dressed in a cardboard tube, painted green, and covered in a variety of twigs from top to bottom, she was expected to remain static for a little under two hours. Her nose never recovered; she'd dropped off halfway through, waking only in time to realise she was going to hit the stage, and couldn't get her hands free to break her fall.

The walk down the various poorly constructed corridors was long and tedious. I wondered whether Nigerian Airways planes were kept as far away from the airport as possible. It's a good job I'm fit or I might not have made it.

Finally at the door I handed over my ticket to the bored steward who pointed me in the direction of the interior of the plane. I found it vaguely amusing as she showed me down the aisle of the plane. I'm not quite sure where else she thought I would go.

I looked around at the seat numbers for 47C and in doing so tripped over a wayward foot which some great oaf had poked out into the path of those in the aisle.

I landed face down in the bosom of the woman I'd tried to speak to in the queue. She sucked her teeth again, more loudly this time.

'Oh, we meet again,' I said, trying to deal with what I found to be quite an embarrassing situation.

I pushed myself up to a standing position using the woman's substantial knees to do so.

'Will you git arf me,' she drawled in a strong accent I didn't recognise but assumed was African of some kind. 'Wart is da mutter wit you?' she said, rubbing down her thighs and blowing out her breath in big puffs, which I noticed smelled of garlic.

Her manner was most unpleasant and I have to admit to being somewhat taken aback. I opened my mouth to say something just as one of the hostesses took my elbow and guided me to a seat some way from the woman I'd just fallen upon.

'Don't take any notice of her,' said the willowy hostess. 'That is Lady Buke Osolase. She was the first African woman to get a university degree and so can be a bit strident.'

'Downright rude, if you ask me,' I said, although not without some regard for a woman who would have had to fight against an even stronger cultural prejudice than I did, one that stated women did not deserve or require education.

I made a mental note of Lady Osolase's name, despite the likelihood my brain would act like an Etch A Sketch drawing pad after it has been shaken, wiping out all notations once laid flat.

I shuffled over to my seat which I was cross to note was in the aisle and not by the window as requested, took off my shoes and settled into as comfortable a position anyone can adopt on an economy flight from London to Lagos.

It was then I noticed a strange smell emanating from the back of the plane, which I would have dismissed had it not been for the comments of my neighbouring passenger.

'What the bloody hell is that awful stink?' said the bleached blonde woman next to me. 'Smells like burning flesh or something.'

I looked round to get a closer look and wasn't entirely happy with the fact I was going to have to spend eight hours on a flight with someone whose dark mouse roots were showing through permed, yellowing hair. Do these people not have mirrors in their houses?

She also had a bright pink hairband featuring two baubles and a daisy, which only added to the general inappropriateness of her dress, particularly for someone who was probably fighting off fifty from one direction or another.

'I'm sure it isn't anything to worry about,' I replied, hoping it would shut her up. I noticed that each finger and one thumb had a cheap ring on it, sometimes two. More offensively she also had false nails shaped into a square at the top and painted fluorescent orange, which quite frankly announce low class like an identity badge. At least she didn't have those ones that look like you've had an accident with the Tippex. I looked at my own neat, pearly-painted, oval-shaped nails and gave myself an internal nod of approval.

'I bloody hate flying, don't you, babe?' said my fellow passenger in the gravelly voice of one who smokes on a regular basis.

'Well, not really,' I said, wondering if my new companion knew Nigeria has the worst air safety record in the world. Darius had told me that fact after some crash where the plane had been declared unsafe but the pilot flew it anyway – into a block of flats killing all the passengers and destroying the homes of many families. The airline's management admitted manslaughter and closed their company, after investigations revealed they were uninsured and heavily underfunded.

'The name's Tracey. Or Trace. Why you going to Lagos, then? Got yourself a bit of black?' she laughed.

I baulked at my relationship with Darius being described as getting myself 'a bit of black', and wanted to argue my case, although I thought an honest explanation of my relationship could be deemed implausible, however vehemently I might have defended it. I also stopped myself from automatically saying I was pleased to meet 'Trace', as I felt quite the opposite.

However I did feel the need to ask why this common-looking woman, dressed in what I thought could only be described as highly irregular attire for her advancing years, was on her way to Lagos.

'Cos me man is out there, hun. I love him like no other,' said

Tracey, turning to reveal a nose piercing which I'd previously thought was a spot. 'Can't do nuffin about it when you want him, know what I mean? He's asked me to marry him,' she said – showing a ring that probably cost less than forty pounds, including the presentation box. 'I said yes, although he's only a baby. Twenty years older than him, I am. The number of people who ask me if I worried about the age difference and how it might affect our future. But if he dies, he dies!' she said, cackling to herself.

I recoiled at the poor elocution of the woman who I'd also noticed had particularly bad teeth and somewhat ravaged skin. Tracey's choice of a short-sleeved top exposing bingo wings of an excessive nature, plus a poorly fitting bra allowing her voluminous breasts to dangle dangerously unhindered, added to my revulsion. She was fitting earplugs from a mobile phone into place when she turned round and asked:

'So what you going to Nigeria for, then, if it ain't a bloke? You one of those church people or summin'?'

If only she knew. I wasn't sure what to say for fear of giving too much away, not only about my relationship with Darius, but also my impending wealth. This woman did not need to know that I was likely to be exceedingly rich very soon. Who knows where it could lead, so I just nodded.

'Yes, something like that,' I replied, and pretended to go to sleep. I still couldn't get the smell from the back of the plane out of my nose and wondered what it was. It reminded me of Christmas Eve five years ago when I put the turkey in the oven on a timer but set it for four hours earlier than I meant to. Colin had woken up choking from the smell of burning. We had pork that year. And I was force-fed humble pie.

CHAPTER TWELVE

When the plane hit some heavy turbulence an hour or so into the flight I was obliged to open my eyes as Tracey was screaming 'We're all going to die' at the top of her voice. Standing in her seat, she was demanding she be let off the plane immediately.

'Get me off this bloody thing. We're going to die, we are all going to die,' she proclaimed to no one in particular.

I would've been quite happy to allow her to disembark while the plane was fully airborne but decided instead to try and calm her down.

'Turbulence is quite normal – it just means the plane is reacting to the air and pressure around it. Nothing to worry about,' I told her, repeating what I'd been told when I first flew. I could remember being scared, but not behaving like a raving lunatic, as Tracey was now doing.

The hostesses showed little reaction to the outburst, bored no doubt by the frequency of such panic, and let me deal with the situation. After a few minutes of talking her through the flight process – as well as pointing out that the stewards were quite happily going about their business, which indicated nothing was wrong – Tracey calmed down.

'I don't know why I'm on this bleedin' thing anyway. Bastard probably won't marry me when I get there,' she sniffed. 'I've only seen him for three weeks in eight months and two of those were when we were on hols in Magaluf. Half the time I don't know if I'm coming or going.'

Then she laughed nervously. 'Actually I always know when I'm coming! One thing the bugger is good at.'

I resisted the urge to concur, adding my own views on the

superiority of shiny black men in the bedroom department and flicked through the in-flight magazine which had mostly been torn apart, rendering it unreadable.

We were nearing the end of the flight before I'd calmed Tracey down completely, as she was prone to repetitive agitation and panic. I'd kept her seated for most of the time, mainly by asking questions about herself, which was a subject she found very engaging. I was about to breathe a sigh of relief when the hostesses started to rush about the plane for no apparent reason. The smell we'd noticed when we first sat down had got worse throughout the flight, and now there was a constant smog around the rear toilets, one of which was blocked and leaking into the cabin, adding further fumes to the already acrid mixture. Despite repeated questions to the stewards about it from various travellers, everyone was assured it was all perfectly normal.

And then came the announcement: 'We are sorry to tell you we're experiencing problems with one of our engines and may have to undertake an emergency landing. Please brace yourself and pray to your god.'

That did it for Tracey. If 'bracing yourself' meant jumping up and down and crying hysterically then she was doing a very good job. I got out of my seat and ransacked the contents of the drinks trolley, to no resistance from the now petrified air crew, one of whom was clutching a crucifix and repeating the Hail Mary over and over. Throughout the aisles Africans were on their knees with their hands clasped together, some were on their mobile phones, despite their use not being permitted in-flight, leaving messages for loved ones. Others were catatonic, staring into some kind of middle distance that offered a neutral solace against the prospect of impending doom. The big black lady I'd fallen into was reciting the Lord's Prayer very loudly from her seat, demanding that those around her join in.

Chucking twelve small bottles of brandy at Tracey, and keeping four for my own internal emergency, I told her, 'Drink this. Whatever happens it might help to be drunk at the time.'

Tracey seemed only too happy to oblige, and between us we necked the whole lot in a matter of seconds, while the plane rumbled and rolled, dropping bumpily out of the sky and eventually heavily, but thankfully not too dangerously, onto the tarmac below.

'We're pleased to report we have landed safe and sound on the main runway at Lagos airport. The pilot would like to apologise for any concern, and asks you to remain in your seats while an external check is made of the plane and suitable arrangements are made for your exit,' said a voice over the tannoy.

All the passengers, when they realised they were still alive and had been given the explanation that a large bird had been caught up in one of the rear engines, probably since take-off, clapped gleefully and whooped with joy. All but Tracey, who looked completely stunned, as if her expectations couldn't have been more wrong.

'Bloody hell. We've made it. Thought we were goners then.'

A fire engine raced to the side of the runway and a team of around twenty officials hurried to the front of the plane. After a few minutes we were told we could leave by the front exit.

My own relief at landing in one piece was palpable, even though I did try to keep my emotions to myself for the sake of dignity and good breeding. There was no need for screaming and crying at the inevitable. But my resolve nearly crumbled when we got out on the runway and felt the searing heat of the tarmac at Murtala Muhammed airport. Walking towards the arrivals area I thought I'd stumbled into one of those refugee camps you see on the Comic Relief films, with so many people sitting around on lumpy luggage.

'Jesus H. Christ, what is this dump?' I heard Tracey shout from a distance behind. Despite all efforts to shake her off, the woman seemed to be following me.

In front of us was a large white building full of people struggling with massive amounts of luggage, in sapping heat and humidity. A throng stood before a varied selection of what looked like makeshift service counters, manned by bored and shifty-looking customs officials who were stopping people at random and taking inordinate amounts of time looking through their cases. Most seemed to enjoy extracting the most embarrassing contents they could find and holding them aloft for all to see.

Scrabble sets, underwear, vibrators and mobile phones attracted the most attention. And anything belonging to anyone who looked like they would play the backhander game of parting with dollars for an easy passage through security.

I couldn't see any type of queue or system when it came to getting out of the place.

'Where on earth are British citizens supposed to go?' I asked one of the passengers in front of me. 'It's chaos. There should be a proper queue.'

'You'll be lucky,' drawled the suited man in response. 'This place is nothing but a scrum. I hope you've got some cash on you, preferably dollars, or you'll never get out the place.'

He pulled out a wad of notes from the inside of his loosely fitted jacket and marched towards one of the customs officers, who appeared to know him.

'Jager, good to see you,' I heard him greet the uniformed man. I strained to hear any more of the conversation but at that point was moved to one side by what I thought might be a police officer, although it was difficult to tell as he was chewing gum and had his jacket open to the third button, which I considered wasn't very professional.

'Here. Over here,' he ordered, yanking on my right arm to get me into the throng of what I assumed were tourists, based on their sheep-like mentality when it came to dealing with the process of getting out of the airport. I found myself wedged up close to Tracey, who was trying to make a call on her mobile phone.

'Bloody thing doesn't work. Been ringing Abassi since we landed and no tone,' she said.

'Well maybe he'll be waiting for you on the other side,' I said, wishing the woman would go away. I felt she was the type of person who created trouble without knowing it.

'Better be,' she replied. 'He owes me five grand.'

CHAPTER THIRTEEN

I walked through the revolving doors from the airport's arrivals area and onto the pavement outside, then wondered what to do. Having managed to deal with the corrupt practices of the customs officers with harsh words and my sternest countenance, I didn't know what to expect next.

I looked at the Western Union address on the email again and tried to see if I could find a map, but there didn't seem to be anything at all. Not even an information desk.

The heat was oppressive and the sheer volume of people in the area overwhelming. So when Tracey came over to ask where I was going, I couldn't help but feel pleased to see her; mainly for the vague idea I might be able to use my new acquaintance as some kind of bargaining tool with the locals.

'I can't get through to Baz at all. The number isn't bloody working,' said Tracey as she bowed her head to pull a cigarette out of a packet with her teeth. As she blew smoke out of her mouth from the first puff she added: 'Bet the arsehole has forgotten.'

As we stood together, asking each other what to do next, a lean and well-dressed man appeared from one of the few clean cars parked outside the arrivals area.

'I think you might be expecting me. Where you looking to go, ladies?' he asked, walking purposefully towards us. He was about six feet tall and wearing well-cut trousers and a brightly clean white shirt that showed off his dark skin. He had a pair of Ray-Ban sunglasses perched on top of his head and dangled his car keys in his left hand, reaching out his right as he approached us.

I noticed how long his fingers were as he touched my arm in greeting: 'I'm Fasina and will be your guide while you stay in Nigeria.'

He had a slight American lilt to his well-spoken, otherwise African, accent, and while I thought his approach rather presumptuous, decided in the circumstances it might be a good idea to have someone with us who knew their way around.

'I'm looking for this address,' I said, showing him the email I'd printed out before leaving home. 'I need to find my friend Darius, or Osezua as he is known here,' I mentioned, hopefully.

I ignored Tracey who took her attention away from her phone for once. She was unlikely to have anything interesting to say so I looked around for someone who might be in authority.

A loud plane took off overhead as she told Fasina: 'I'm looking for Abassi Osolase. Do you know him?'

He seemed to smile to himself as he looked carefully at the address he had been shown, but I put it down to the fact he had as low an opinion of Tracey's appearance as I did.

Fasina moved close to us as if in conspiracy.

'No problem, my ladies, you're safe with me. I know everyone. Come, I have a car with air conditioning. And put your phone away, it will get snatched here. There are big problems with crime and many thieves.'

That was enough to persuade me to trust this man. He knew the dangers and was well-spoken. After some negotiation he said he'd charge us four thousand naira, just over fifteen pounds, to take us to our destinations, which seemed a fair price – particularly if he was going to put me back in touch with Darius.

If hope could rise it was doing so in my nether regions. I was sweating profusely, so much so that my knickers were stuck to my bottom and I was sure I was developing an unsightly damp patch. I desperately wanted a shower, something to eat and a change of clothes. I started to feel completely out of place. Which I suppose I was.

Meanwhile, Tracey seemed to be happy to come along for the ride, and while Fasina placed our luggage in the boot we got comfortable in the back of the old, but classic, Saab estate.

As we drove away from the airport, I looked at the vast numbers of people who were spilling out of the airport without any sense of order. The crowds were untamed, animate and busy. It was almost impossible to think one country could find enough for so many people to do at one time.

Fasina talked throughout the whole journey about Nigeria, its people, customs and expectations. He also claimed Nigeria was on its way to destruction, that the resources of the country were being looted by the same people who had a duty to protect and preserve it.

'We cannot continue like this,' he said. 'The World Bank actually warned us to focus on managing resources and plan ahead, but our leaders – most of them self-appointed and selected – have no respect for our system and state.'

I thought he was on a bit of a soap box. It wasn't any different to listening to some of the bridge club members going on about leftie liberals and the need to bring back national service. It wasn't my place to comment, and Tracey was preoccupied with her non-existent phone service.

'They abuse, exploit, disrespect and manipulate our processes, policies, systems, laws and procedures to maximise their own gains and to take undue advantage of the nation and the people,' he went on.

'Thieves run our nation and control our resources while the majority of our people wallow in abject poverty; many are hopeless. Does the sight of a homeless, helpless and jobless youth not worry those who lead us?'

He then went on to talk about something called the Ribadu Report, which I'd little interest in, but I felt I had to feign some interest while Tracey made it clear she wasn't going to listen to anything about this man's country, so obsessed had she become with trying to make her phone work.

I wasn't quite sure of his point. His tirade went on to cover fuel scams and the dirty deals of Nigeria's oil ministers.

'The current band of thieves must not be allowed to go unpunished. The civil society must be active and take the front seat in ensuring every penny stolen is recovered, the thieves punished severely, and the funds used to make the nation better,' continued Fasina.

I half-listened but found my anxiety about finding Darius growing with every minute. I wasn't terribly interested in supposed corruption, as it really had nothing to do with me. I was just looking for a friend and wasn't bothered about how these people ran the country, which felt a long way from the suburban glades of Surrey, England.

I took in the scenery as we drove through Lagos, which was a world entirely different to anything I'd seen before. What started as a journey through an apparently prosperous area changed abruptly as we drove past dark and dirty alleys barely wide enough for two people to pass. Where before I'd seen suited men going about their business, the people in the streets were looking downtrodden and undernourished. Children weren't playing, but carrying large pots and packages on their heads, taking part in activities that would be alien to any of the children I've known.

Tracey had put her headphones in and didn't seem to notice what was going on, so I continued to concentrate on the journey, making a mental note about the differences between home and Lagos. It was quite difficult to find appropriate comparisons, as I asked myself if parents cared about their offspring in any way or just needed them to fetch and carry. What about supermarkets or schools? Did anyone play golf? Did teenagers have computers? I thought fondly of Tom at that moment and felt some guilt I hadn't told anyone in the family that I was going on a trip – quite an unusual one at that.

After a few minutes in my own thoughts, I noticed Fasina had gone quiet but reckoned maybe he'd had enough of talking to us, particularly as my companion wasn't responding at all, unless singing along to a pop song out of tune counted.

Twenty more minutes into the drive I saw a sign for Manita and was surprised to find we were entering a district that appeared to be built on stilts, elevating all the buildings above a shallow lagoon. The roads were narrow and the houses derelict. There were very few cars, which I assumed was down to poverty.

Fasina piped up at this point and became highly animated.

'Fishing families have lived here for more than 120 years. There are more than a quarter of a million people here, neglected if not despised by the city's rich people. Look how they are living, having had to make their homes above water.'

He was pointing to a group of people squatting around some wire baskets, sorting fish with bare hands and discarding heads, tails and fins into a rotting and fly-infested pile. The ground was dusty and rough. Children sat by, watching the adults work.

Fasina went on to tell us that in the summer over one hundred officials arrived and demolished dozens of the wooden houses that lined the canals.

'They had just a couple of days' notice. They told the people to go back where they come from. But they were born here. The governor promised schools and hospitals at election time and everyone voted for him,' he added. 'Nobody ever mentioned they would lose their homes.'

I remained silent as an indication of my boredom, although I don't think our guide cared too much. It was obviously a subject close to his heart, if far removed from mine and even further removed from Tracey's.

I'm not one for politics at the best of times, the annual general meeting of the Farsham District Council being about as lofty as I can aspire to. Frankly I think it's up to these people to get themselves out of the situation they found themselves in. I didn't want to listen to this bleating, I just wanted to find Darius.

Fasina stopped the car.

Finally Tracey decided to join the communicating classes by speaking.

'Where the bloody hell are we?' she shouted a bit too loudly, as people tend to when talking with earphones in.

I was thinking the same but wasn't sure how to ask our self-styled guide. He behaved as if he knew where we were going and we'd shown him the address we needed to find. He hadn't said he didn't know it.

'We get out here,' said Fasina, taking the luggage from the boot and heading towards the canal before pointing to a canoe. 'The car won't take us any further this way. Get in, ladies.'

I was horrified. Boating of any kind isn't an activity I enjoy. Even first-class cruising still involves floating on a large piece of metal which, if it sinks, leaves you with nothing but miles of cold and dirty water to deal with.

'Where are you taking us?' I asked, trying to make sure my voice didn't squeak with concern. 'Is this where I will find the Western Union bank and be able to get in touch with Darius?'

Fasina didn't reply, but just marched speedily towards the canoe, with both suitcases weighing heavily at the ends of his slim arms.

Tracey looked agitated and took out another cigarette from her handbag, lit it and stood stock still.

'Something ain't right. I can feel it in my water,' she said, dragging as much smoke into her lungs as she could. Her eyeliner and mascara had begun to melt and spread under her eyes, making her look a little like a tired koala – one from Essex.

'You have nuttin' to worry yourselves about,' said Fasina, slipping into more of an African lilt than had been noticeable when we first met. 'You are talking to me now!' he said with a big smile. 'I know where to take you. Have some faith, oh yes. Faith is good.'

Having given up church some time ago on the grounds of hypocrisy, mine as much as anyone else's, I wasn't a great believer in faith. In fact I'd given up on most things faithful for some time. However, I had little choice other than to follow this man, who did, after all, seem quite pleasant if now a little distracted. And well dressed.

Tracey wasn't at all sure so I put on my best confident demeanour and led us both to the canoe, telling her on the way that I was sure everything was fine.

It wasn't easy getting either of us on board. My balance got the better of me and Fasina had to hold most of my weight, even though it's only around nine stone, as I slipped and slid like a newborn foal into one of the seats. Tracey was wearing wedge shoes with six inches of heel, which I thought were entirely unfit for any purpose, unless working in a lap-dancing club. She'd been teetering along with some difficulty throughout our entire journey, but it had all got much worse as we reached the muddy banks of the canal.

'Just take them off,' I said to Tracey, trying not to show my irritation with her as she settled into her seat at the front of the canoe.

'Why you even think that things that look like correction boots are suitable for travelling is beyond me,' I commented, pleased I'd decided to wear my sensible flats, although even Clark's best still rendered me helpless when it came to negotiating my way off terra firma.

'These are my shag-me shoes,' sniffed Tracey, whose blotchiness was increasing with every ounce of effort. 'Baz likes them.'

Probably because it means you have no way of escaping while you're wearing them, I thought, as I turned my attention to Fasina who was rubbing his arm where Tracey's cigarette had burned him while he'd been helping her onto the boat.

'So where are we and how long will it take us to get to civilisation?' I said, noting that Tracey's feet, now bare, were very pale compared to the colour of the rest of her. And there were brown streaks leading from her ankles to the bottom of her mid-calf trousers. It took a while to work out it wasn't a skin disease but the result of a home-applied fake tan.

'We're nearly there,' he replied. 'We can't drive this way by road without a four-wheel drive. The boat is our best transport.'

Fasina hastily moved along the vessel and started to punt us along the narrow channel at good speed for a man who lacked obvious muscle. We passed hundreds of wooden shacks perched above the water, which were occasionally connected by weak-looking bridges. I thought how I'd be worried walking along them with Darius who was, after all, a man of sturdy build and therefore some considerable weight – particularly in comparison to the man now before us.

Some of the boats were covered with tarpaulins and Fasina

explained that families who'd lost their homes lived on them now.

'We don't need a government any more. They take our homes. We have our own system now.' A shiver ran down my spine, for a reason I couldn't explain.

After about twenty minutes of silent punting, he stopped the boat and moored up close to an area that appeared to be surrounded by a mud wall about seven feet tall. There was an archway made of brick, beyond which five or six shacks were apparently linked together with makeshift corridors, covered with struts of cane, tarpaulin and in some places, plastic sheeting. It looked dark and empty, but as Fasina tied up the canoe and was helping us out onto the bank a giant of a man, dressed in a green cotton shirt and wearing a skull cap, came towards us.

'Ladies, welcome,' he said in a manner that was anything but welcoming.

Fasina shook the man's hand vigorously and introduced him as Chike, pronounced 'cheeky', which seemed incongruous for a man with heavily bloodshot eyes, drooping jowls and a scar running from the bottom of his lip to the side of his ear.

Tracey and I looked at each other. If she was as nervous as I was, she hadn't voiced her opinion as yet. She moved closer to me so she couldn't be heard by the men as she whispered:

'I don't know about you, but I don't think these guys are going to find us our men. We need to get out of here. They are creeping me out.'

Regardless of my view of this peculiar woman, I agreed she had a point. It was difficult to know what to think, but I knew we needed to do something. I tried to keep an open mind as to what. Throughout the journey here I'd questioned if we were really on our way to our desired destination but could see no reason why we wouldn't be. What would someone like Fasina want with me and, more relevantly, Tracey?

But there'd been a distinct lack of banks, roads and the normal tourist facilities I'd come to expect when accompanying Colin on his many business trips. It was worrying.

'Listen here. We really don't want to put you out but I'm not sure we are in the right place to find our friends. I need to find the Western Union bank where I'll be collected and can get on with why I came here,' I said, thinking I'd been incredibly diplomatic and persuasive.

Fasina and Chike looked at each other before bursting out laughing and 'high-fiving' each other.

The sweat on my bottom was starting to cool and as I thought about damp patches I worried about wetting myself, remembering I hadn't been to the toilet since the vomiting incident. Not only that, I'd developed wind from a combination of my recurrent diverticulitis and the flight – and was getting stomach cramps from trying to hold it in.

'You come with me,' said Fasina, grabbing both of us firmly by the arms. He'd stopped being the polite and enthusiastic guide and adopted what appeared to be a snarl.

I pulled back, bringing Fasina to a halt: 'Now, young man. I don't know who you think you are but that is no way to speak to ladies. We don't want to be here and so must insist you call us a taxi so we can get away.'

At that point Tracey threw up. Possibly because of the brandy from the plane or maybe from fear, but either way she narrowly missed Fasina's shoes. I briefly noticed the lack of carrots before I stepped away quickly. In a bid to escape the embarrassment of the situation I went to ask Tracey if she thought her phone might work sufficiently to make a local call for a taxi. As I went to speak the men moved forward quickly, grabbing both our arms around our bodies and dragging us to a shack behind the main entrance area of the buildings. Tracey squealed as Chike pushed her along, using all the force of his knee against the back of her thighs. She was still barefoot, so her attempts at stamping on his boot-clad feet had no effect. She did, however, manage to get a bite of his forearm, which might have been noticed had she paid more attention to her dental health in the past. I heard a crunch and she spat out what looked like a crown onto the dusty floor.

'Get off me, you fucking brute. I'll do you for frigging assault, you motherfucker,' said Tracey, sporting a very noticeable gap in the front of her teeth.

Chike kicked her harder at this point and grabbed her hair, pulling her head backwards before throwing her onto the floor inside the shack.

'Get in there and shut up,' he shouted before turning on his heel.

Fasina was a little more gentle with me, either out of deference for my age and class or possibly because he was concerned about experiencing any further issue from our stomachs. I didn't struggle, deeming it pointless in view of his superior physical strength, but he still used more effort than necessary to push me into the room with Tracey before quickly pulling the door shut behind him.

The next thing we heard was the sound of keys in the padlock that had been hanging off bolts to the side of the door and Fasina's voice.

'See you later, ladies. Make yourselves at home.' Then he laughed and his footsteps disappeared into the distance, leaving us two unlikely room-mates looking around our new accommodation with mutual disgust.

Tracey reached round to her side to get into her shoulder bag for another cigarette, only to find the packet was missing.

'Bastards,' she spat. 'They've got me fags.'

CHAPTER FOURTEEN

The shack was made of various types and shapes of wood and was reinforced with steel struts, held together with bolts and brackets and covered with chicken wire. As much as we tried, using all the brute force I and my shoeless companion could muster, we could see no way to force an exit.

There was a pile of blankets and two mattresses in one corner, a small chair in another, and a large washing-up bowl and a jug of water on a chest that should have contained drawers but was empty. Strewn across the floor were a selection of old British newspapers and magazines, cigarette ends and dirty mugs. A light bulb hung from a pole stretched below the ceiling and dimly lit the room.

'This is just outrageous,' I said to Tracey, who was pacing up and down the twenty square feet or so that was available to her.

'What the hell do these people think they are doing?' Tracey said, crying and making even more of a mess of her make-up.

I felt for her a bit at this point, particularly as it seemed she had still to notice her missing tooth and the extremely unattractive spike left in its place. Despite the bluff and bluster, and the badly disguised advancing years, she seemed quite vulnerable, if incredibly thick.

'Well, I may be being a tad pessimistic, but I've a suspicion we've been kidnapped,' I said, aware I might have been stating the obvious, but apparently not.

Tracey wailed at this information, which she clearly hadn't considered properly. Big sobs left her heaving body, forcing her bosoms to move independently of each other, in different directions. I marvelled at the sight, having only ever had marginal movement in my own 34B bust, even when breastfeeding for the few short weeks I managed it with each of my children – apart from Patrick, who had the habit of biting.

'Well there is little point crying, that won't get us anywhere,' I said, while trying to think. I'd already worked out I was probably the only one out of the two of us who might be capable of such a function.

'What about our luggage?' sobbed Tracey? 'I need my make-up and my sleeping pills.'

'Sleeping pills? What do you think you will need those for?' I asked. 'You reckon you can settle down on this infested mattress for a full eight hours?'

Tracey looked around gloomily and acknowledged that the pills weren't maybe as necessary as the make-up.

'I can't let Baz see me like this. He'll never marry me then!'

I suspected he was unlikely to see her in any state at all and had no intention of marrying her, particularly now he'd fleeced her of five thousand pounds. I wouldn't be so stupid as to be conned by any man into believing they were going to marry me.

'Where did he say he'd meet you?' I asked, mainly to make conversation rather than out of any real interest. At that point I'd started to worry how the bloody hell I'd got into such a mess. More importantly, how I was going to get out of it.

'At the airport,' Tracey replied despondently, possibly because she may have finally twigged that particular beau had sailed.

I kept my thoughts about Tracey's stupidity to myself. I could bring them back once I'd found a way out of our predicament.

'Well, maybe he got held up for some reason and is on his way to find you right now,' I said, as I looked around the shabby quarters for anything that might offer a degree of comfort.

It wasn't so much that we needed somewhere to sit and, God forbid, sleep – we had no idea of our fate – but more pressingly I was concerned about toilet requirements. The more I thought about it the more urgent my requirement became, and so in a bid to distract myself I spent the next hour or so trying to move mattresses and blankets into some kind of makeshift bed. It wasn't easy, and after some puzzling I came to the opinion that the only way we would both be able to get any rest at all would be to share sleeping space. The mattresses and blankets were insufficient to make two separate beds, and so I devised a double arrangement where we could share whatever covers were available.

Sharing a bed with Tracey was a prospect that filled me with absolutely no joy, particularly as she had taken to smiling gap-toothed on every occasion she glanced over at me. I'd only ever shared with Colin and Darius (even my children were banned from such sacred space) so the anticipation of potential embarrassment was excruciating.

I just hoped that Tracey, having given in to her fate and sitting cross-legged on the floor in an apparent daze, wasn't the touchy-feely type likely to make physical contact when least expected.

I settled down onto the bedding arrangement and wondered again what we were supposed to do about toilet requirements. My bladder was stretched full to the point of being painful, and my bowels were clenching in the knowledge they needed imminent emptying.

Despite our repeated hollering and shouting through the door of the shack, no one appeared. There'd been no sign of the men who brought us here and no apparent sign of any life at all.

'I really need a pee,' said Tracey, as if reading my thoughts. 'I'm just going to have to go in that bowl,' she said, getting up and staggering her way over to the corner where I'd placed it.

The thought of public ablutions filled me with horror and reminded me of those awful women in the swimming baths who take off their costumes in full view of everyone. It's always the ones with the worst bodies who are prepared to display them: warts, veins, stretch marks and all.

'Oh goodness me, we aren't animals! Can't you wait?' I asked. 'Human rights law states that we must be treated humanely,' I said, reminding Tracey that there were legal procedures in place for every person on the planet. 'Someone will have to come and look after our needs soon,' I added, before wondering if we would see anyone other than each other ever again.

It was too late for any pleas of decency. Tracey had dropped her trousers and knickers and was on her way into the crouching position.

I felt my own need for release increasing as I heard Tracey go about her business, and was horrified to think that I might have to do the same thing if I was to get the relief I so desperately sought.

The thoughts flew from my mind when I looked around to see that Tracey was standing above the bowl, holding her knickers forward and shaking her lower self about in a rigorous fashion.

'No toilet paper,' she grinned, exposing her toothless spike in its full glory. 'So I'll have to drip dry!'

I was completely taken aback. Not only by the actions but the fact that Tracey had no pubic hair, other than what looked like a thin brown line running down the middle of her mound. I found the sight most peculiar and wondered what sort of problem she had that would cause hair loss in that region. Perhaps she had been dying it the same colour as the hair on her head and it all fell out?

Dismissing the vision I made my way over to the corner. What was sauce for the goose, and so on . . .

'Out of the way, I need to go,' I said, contemplating my own genital area which was, in comparison, trimmed to prevent overspill and decidedly grey. At least I'm not bald, I thought as I lowered myself into a crouching position before releasing not only my bladder but a huge stool that splashed loudly into the bowl.

'There's no shaking that off!' laughed Tracey, turning towards the pile of papers that sat neatly on top of the chest.

Tearing off a page from OK! magazine, she walked over to me as I struggled to maintain privacy while wobbling about over the now full bowl.

'Here you are, I use old mags all the time when I forget to buy bog roll. This one's got Kerry Katona on it at her first wedding. Shows how old it is.'

I was mortified. I'd hoped to hang on a bit longer, but nature took its course without so much as a by your leave to my dignity. I cleaned myself as much as I could with the glossy remnants of Ms Katona's nuptials. I couldn't help but pause briefly to note the youthful and misplaced ardour of her husband's face.

Having pulled back my lower clothing as effortlessly as I could under the circumstances, I made my own way to the paper pile, returning to cover the offending bowl with two pages of obituary columns from the *Daily Telegraph*.

I thought this was about as low as I could go, but just as I was feeling myself fall into a pit of despair, the door was unlocked before it flew open and a man dressed in a military guard's uniform marched in with a tray carrying two mugs full of steaming liquid, a bowl of eggs and four oranges.

He was young, about thirty, shorter than the two men from earlier and was wearing full khaki uniform with a massive belt that was too big for him. Where he had pulled it tight around his small waist it had bunched the waistline of his trousers and left a good six inches of belt dangling freely in front. He had a baseball cap that partially covered his eyes, meaning he had to tilt his head up to see in front of him, and red Converse boots, giving away the fact his military status might not be genuine. I thought he looked a little like Darius, but smaller. Much smaller.

'Here – food,' he grunted as he sniffed the air and looked with disdain in the direction of the bowl.

'We need to make arrangements for the toilet and access to a telephone,' I said to him as sternly as I could muster. He looked slightly put out by my assertion, which I thought was a good start. He had a large chain attached to his belt loop which held a key ring, but there was only one key, which I suspected was to our quarters.

'You cannot keep us here and will not keep us here,' I added, moving towards the fake guard with as determined steps as I could, which seemed to unnerve him further. 'Do you understand me?'

I had the advantage at this point, so glared at him, trying to meet his eyes which had been gradually hidden from sight as his oversized baseball cap, featuring a Manchester United Football Club emblem at the front, fell down his face.

'Maybe he don't speak English, hun,' said Tracey, who had tried to move towards the door before the guard kicked it closed with his foot and stood in her path.

I thought that was a touch of the pot calling the kettle black, and then laughed to myself at the irony of my observation. I continued speaking to the guard whose initial attempts at looking in control were slipping with every word.

'Now you must tell me why we're here and when you're going to let us go. We cannot tolerate being here any longer and will report your superiors for false imprisonment,' I demanded in my best magisterial voice.

The guard continued to look around the room, sniffing as he did so until he found the source of his consternation.

Placing the food tray on the floor, the guard walked over to the bowl, removed the paper and, on witnessing the contents, picked it up and carried it with him as he left the room, closing and locking the door behind him.

'I'll be back,' he shouted through the door, leaving us wondering if that could be a good thing.

'Hey, come here now,' I shouted through the door. 'Where's our luggage? And I want to make a phone call.'

'And I want clean knickers, fags and my make-up,' said Tracey who was busy inspecting the contents of the mugs. She sniffed cautiously before taking a large gulp – an act she quickly regretted. 'Yuk, that's disgusting,' she wailed, spitting the contents to the floor. 'It tastes like pig shit.'

Trust Tracey to moan about everything. I was just fed up that the guard had paid no heed to me. Perhaps had he not had to deal with my excrement he might have paid me more respect.

I was hungry, and as I'd no reason to respect my companion's view on cuisine, decided to give the contents of the mug a try. I made a face at the peculiar earthy taste of the concoction, but was determined to show an open-minded appreciation of foreign food, and so continued to drink.

'Well, this is all we've got by the looks of it, so we might as well make the most of it,' I said, as much to convince myself as Tracey, who was sobbing again.

'This is your bloody fault,' said Tracey, as she sniffed and rubbed her arm across her runny nose. 'Why did you make me get in that car?'

I couldn't recall making anyone do anything.

'I thought your boyfriend was going to pick you up. You didn't have to come with me,' I said, thinking her plight could have been worse if she hadn't been with me. I decided to try and keep the peace and find a way out of this mess.

'Whatever's happened we're here now. Let's see what they've given us.'

I've never actually tasted pig shit but did have to concur with Tracey – the flavour was like nothing I'd experienced before. Turning my back on this new culinary experience for a while, I cracked open the shells of the eggs and was delighted to discover they were still warm and not quite hard boiled – just as I liked them, although I was miffed they hadn't bothered to bring us any salt or a teaspoon.

'Come on, eat something, Tracey. You have to keep your strength up. The oranges smell divine,' I added, as I pressed the dimpled flesh to my nose, taking in the fresh, fruitful aroma.

Suitably convinced, Tracey joined me as we devoured the eggs and the oranges before turning our attention again to the mugs of whatever it was we'd been given. Neither of us could decide if it was soup, gruel or something completely alien.

'It's probably a local drink of some kind,' I said in a bid to remain positive. The last thing we needed was to be at each other's throats.

Tracey had settled down a little and had stopped sniffing quite so much. Her nose was bright red while her nostrils shone with untamed snot. Her eyes, still stained from mascara and tear-diluted eyeliner, were swollen and misted. But she seemed, if not cheerful, resigned.

Both of us decided that after our adventures so far, we needed food. In the absence of any alternative we managed to finish the contents of both mugs, silently and with increasing relish as time went on.

'It ain't that bad really,' said Tracey.

We were both silent for a while. We didn't know the time as neither of us had been wearing a watch, and Tracey usually relied on her phone which had been taken.

'I'm cold,' I said, as I noticed the room getting dark. Daylight seemed to disappear quickly.

'Me too, hun,' replied Tracey. 'And I'm a bit shaky.'

My thoughts were untethered and floating around in my head. My legs were weak, and although they felt heavy the rest of me felt incredibly light. I flopped down on the bed and held my hands tightly together for comfort.

'That's a bit strange,' I tried to say but my tongue swelled up with every word.

My mind was full of random ideas, none of which I could grab hold of long enough to articulate, even to myself. I came up with solutions to problems I didn't know existed, and then as quickly forgot them.

'Soup. Is it soup?' I heard myself saying, but thought it was an animal talking to us from the corner of the room. 'Did you see that?'

I pointed to the corner of the shack where I could see a unicorn sitting on a stool, playing the ukulele. My thoughts drifted off again and I was dreaming of chocolate.

I started to laugh and couldn't stop. It was uncontrollable, and the more I laughed the more I thought about chocolate. What I wouldn't do for a Malteser. What I hadn't done for a Malteser.

Tracey had been briefly asleep and my laughing woke her up. That made me laugh even more. So much so that I held on to my sides in case my ribs popped out. My chest could barely hold my breath. I'd never laughed like that before. It was most peculiar.

'See what?' said Tracey. Her eyes were barely open and her pupils were like big black rings. She tried, but failed to rest her weight on her elbows and ended up with her face in the pillow.

My head was scrambled. I tried to focus on my thoughts, but every time I grasped hold of one that made sense another would get in its way. My body could float away to an unknown galaxy at any point and there was nothing I could do about. At one point I was convinced I was actually on a moon – one made of Victoria sponge cake and chestnut macaroons – and rather liked it.

'I wish I had something sweet,' I said to Tracey, as this was a recurring thought I couldn't shake off, despite normally being quite moderate in my calorie intake.

She was still wrestling with her own body weight as she tried to turn over onto her side. After three attempts she propped her face up with a folded arm.

'I've got a Galaxy bar in my bag if only those creeps would bring it back. And my fags. I need a fag. Even a Silk Cut would do,' she said, as she fell into a fit of giggles, soon to be joined by me, for no reason I could work out.

Tracey tried to sit up again and managed to push herself onto her left arm, bringing her right hand across her face to wipe spittle from her mouth. She squealed.

'What the hell?' she cried. 'What's this in my mouth?'

She tugged at the spike that held her absent crown and, for the first time since its loss, wanted to know what had happened.

'Where's my tooth? What's happened to my tooth?'

I thought of the unicorn again, taunting us with Tracey's tooth, and started to roll about with laughter, unable to retain any sense of empathy.

'The tooth, the whole tooth. Nothing butts the tooth!'

'Fuck, fuck, fuck. It'll cost an arm and a leg to get that sorted. Bastards,' said Tracey, as she started to laugh so hard I thought she was going to cough up her lungs. That's what a lifetime of smoking does to you. 'It serves me right for eating too much chocolate and rotting me teeth,' said Tracey. 'Oh, chocolate. Wish I hadn't said that.'

'Me too,' I said, wiping my eyes of tears of laughter.

'I could just eat a family-size bar now,' she added. 'Or a furry rosher.'

'What's a furry rosher?' I asked, feeling the need to know.

'Those chocolates you get at Christmas. With gold paper. Bit like Ryvita covered in Nutella,' Tracey replied.

'Ah, Ferrero Rocher,' I clarified.

'S'what I said, innit?'

'I think we've been drugged,' Tracey added a moment later, before falling back onto the mattress and closing her eyes. 'What is this shit, man? Nothing like I've ever had.'

I drooled, barely able to speak and having to hold onto the floor with both hands for balance, even though I was lying down.

CHAPTER FIFTEEN

I woke abruptly, halfway through a dream where Colin was telling me how stupid I'd been. I was about to get indignant when vague memories, which I'd hoped were part of the dream, started to surface.

I saw one of the men kick the mattress, and when he realised I was already awake, he smiled broadly – revealing a lovely pinkness of the lips that reminded me yet again of Darius.

Tracey was still stirring, making muffled noises like a cow in labour, although I forgave her on the basis that if she felt like me she would be still muddled from the effects of the previous night's drink.

The guard nearly lost his balance trying to negotiate a tray of eggs and oranges, two chipped Coca-Cola glasses filled with water and a bucket, with a lid, which he carried over his right arm. I stifled a laugh.

My dreams had been vivid and multi-coloured, which on recollection might have had something to do with the drugs we'd inadvertently taken. But they didn't add any colour to Colin's personality. Even in my wildest dreams he was still permanently affronted by the way no one, particularly me, seemed to take him seriously enough.

Tracey had said last night she thought there'd been something in our drinks, and I suspect she had an inkling of what it was. She was far more familiar than I with the feelings of disorientation and euphoria, neither of which have been my regular companions. I also remembered the lack of toilet facilities, so thought I should make my feelings known to the guard again. He'd already shown signs of weakening to previous demands, so a bit more work and I reckoned I could crack him.

'Now, unless you want to clear up after us again I suggest you find a way we can use a toilet and a shower,' I barked at him, as I tried to untangle myself from the blankets and Tracey's right leg, which she'd hooked over mine in the night. Thankfully I hadn't noticed at the time. 'We might not be so tidy about where we do it in future.'

The guard looked uncomfortable, particularly after Tracey awoke abruptly, sat up and then smiled at him full on. She'd worked out the sight of her toothless grin might not be as attractive as she'd like, but it did have some power – if only to shock.

I wanted to tackle the drugs issue but thought it might be best to leave it until another time. I needed to quiz Tracey about what she thought we'd been given, although in principle I'd already decided I wasn't entirely against it. My sleep had been unexpectedly marvellous, which considering our circumstances was surprising. Although I was trying to maintain dignity, my anxiety levels were high. We didn't know why we'd been locked up by these people, what they wanted, or indeed if we would get out alive. Maybe all kidnapped people were drugged to ensure they didn't wail through the night, or cause their captors any problems. Thinking about it logically, that made some kind of sense.

'You look kinda cute,' Tracey said to the guard as he placed the tray on the chest and backed towards the door. If he found me scary he was almost apoplectic with terror now he'd seen her spiky grin and wobbly bosom.

'We will arrange for proper facilities,' he said, letting the bucket fall from his arm and onto the floor. 'This will do you for emergencies. I just need to get s-s-someone,' he stuttered, before making a swift exit.

'He'd better mean it. I stink,' said Tracey.

We'd just finished eating our breakfast of slightly runnier eggs and oranges when the guard returned with a larger but similarly aged male, also dressed in the khaki clothes masquerading as a uniform. Both were carrying handcuffs.

'Here,' said the first guard. 'Come with me.'

He came over to me and locked one of the rings of the cuffs over my left wrist. As he did so he smelled very welcoming. I would like to say a manly smell, but it wasn't redolent of Darius, who wore a distinctive aftershave advertised by muscle-bound surfers. It reminded me of something very familiar, which made me feel safe. I also noticed he'd shaved and had decidedly clean fingernails. This was a fact I found surprising.

The second guard, around four inches taller than the first and with noticeably light brown eyes, put the same kind of handcuffs on Tracey, who seemed to be somewhat entertained by the experience.

'This is all a bit *Fifty Shades*, innit?' she said to the new guard, who had a firm chest exposed through his largely unbuttoned shirt. It was hairy but with tight curly black hairs rather than the thatch of untamed grey wire I was used to with Colin.

'You into a bit of S & M, Cynth?'

'What are you talking about? Do you mean M&S?' I said.

Tracey laughed, trying to cover her mouth as she did so, but the weight of the guard's arm cuffed to her wrist prevented her.

'Sadists and stuff. *Fifty Shades of Grey*. Don't tell me you ain't read it. Everyone else has. Rich boy meets hot chick, he ties her up and they shag. No foreplay, as he's so hot she orgasms just by looking at his trousers. That's about it really.'

I was frankly surprised to hear Tracey had read anything and wondered why *'Shades of Grey'* reminded me of her pubic region. I dismissed the thought of no foreplay. It reminded me of Colin.

Before I could think any more about sadists, sex and trousers capable of inducing orgasm, I was tugged out of the shack and along one of the makeshift corridors to what looked like a camper's toilet area within a muddy cave.

There was a wooden bench with a hole cut into it placed over a gap in the stilted floor which I assumed perched over the lagoon area below. To both sides of the caved area were two watering cans filled to overflowing with water, placed next to wooden slatted blocks. Each block had a back scrub and some washing-up liquid on the floor next to them. I noticed one of my towels, which would have been in the luggage they took away from us, was hanging on a hook on the wall. Logic suggested the beach towel hanging on the other side belonged to Tracey and I guessed this was what was going to pass as a bathroom.

'So how are we going to get washed while we're tied up to you?' I asked of my guard, who at least looked a bit embarrassed by what he was showing us. 'This is very improper.'

The guard shrugged and placed his free hand over his eyes as if to suggest he wouldn't be looking. He seemed very sweet, and there was definitely an air of Darius about him – his skin was shiny, his lips pink and his teeth white. I couldn't help but find him attractive, regardless of the underlying terror of the situation.

Desperate to go to the toilet, and keen to avoid the embarrassment of yesterday, I remained calm as he escorted me to the wooden slat where I managed to pee. Tracey's guard followed us over to the bench, which meant she had to follow too. He wasn't as gentlemanly as mine, and didn't bother to avert his eyes while she loudly and fully carried out her evacuations.

'No ruddy paper,' she shouted out to anyone who would listen.

The fact the guard fixed his gaze on her throughout didn't seem to bother Tracey, and as I considered how I was best going to get myself washed, Tracey had stripped to her knickers, having thrown her clothing to one side, and was busy pouring water over her naked body, sluicing under her arms with cupped hands as she caught the flowing water.

'Get in there,' she growled as she rubbed away at bits of her body, including between her buttocks.

Her guard was captivated, which appeared to be Tracey's intention. She was swaying her body around as she sang 'Sex on Fire', occasionally moving provocatively towards her captor.

'What's yer name, babe?' she said, thrusting her hips towards him as she rubbed her hands down into her knicker area, highlighting again the pencil line strip of pubic hair.

Her guard looked nervous. He turned away to look for reassurance from his colleague, who I'd noticed was being very deliberate in keeping his eyes averted from my own body. I was topless, but had turned away from any potential audience so all they could see was my shoulder blades.

'Come on, don't tease. You know you wannit,' continued Tracey.

'Stop,' said her guard. 'I have girlfriend. We get married. Soon.'

Tracey snorted.

'Me too, babe. But all the time I'm here I ain't gonna find me man, am I? So wise up and give a girl a thrill,' she said, spilling more of the water over her breasts, causing her nipples to harden.

I overheard the guard saying something in what I assumed to be a Nigerian dialect under his breath and trying to make the sign of the cross on his chest, but his tethering to Tracey meant he looked like a badly operated puppet.

Wanting to say something to calm the situation, I turned round absent-mindedly before realising I'd given my guard a full-frontal view of my naked body. He couldn't help but look at me and I was quite delighted to note he didn't seem disgusted.

'You have beautiful breasts,' he said, lifting his hand slowly to touch one of them.

At first I was shocked but was pleased he'd noticed I'd kept myself in good shape. All those years of thrice-weekly swimming sessions, coupled with regular Pilates evening classes, had done their trick.

I did think it would be appropriate to have some kind of conversation before I could get to the point of allowing this physical familiarity.

'But I don't even know your name. This is highly irregular,' I said, thinking how bizarre my life had become in a relatively short space of time. I wondered what Colin would think of this new-found Cynthia. I also wondered if it was possible to turn into a sex maniac at the age of sixty.

'I'm Gowon,' he muttered, bringing his hand to rest around my nipple.

'How do you spell that?' I asked him, as it sounded like 'go on', which I very much wanted him to do.

Far from being scared or angry, I found the delicate touch of this young man's fingers very sensual and figured I might as well make the most of it.

My abdomen clenched with arousal and the attention Gowon was giving me was being welcomed by my skin, which he caressed with soft and expertly manicured hands. I looked over to the other side of the room to make sure we weren't being watched. It's one thing to get up to no good but quite another to do so in front of an audience.

Tracey was engrossed with her latest victim, teasing and tempting him in every way she thought she knew how, as she went about washing her voluminous body. It didn't look like she was having much success, as the guard flinched with every one of her movements. But it was keeping them occupied.

'I will bring more clothing for you,' said Gowon, pressing his body against mine so I could feel his hardness pressing against my hip. The strange tingling could have been the recurrence of the groin injury, but I was sure the throbbing came from Gowon, not me.

'You're a sexy mother,' he said.

The reference to parenthood gave me a moment of guilt which I soon abandoned as I heard a squeal from Tracey and then a thump. As I looked round I saw the other guard was kneeling on the floor, his arm in the air where it was attached to her via the handcuff.

'Dirty pervert, tried to touch my tits,' she said, swinging round to look at me, giving the impression that if butter did melt in her mouth, she'd swallow it.

She'd whacked him one and his nose was bleeding.

'I really don't think that's the way to get what you want,' I said to her, looking back to Gowon whose erection was still very evident, should one be bothered to look. 'You'll get yourself into trouble if you're not careful. You were leading him on,' I said, basking in the warm glow of knowing I still had plenty of life in me, for an old girl.

'She a beetch. Silly beetch,' said Tracey's guard. He was holding his nose with one hand while the other was swinging about, being attached to Tracey's every erratic and infuriated movement as she dressed herself.

She tried to manipulate her bosoms into her bra by shaking them vigorously, while bending forward to shackle them in place – which had her guard bending down as well, making him look as if he was bowing to an invisible crowd in front of him. She'd undone her hair from the ghastly daisy-clad band and was flicking it around as poodles do when wet, with droplets of water flying through the air and mostly onto the guard's face. When he wasn't bowing he was blinking, at the same time as attempting to stem his nosebleed.

'Come with me,' said Gowon, wrapping me in my towel. He was clearly uninterested in what was happening on the other side of the room. 'I fetch you clothes.'

He led me back to another shack some distance from the one Tracey and I had been incarcerated in. It wasn't much better than ours, other than it had a small TV in a corner, proper beds with clean bedding and a portable gas stove, no doubt used for boiling our eggs. What I did notice was my suitcase, which had obviously been rifled through for anything of any value. It was then I knew what Gowon smelled of, as the evidence was straight in front of me.

I'd worn Chanel N°5 since Colin bought it as a wedding day gift. He continued to buy it due to not having the imagination to think of anything else more original. Gowon had been using it, with what I admitted were quite powerful results. I'd been lured into a sense of safety by my own perfume!

He sorted out a pile of clothes, which he passed over just as the other guard came tumbling in, holding his nose with both hands. I couldn't see Tracey but I soon got the impression he wasn't prepared to have any more to do with her than necessary.

'That woman hit me!' he said, clearly wounded on more than a physical level. 'She's mad!'

I glanced up at Gowon, who was looking admiringly at me. He was probably glad to have got the sane one of the two of us to deal with. I was staying sane amidst the horror of the situation mainly because I was rather thrilled to confirm my allure to younger men, even if this one had taken me hostage. He could do what he liked, within reason.

The other guard threw Tracey's belongings out of her cases and handbag. I could see they'd gone through all our paperwork, which had been spread across one of the beds. They'd also smoked some of Tracey's cigarettes, as the ends were stubbed out on a plate next to a pile of eggshells. It seemed that even the guards were on a limited diet.

Maybe I should teach them how to make an omelette, I thought.

'Could my friend have some clothes as well, please?' I asked Tracey's guard, as Gowon piled my clothes into my arms. He sucked his teeth and held his head in his hands, occasionally swiping his wrist past his nose, which was still bleeding.

Gowon went to Tracey's case and pulled out a pile of clothing, most of which looked like very small knickers. He placed them all on top of my own pile, which was far more suited to foreign travel, although perhaps not ideal for living in a shack as a prisoner.

As he led me back, still locked into the handcuffs, men could be heard in the direction of the canal. They were talking animatedly but I couldn't work out what they were saying. I tried to turn round to catch sight or sound of them but Gowon increased his speed to get me out of the way as quickly as possible.

Once we got to the shack he pushed himself against me while unlocking the door. It wasn't an unpleasant experience and I smiled at him. As I did, I thought I could see him blush, although it was difficult to tell beneath the dark skin.

'See you later,' he said as he unlocked the handcuffs, closed the door behind him and blew me a kiss. My insides turned excitedly at the gesture.

Tracey sat with her hair in a big mess on top of her head, wrapped in her towel and holding her dirty clothes.

'What was that all about?' I asked her, as I placed my clean clothes in a pile on the chest and put her items on the chair. 'Hitting the guards isn't a very good idea. Not if we want to get out of here.'

'Well, flirting in the shower isn't the best trick either,' replied

Tracey as she flicked her hair around with no apparent result.

I stopped briefly in my tracks towards the chair. I didn't want someone like her judging me on my social etiquette.

'I'm just trying to get him onside,' I answered, climbing into my clean clothes and hoping my tone gave the impression of someone trying to save themselves in dire circumstances, rather than that of a woman with very loose morals. 'If we have any chance of getting out of here we need a friend. I don't reckon any of yours are going to turn up, after all.'

The sound of the men could be heard again. They were talking loudly, and this time and I recognised what I thought was Chike's voice saying that something had to be done.

'We need to use the details. We can't keep them here for ever,' his deep Nigerian accent lilted.

As the voices got nearer we heard the door's padlock turn and the two men, followed by Gowon, came into the shack.

'Ladies!' smiled Chike, looking more menacing than friendly. 'Well, what have we to do with you?' he said, looking at each of us in turn. His smile turned to a snarl and he walked around the shack as Fasina sat on the one seat and Gowon stood by the door.

'We need to get you out of here but that is going to cost someone some money. So let's hope your families care enough to pay up. Then you will be free to go,' said Chike, smiling again.

He walked very close to me and placed his face in front of mine.

'And if they don't care . . . we'll have to find other ways to get what we want.'

Tracey looked shocked. Although she'd understood we'd been kidnapped she didn't understand the concept of ransom. I also suspected she'd have to think hard about whether there was anyone who'd be prepared to pay for her release. I couldn't imagine there was anyone at home relying heavily on her input for their survival – emotional, physical or otherwise.

I knew, on the other hand, I'd be released as soon as Darius found out what had happened to me. He would, of course, be waiting at the Western Union bank and he'd speak to these people, his people, and all would be sorted out.

'Well I'm sure that won't be necessary,' I said as I tried to make eye contact with Gowon who had been staring at the floor since he had come in. 'I think you will find everything can easily be sorted out.'

Chike smiled and did a little hopscotch skip across the room, nearly falling into Gowon as he caught his right foot behind his left leg.

'I very much hope so, my dear ladies. Time is money and we have plenty of time.'

As the three men left the room Tracey and I remained silent as we took in the implications of our kidnap. For the first time since we arrived I felt out of control – like my life was hurtling towards a precipice. I knew I needed to remain calm, but worry was biting at my heels like a snappy dog.

'What do you think is going to happen to us?' said Tracey. 'What if they don't get what they want and decide to kill us?'

Her words opened up a flower of possibility I hadn't considered in any depth. I addressed the rising panic by focusing on my breathing, an act that reminded me of childbirth. I thought of my family and what they would, or wouldn't, be willing to do to rescue me.

'Let's hope someone knows what's going on,' I said. 'Or we could be here for a very long time.'

CHAPTER SIXTEEN

We'd been kidnapped for five days, and each day had passed much as the other, but this one felt heavier than the last. I couldn't decide if it was because of an accumulation of drugs or whether the novelty of staying in the shack was wearing very thin.

Both of us had had time to think. Tracey mainly about the state of her hair and nails, and whether she'd qualify to go on *Big Brother* after our ordeal.

'It's much the same as being here,' she said, attempting to educate me about a reality television programme that sounded about as entertaining as watching paint dry.

I, on the other hand, had time to reflect on my lovely middle-class life, and wondered why I'd done nothing of any note with it. I could have had a career, written a book, learned Spanish or completed a marathon. I also thought that through my own force of will and personality I could chart my own path through life. Having been pulled dramatically off the course I thought I was taking, I was aware of the fine line between my comfortable life and what could become a living hell. If I'd learned anything it was to accept this adversity with dignity.

None of the days could be described as my ideal but no one could say we'd been particularly badly treated or abused in any way, although I was getting tired of the state of limbo – and the conversation, which would always be limited with only one other person to converse with. I could have been persuaded to watch *Loose Women* or start making my own greetings cards, I was that bored.

We were woken up by the delivery of the usual fare of eggs and fruit. My clothes were feeling very loose, and Tracey looked like her face was about to slide off from lack of nourishment, suggesting we'd both lost a fair amount of weight.

'I'm getting really pissed off with this now,' she said. 'Why doesn't someone come and find us?'

I sensed Tracey was suffering anxiety of her own. She'd expressed feelings of denial, sure we would be rescued at any moment, followed by thoughts of murder, torture or being locked up for decades with no one knowing where we were. I'd had my own concerns about all of those things but decided not to voice them to my fragile companion. Out of the two of us, I was the one to be relied on in a crisis.

'We won't be here for ever. There's no point in them keeping us much longer,' I said. 'We're no use to them other than as a bargaining tool for cash.'

Tracey lifted her jowls up on either side of her face as if checking whether a facelift might be necessary. I was glad we didn't have a mirror in the room.

'What if they decide to torture us?' she said.

The thought had crossed my mind but I decided it was unlikely. They'd shown no real signs of aggression and didn't appear to have weapons. The very fact we were imprisoned had an implied threat, but what would they do? Shoot us and throw our bodies in the water to be eaten by the fish they pull out to eat? That wouldn't achieve their goals. Although I thought it unlikely, I also recognised I was avoiding the issue and allowing hope to override any such possibilities.

'They are looking after us to some degree,' I said. 'They wouldn't be feeding us and keeping us clean if they didn't care about our welfare.'

'They ain't keeping us clean. Cold water and no bloody bog roll. I just want a nice hot shower and some smoothing serum for my hair,' said Tracey.

I said I doubted they'd be able to offer either of those at the moment, but maybe we could ask. We needed to keep up our spirits and a positive atmosphere, and the hope of any improvement in our conditions could help greatly towards that.

I peeled open one of the eggs and bit the glistening white top off it, revealing the sticky orange yolk beneath. If I had to eat just one thing over and over again to prevent starvation then egg was probably the best option.

'It's not my obvious choice of diet but it seems to be working. We both look like filleted anchovies,' I said.

Tracey flicked her hair about to get it away from her eyes.

'Eh?'

'I think we've lost weight,' I said, partly to distract her from melancholy. Any focus on her would do that.

Tracey looked pleased.

'You reckon? Hope I don't lose it off me tits.'

'Well it wouldn't hurt if you did. You've plenty to go round,' I said.

Tracey laughed. 'Certainly more than you have, that's for sure.'

I felt like telling her that Gowon thought my breasts to be particularly beautiful, but as she likes to steal the sexual thunder I thought that might give her the competitive opportunity she thrived on. I didn't want her as an enemy.

When it came to washroom time, Tracey's guard was conspicuous by his absence. Perhaps he'd been frightened off by her right hook.

'I will take you both today,' said Gowon, handcuffing Tracey but letting my hand remain free. I hoped his statement wasn't meant quite as it sounded. He might not be the man I wanted to spend the rest of my life with, but I'd no intention of sharing him, particularly with Tracey.

We got to the other shack and he attached her to one of the struts against the wall.

'Why ain't you letting me go too?' said Tracey, pulling at the handcuff until it rattled the walls. 'That ain't bleedin' fair. What's she got I ain't?'

I wanted to tell her 'pert breasts and a personality to match' but that was just being childish, so shrugged at her as if I'd no idea.

'Please let her go. She won't do anything silly,' I said, thinking that everything she did had a tendency towards silliness.

Gowon went over to her side of the wash area, took off her handcuff and pulled across a makeshift curtain.

'Stay there and don't go anywhere. If you do I will not trust you again,' he said, walking away to leave her to wash.

'Cheers, mate,' I could hear from behind the screen.

By this time I was sluicing myself with water from the can, which I noted had been warmed, although the heat during the day was almost suffocating. Gowon handed me my own shower gel and shampoo, which he must have retrieved from my case. He gave it to me as if giving me a present, but I tried not to be cross with the gesture of handing me my own goods. He didn't have to do that, I suppose, so I was grateful for such tiny home comforts. The smell of the gel reminded me of my bathroom at home and I wondered if anyone had thought to go and water my plants.

Tracey was singing 'Somewhere over the Rainbow' on the other side of the shack and I could hear the slapping of her flesh as she washed, an activity that seemed to be occupying all of her energy.

I felt free to allow Gowon to move his hand around my body as he wanted to. It reminded me of Darius and how he'd thrill my senses with his large, capable hands. He didn't have a huge amount in common with him, other than the colour of his skin and country of birth, but they did both have clean fingernails. There's something about that level of hygiene in a man that's very attractive.

'What is it you do to me, Cynthia?' said Gowon as he reached down into my knickers, where he caressed the tops of my thighs, prising them apart with a tightened fist. He rubbed gently, moving more slowly each time towards an ache which had been developing since his first touch. He spent some time using the middle finger of his right hand to excite me and I was conscious of his cleanliness in that department. I may not have been so willing had he shown signs of grubbiness. When I thought I was going to have to beg, he slipped his finger inside me, moving it rigorously up and down until I felt my knees buckle with pleasure. I could see his erection beneath his combat trousers but decided to do nothing about it – and he didn't seem to expect anything.

Strangely satisfied and wondering why imprisonment and potential jeopardy excited me, I allowed him to dry me with my own towel before I got dressed.

'Thank you very much,' I said, and I think I meant it.

Tracey emerged from her private area and Gowon snapped back into professional mode. Instead of leading us back to our own shack he told us to get dressed and then walked us to the front of the settlement.

'Hey, where are you taking us, big boy?' said Tracey, doing the usual thing with her wet hair.

'The boss man wants to see you,' he answered, before leading us to the guards' shack.

'Good morning, my ladies,' greeted Chike, who was lounging in a large armchair and watching a small television screen that was playing cartoons. 'How are you today?'

'Fine, thank you very much,' I answered, 'Although we'd really like to know when we're going to be released.'

'Ha ha!' said Chike. 'That is the twenty-million-dollar question! You might as well ask me how many mobile phones are in the sea or whether Jesus had bunions. You are very funny!'

He stood up quickly and banged his fist on what passed for a table in front of him. It was actually a door balanced on two cut-down oil drums and wasn't secure – so the contents of his mug went flying across his side of the room, adding to the stains on the front of his combat trousers. He kicked the mug away as he walked round the shack.

'Your people are very slow. They do not understand they need to pay us, and if they don't you won't be singing songs to your grandchildren!'

Just as I was thinking that I've never been moved to sing a song to anyone, let alone my grandchildren, Tracey started to sob again. In the background the TV was blaring out *What's Up, Doc?* which seemed appropriate, bearing in mind her clear need for some medical assistance for her hormone imbalance.

'What is it you want from us?' she said, having missed the obvious.

'Your friends and family need to pay us what we have asked and you will be free to leave,' added Chike, smiling his snarly smile.

He moved across the room and stared into Tracey's eyes while inching his body closer to her.

'Personal space, if you don't mind, mate. Get any closer and I'll be brushing your teeth with me tongue,' she said.

'I am not interested in you,' he said, spitting as he spoke. 'You have nothing for me. Yet.'

Then he moved to me.

'You have an interesting family. I think you could be of much more use. Tell me about them.'

I spotted beads of sweat forming on his brow and wondered how confident Chike was about getting what he wanted. I didn't know what to say for fear of putting my children and grandchildren in jeopardy, but then I couldn't see how I would do that just by giving these people basic information.

'I have four grown-up children and a number of grandchildren, boys and girls. The oldest is eighteen and the youngest is five.'

I couldn't calculate quickly enough how many there were exactly, so I just hoped he didn't ask for any more detail.

Chike wasn't listening. He was removing a cigarette from a packet that Tracey recognised as hers.

'Help yourself, why don't you?' she said to him, shutting up after he handed her his lighted one and got another for himself. She took a deep drag and coughed.

'Tom is your grandson, I believe?'

How on earth does he know that? I thought.

'And you have a friend called Bob and another called Darius,' added Chike, looking menacingly at me. 'You bank with NatWest and live in Surrey, England.'

I felt like I was going to be sick, but as his words sank in my hopes rose. *Darius must know where we are.*

'They need to hurry up with our fees for your release. They have three more days,' he said.

Tracey's mouth fell open.

'And then what?' she asked.

Chike laughed at her.

'What do you think, my little yellow-haired friend? We have tea and talk nicely about books we have read or the politics of Africa? Maybe I could take you out for a nice dinner?'

'You're not my type,' said Tracey, taking another puff on her cigarette before throwing the stub onto the floor, where Gowon crushed its life out.

'I'm sure they're doing everything possible,' I said to Chike as calmly as I was able, which wasn't easy as my legs had turned weaker than a new born foal's and I felt I could drop to the floor at any moment. 'My family will know what to do. They are very reliable and can be trusted to do the right thing.' *Usually.*

'They had better be, Mrs Cynthia Hartworth. We're relying on them for our future and you are relying on them for yours. Let's hope they are intelligent people who know what they have to do.'

Tracey looked over at me and was as white as a sheet. I couldn't work out if it was shock or the effects of the nicotine, the first she'd had for some time.

'They'll all be dealing with it professionally and properly,' I said, hoping against hope that was true. I got the impression Chike was getting impatient, and although he hadn't made any direct threats I wondered what his plans were in the event he didn't get what he'd demanded. Would he get frustrated and take it out on us? I didn't like the thought of what he might do and tried to prevent my mind playing out my untimely demise in full Technicolor. I'd heard of hostages being beheaded or shot, and wondered how much it would hurt. I visualised a bloody end and dismissed the vision as nothing more than panic. I couldn't allow myself to think of such things.

'You say you've been in touch with my family, and they'll be doing everything in their power to secure my safe release,' I added, wondering if I needed to cross my fingers.

I knew Darius would come to find me but couldn't work out how these people knew about Tom or why they would want to contact Bob, who I hadn't seen in goodness knows how many years. Bob might have been keen for a meeting, but I didn't think he'd be quite so committed if asked to cough up his life savings for my release. It would be an interesting test of his intentions, however.

'What fees have you asked for?' I asked, but didn't get a reply. I hoped they were reasonable and could be met from the funds I was expecting from Darius.

Chike slumped heavily back into his chair and turned the volume up on the television, indicating our meeting was over. Tracey's cigarette had caused a major coughing fit. Her eyes were watering and she was still sniffing from her previous sobbing, so Gowon handed her a paper handkerchief. I noticed the distinctive National Trust print on the packet, which gave away the fact it had been liberated from my handbag, wherever that was.

'I'll take you back,' Gowon said quietly.

Once we were on our own I processed the information we'd just been given; I couldn't understand it, although I was confident that we weren't going to be in captivity for very much longer. These people had been in touch with my family, so it was only a matter of time before something happened to finish this entire episode. Tracey wasn't so sure.

'They're just messing with your head. They probably looked you up on Google or something and got details of your family,' she said.

'That doesn't explain how they found out about Bob, who I have only been in touch with a couple of times by email – or my grandson. He's not even on the electoral list yet so he doesn't exist,' I said, more to myself than her. 'But if they know about Darius, he must know about us and where we are,' I added.

'Let's bloody hope so,' said Tracey.

Some hours later, as the night drew in, we could hear shouting and car doors banging. We couldn't see if people were coming or going, but guessed by the increasing volume from our captors' shack that the numbers were increasing. We hadn't been given any supper and both of us were hungry, which is what made Tracey a bit tetchy.

We both tried to look out of any gaps in our shack walls to see what was going on but other than the occasional flash of light when car doors were opened and closed there was nothing to be seen that gave any clues to the activity.

We'd just about given up on getting any food when Gowon brought us the usual round of eggs and our night cap, which we were grateful for. He also pulled out a packet of pine nuts from his pocket and placed them in front of me.

'A present from my brother, he brought them to me today. They are for you,' he said.

'That is very kind,' I said, and wondered if I could extract any further favours.

'We do appreciate your help as it gets very dull trying to pass the days in here,' I said to him. 'It would be really good to have some newspapers or more magazines, and I'm sure you're the man who can get them for us.'

Gowon visibly swelled with the compliment and I felt sure he'd do what he could to help us, particularly after he blew me a kiss on his way out of the shack.

'Leave it with me,' he said.

The nuts made a change, and although Tracey complained they were getting stuck on the metal pin that used to be a tooth, she was happy enough to share them with me.

'He's a bit young for you, ain't he?' Tracey said after another game of 'pin the tail on the donkey' which we'd fashioned using one of Tracey's earrings and a picture of David Beckham, torn from OK! magazine.

'That would be a matter of opinion,' I replied. The washing rituals had become more exciting as time went on. Gowon seemed to want little in terms of his own physical satisfaction, and was a gentleman in the truest sense of the word. I suspected he'd been brought up around women or animals, as he had a definite nurturing side. It might even be a Nigerian thing, as Darius was equally as attentive, unless I was comparing all men to Colin, whose knowledge of female anatomy was limited to scratching around my genitals with warty hands and a definite sense of impatience.

Even though it took enforced captivity to produce a peculiar and unplanned physical relationship with yet another young Nigerian, I admitted to quite liking the activity, although I was getting concerned about how I was going to get out of the place. There was only so much fascination dalliances with a stranger could provide when faced with a lifetime of incarceration, or worse.

In the meantime it made sense to welcome the sexually charged distraction, as life stuck in an African hut with a woman with negligible conversation and an increasingly bad mood brought on by enforced nicotine withdrawal, was beginning to pall.

'You're a good-looking woman 'n' all that, but I don't get what he'd see in yer,' said Tracey. 'You'd think he'd go for someone a bit younger?' she added.

Her comments suggested a little bit of jealousy so I ignored them and the ensuing frostiness they brought to our quarters. While I felt like telling her men usually preferred something with a bit of mystery rather than a 'what you see is what you get' approach, I knew we needed to work together, firstly to stay sane while in captivity, and secondly to get out alive. Not only that, she was only nine years younger than me so it wouldn't be long before the diamond birthday would hit her like a jack out of its box.

'Perhaps I remind him of his mother,' I said, laughing to myself that he was probably the child of a massive great African woman with a shelf for a bottom and big white tombstone teeth.

'Yeah, that could be it,' said Tracey, as she stuck her earring into David's eye.

CHAPTER SEVENTEEN

If Tom, Darius and Bob had all been contacted by this gang, how come they found no one to connect with Tracey, not even her so called fiancé who had disappeared off the face of the earth, I wondered?

I questioned if he really did exist and what her background was. There are few people who have so little contact with their relatives they can't be found in emergencies.

'So how did you meet him?' I asked one morning, during a moment when I thought our various predictions of our destiny could spiral into madness. I was fairly confident Darius would find us soon but Tracey's view was that Africans are cannibals and our captors were just waiting for a few onions and a big enough pot to make us into stew.

Making conversation could be hard work, bearing in mind the limitations of my fellow prisoner's interests, which were restricted to a few subjects, mainly clubbing, the size of her widescreen plasma television and how many men she'd been on a date with who she later found out were married. I would surprise myself at the topics I could drag up to discuss with someone who probably had no idea about how to make a béchamel sauce.

'On the internet,' sniffed Tracey. 'PlentyOfFish.'

I was confused. All we'd eaten since our arrival had been boiled eggs of varying degrees of hardness and some fruit.

'We haven't had any fish,' I said.

Tracey screeched with laughter, forgetting the gap from the loss of her false tooth.

'No, silly. It's the name of a dating site. It's like, more fish in the sea. PlentyOfFish,' she giggled in her throaty fashion. 'We got on really well from the first message. He likes loads I like. Even techno and trance, and he thinks I'm well fit.'

I held back the immediate comments I had about grammar and decided to avoid any questions about the meaning of 'techno and trance'. I suspected they were both something to do with drugs.

'I met Bob online,' I threw into the conversation by way of association. I didn't want to feel totally left out in terms of my willingness to grasp some concepts of the modern world.

I desperately wanted to talk to someone about Darius. He filled my waking moments, and some of my sleeping ones, and my awakened sexuality was as strung out as a politician's speech.

'Hey, go Cynthia, high five!' said Tracey, holding her right hand up in the air. I ignored the gesture, mainly because I didn't really know what to do and suspected the whole process was a bit vulgar.

Tracey let her hand drop. 'You're supposed to hit my hand with yours. High five, geddit?'

I didn't get it and so continued with the interrogation. Her story was fascinating in the same way as watching a car crash. You just can't help wanting to know more – and whether or not anyone dies.

'So when did he ask you to marry him?'

Tracey looked up towards me, and as her face became partially shadowed by the light from the unshaded bulb hanging from the ceiling, I could see dark circles under her eyes and sagginess in her cheeks only a lifetime of nutritional deprivation can produce.

'Three weeks ago. He told me to come here as he has family business, and then we'll get married at home,' she replied.

She told me she'd had a daughter when she was eighteen, but rarely saw her as she'd married some 'posh git' as Tracey called him. I gathered the son-in-law didn't approve of her, so she was banned from visiting the house. Tracey had tried to keep in contact but her daughter got busier and Tracey found repeated rejection too hard. She didn't express it like that, but I understood what she was saying; sometimes it's easier to take yourself away from the firing line, particularly with families.

Tracey went on: 'That's why he needed the dosh. So he can sort out stuff here and then come back with me for the wedding. He can't just walk out on his family.'

I was sympathetic to Tracey's feelings, considering how I'd reacted upon hearing of Darius's predicament.

The door opened and I assumed it was going to be Gowon, but instead Chike walked in, carrying a small plastic bag.

'Morning, my ladies,' he said, grinning widely. 'I have a very important question for you.'

He spun around and then sat down on the one and only chair, while Tracey and I remained sitting on the mattress. Chike rummaged about in the bag and pulled out a mesh canvas, some woollen yarns and a selection of needles.

'How am I supposed to finish this?' he shouted, throwing everything on the floor.

He held his head in his hands and started to cry, which I found most disturbing. I went over to the pile of material and sorted through it. There were two needlepoint patterns. One called 'Baa, Baa, Black Sheep' and the other 'Groovy Frog'. They'd both been partially completed.

'I think you need some black yarn,' I said to him, not quite sure how to attend to the requirements of a frustrated needle-pointer.

'It isn't just the yarn. They sent me no finishing materials. You can't trust the internet!' he said again, sobbing.

Tracey was stunned. She looked between me and Chike and back again, rolling her right index finger round her temple to indicate she thought he was mad. I suspected the same but felt it necessary to humour him. He had the key to our shack, after all.

'Well, let's see what we can do,' I said.

Chike lifted his head and stuck his bottom lip out and sighed.

I picked up one of the needles and threaded it with a dark brown yarn which could pass for black and started to stitch some of the sheep onto one of the canvasses. Chike watched like a small child, occasionally breathing in very deeply as one does when emotionally distraught. After I'd done an outline of one of the sheep I handed it back to him.

'Look, you can finish the sheep in brown and it will look just as good. Then you can frame it with some wood. It will be fine.'

Chike put everything back in his bag, stood up and walked across the shack. As he was walking through the door to leave he turned and pointed to Tracey.

'You. Bad girl.'

'What does he mean by that?' she asked. 'And what was all that about?'

I couldn't answer, as I was as taken aback as Tracey. I showed her the needle I'd managed to keep from Chike's sewing kit. It was the largest there, and I wasn't sure how I could use it, but it was something.

'What yer going do, stab Gowon with it?' she asked, half laughing and making her way over to the bucket which had now become our water closet. We'd even managed to hitch up a bit of bedding to allow some privacy.

Shouting from behind the sheet she said: 'I wonder what he'll come up with next? Maybe he does ballet and owns a My Little Pony, too.'

I thought back to Jonjo, who'd always shown a pronounced feminine side, displaying interest in Barbie dolls and making fairy cakes at an early age. Both activities were discouraged by his father.

'He might just find needlepoint relaxing,' I suggested, not really convinced by my own argument.

'Perhaps his mum wanted a girl,' said Tracey as she reappeared. 'Or he's a poof.'

We talked a little more before she brought the conversation back to Baz and how he was just what she was looking for. I mentally agreed that he had a pulse and no understanding of the British class system, which would both be advantages.

'So, what you looking for in a man?' she asked.

'I'm not looking for anything. I was married for nearly forty years and that was enough,' I replied, and then moved away from discussions about meeting men and instead cobbled together a story about working with management consultants on an education project involving Nigerian children.

I struggled to recall some of the information Darius had given me about schools and teaching in his home country, a topic he felt passionate about and would often discuss with me during our meetings. I wasn't particularly interested, especially if it delayed the onset of physical activity, but one thing I did remember was that he'd been sent to a private college and had ended up taking his degree at the California Institute of Technology. He got interested in computer science when it was introduced to his syllabus early on in his school career.

I'd been surprised at the level of education available across the whole country, considering how many people still lived in conditions of poverty. I'd taken note of the subjects he'd learned – English being another important part of all Nigerians' education – and the importance his family placed on that learning. The name Loyola Jesuit College in Abuja came to mind more clearly than I expected, so I used this in passing to add credibility to my story about working with top business people to bring high-quality teaching to the Third World.

'We're working with the best minds available to help bring the standards of education to where they should be, particularly for women,' I said, feeling that I sounded very knowledgeable.

I'd added the last bit of information more for effect than out of any real desire to promote a leaning towards equality, but as Tracey hadn't acknowledged any of the references, only occasionally nodding to indicate that she was listening, I didn't think she'd notice.

However her response took me by surprise. She started to move animatedly as she had registered what I said.

'Women go to school in Nigeria,' Tracey stated with confidence. 'Baz's mum got a degree, so they must do.'

My mind whirred with a vague feeling that I ought to find some connection with this latest remark but I was too busy feeling relieved. My tale had been convincing enough that I didn't have to divulge any of my personal secrets.

'That's interesting,' I said to Tracey, concealing the fact I thought anyone who was associated with her was unlikely to have a degree. Anything beyond a couple of CSEs in Drawing and Woodwork would be a stretch.

'Yeah, he was going on about it when we were on holiday. He thinks all women should get exams and that, so they can work and earn good money.'

I bet he does, I thought. What more would a con man want than a besotted woman with great earning power? But at the same time it was a sentiment I wished my father had encouraged when I was younger; then I might have been able to do something interesting with the last forty years of my life, instead of giving up all my time and energy to convention and conformity. Family life is great, but once it's all over the nest can feel very empty. It would be good to have another identity apart from wife, mother, grandmother. Prime minister, doctor, professor. Even plain old Mrs Hartworth would do if it was followed by some kind of explanation of my worth.

Despite my private thoughts about our differences, which I concluded were very numerous, it was good to have someone fairly manageable as company. It had occurred to me once or twice that it could've been worse and I could be stuck with Mavis, or that awful woman from the Advanced Driving course. At least Tracey didn't have a clue how to argue with me, which was comforting. The whole situation could have been so different if I'd to mentally parry my way round the confines of an African hut with a bigoted old bat from the bridge club. Things weren't too bad considering the two of us had no idea why we were captured, who by and what they wanted.

The other contributory factor in our ability to remain calm and congenial was the nightly herbal drink which had the very welcome effect of allowing time to pass pleasurably, often with some hilarity brought on for no apparent reason, followed by deep sleep. I decided we should be grateful for the wide availability of drugs in this country, otherwise neither of us would get any respite.

'Well if you are to get married we must get you out of here,' I said.

Problems are just challenges, as Colin used to say, and so we needed to find a way to get out of this shack. I just had to convince Tracey to follow my plans and then we could make an escape. An idea was beginning to develop.

'And I think I know how to do it.'

'Really?' said Tracey, looking up from where she was sitting cross-legged on the mattress. She'd been picking the remaining varnish from her thumbnail, leaving a small mountain of purple dust on her very grubby white leggings.

'Well it might take a bit of work but there is method in my madness,' I added, aiming to appeal to Tracey's determination.

She sighed and looked despondent. I'd expected this, but now I was sure she wasn't someone who coped well with challenges – and if she did they probably defeated her.

As if confirming my concern, Tracey said, 'I've no idea how you think we're going to get out. We've tried getting through the door. We're locked in and I don't know how we are going to escape unless we drug the guards.'

'Well, there is that,' I said, adding some further ammunition to the plan I was brewing up, loosely, in my head. 'But I think we both have something we can use in our bid for freedom,' I added.

I paced around the room as the plan took on its own life. I looked through the spyhole in the door, where I saw our captors handing round what looked like a cider jar, each swigging from it in turns.

'Gowon is young and has a clear interest in me,' I said, rejoicing in the continued pleasure I found in my latent sexual awakening. After so many years in the desert of desire it was an expected bonus to have experienced not one, but two dalliances, and both with younger men. Who also happened to be black.

'If he considers me with enough interest then it could help us get out of here,' I said, smiling to myself as I thought of the latest washroom escapade involving a banana – which had been served up a few hours later with our evening eggs.

Tracey pressed her lips firmly together, a habit that had formed over the past few days because of the tooth incident, and frowned before replying.

'Well I think I look pretty good for fifty-one,' she muttered, which seemed a rather inconsequential comment at the time but made me think. I wasn't so sure 'good' was a description I would use for Tracey. She might not look like a normal fifty-one-year-old, but did look remarkably like one of the grandmothers from that dreadful programme, *Big Fat Gypsy Wedding*. I only saw it the once when I couldn't find the remote control and was astounded at how people of a certain age were dressed. But they are travellers, so I suppose they don't get to buy many good clothes as they wouldn't have anywhere to keep them.

I didn't tell Tracey what I really thought, because we needed to stick together if we were going to think of a way to get out of our prison. Commenting on whether or not she could pass for someone younger, one of Tracey's favourite topics of conversation, wasn't really an option.

'Yes, yes,' I said, hoping that she'd forget the fishing line of a statement she had thrown to me in the hope of hooking a compliment.

'I've thought of something but I just need to work through the details,' I said.

Tracey looked pensive.

'The guards are here most of the time, and even when they aren't, Chike and Fasina show up, and I wouldn't want to get Chike cross. After his hissy fit over his bloody sewing, I reckon he's the type that could murder you for no reason,' said Tracey.

I sat down on the space beside her and patted her knee.

'We're going to have to be resourceful,' I said, picking up the banana skin from where Tracey had finished eating, placing it on the tray beside her.

I explained my plans, in the best way I could to someone who probably wouldn't understand them, when there was a loud hooting and the sound of a car making its way up the narrow pathway behind the shacks. It screeched to a halt before Chike and Fasina's voices could be heard.

'We have it, we have it,' shouted Chike. 'Party time,' he shouted again, and within minutes the area outside the shack sounded like a carnival. There was cheering and clapping and the distinct tones of *Max Bygraves' Greatest Hits* pumping through the car's stereo system.

'It sounds like they've something to celebrate,' I said to Tracey, who'd stood up to see if she could catch a glimpse of what was going on through the gaps in the door.

'Looks like they have some people with them,' she said, squinting as she peered through the small gap she'd managed to expand just below the hole that had been gouged out for the padlock bolts.

The music got louder and I put my hands over my ears. I have a sensitive reaction to most music, finding much of it superfluous to my life, but particularly that of Palladium-style crooners with absolutely no classical training. Why on earth were they listening to Max Bygraves in this day and age?

The noise was deafening and went on for some time before Gowon made his way to our shack, via the usual ritual of padlocks, to bring us the nightly cups of herbal tea and a selection of newspapers and magazines. I noticed one of them was *Needlepoint Monthly*. He was smiling at both of us as he put the tray down.

'What is going on? Why such frivolity? 'I asked him. As I looked at him I thought he was a bit drunk. His eyes weren't focusing, and when he spoke it was with a bit of a slur.

'You've brought us good luck. Things will happen soon,' he said.

I swelled inwardly. This must mean Darius had come forward to save me and we were to be freed. My logic had been skewed by over optimism, but I didn't let a lack of knowledge about the facts get in the way of my sense of hope.

'The boss is very pleased,' said Gowon, who clearly shared the same optimism about a great outcome.

'What's happened?' asked Tracey, hopeful for the first time in a while that it might be news of her fiancé.

'Is it Baz? Obassi?'

Gowon shifted on his feet and rubbed the side of his face with his right hand, which still held the padlock key he had let himself in with.

'I do not know for certain, he said. 'But I know the boss man is pleased. So we are pleased.'

'Does that mean we will be released?' I asked, as anticipation rose like mercury in a sauna's thermometer.

'Oh God, I hope so,' said Tracey. 'I want out of this hole. I need to get my nails done, my hair sorted and a new tooth, and I want some decent grub.'

Gowon ignored her and looked kindly over to me, moving his eyes up and down my body and allowing his eyes to meet mine. I thought they looked a bit watery and couldn't work out if that was the drink or emotion.

'Big boss is very happy. But you're not going anywhere. You bring us the luck. So we wait.' Then Gowon turned and left, locking us in without any further explanation.

I eyed up the door and my thoughts crystallised further. I had a plan to get us out of our imprisonment but needed to think very carefully and make sure Tracey was fully capable of following my instructions – something I wasn't one hundred per cent sure was possible.

CHAPTER EIGHTEEN

The magazines provided much-needed light relief. Reading that Bernie Ecclestone spent £12m on his daughter's wedding led to some animated discussion between the two of us. Tracey thought it was quite reasonable to spend that kind of money on one event, if you had it, whereas I could only refer to Bobbie's wedding, which involved a parsimonious meal of sausage and mash in a damp marquee on a Sussex farm. We were still discussing the details while we were waiting for our (late) breakfast when Chike burst through the door.

'Get up, get up!'

He seemed very agitated, and I reminded myself not to show fear and remember hostages are generally worth far more alive than dead. It also occurred to me that a man with a passion for needlepoint might not have quite the killer instincts you'd expect from a kidnapper.

'You need to come with me – now,' he said, as he marched around our bed, kicking the mattress with his booted feet.

'What's up with him?' said Tracey, as she hauled herself to a standing position dressed only in pants and a bra. The night had been particularly close, and if we'd had a window we would've opened it.

'Don't speak!' shouted Chike. 'Come with me.'

Tracey looked over and uncharacteristically shrugged before crumpling up her face as if to cry. She didn't, but took a deep breath and let it out in one juddering go. It was difficult to anticipate how she'd react to anything. I sometimes wondered if there were three personalities in our shack: me, her and her hormones.

Chike held the door open and gestured for us to move through.

He hadn't handcuffed us or offered us the option of breakfast or the washroom. Thankfully we had our bucket to use for early morning and the inevitable middle-of-the-night excursions that seem to hinder a full night's sleep for many women over forty-five – and the lid made a difference.

'Move. You must come.'

Thankfully I'd already dressed and so could make my way towards the door while Tracey struggled to wiggle herself into her leggings and a strappy top that looked like it'd been torn off her shoulder in a fight with a hungry goat.

When we got to the guards' shack there was a video camera set up on a tripod. It was like nothing I had seen before. Much larger than the camera Tom often used, it was pointing at two seats in front of a draped white sheet, hanging loosely over the back wall. Fasina was fiddling about with some sheets of paper.

'Your people need to know you are in danger,' said Chike. 'Tell them to send money now.'

Tracey said, 'I thought you'd already found our families and they were going to get us out of here.'

Chike sucked air through his teeth and pursed his lips. It made him look like a ventriloquist's dummy.

'You,' he said, pointing a stubby finger at Tracey, 'have no family – you are worthless. But Mrs Hartworth here is a wealthy woman and has people who want to get her back, so will pay.'

I sincerely hoped Tracey could hang on to her limited self-esteem at that point to prevent a further outburst of tears. It seemed she could, as she was busy eyeing up the cigarettes Fasina held in his hands.

'Could I have one, please?' she asked in a childlike voice. Fasina passed them over and threw her a lighter.

As she lit up, Chike snatched the papers off the table and thrust them into my hands.

'You read this, to the camera,' he said, shoving me across the room towards the chair.

I looked at what was written and knew I would find it difficult to read the words that had been written for me.

'Are you sure?' I asked.

He pushed me down on the chair and indicated to Fasina that he wanted him to start filming.

'Speak. Tell them what is written on the paper,' barked Chike.

Fasina was told to only film my face and nothing else. He didn't want any viewers to see I was reading from a script.

I faltered with the first sentence because I found the writing difficult to understand; partly capital letters and partly scribble, it was like my doctor's writing on a bad day.

'My dearest family members,' I read, trying to sound as plausible as possible. I didn't want to annoy Chike when he was showing signs of psychotic behaviour. 'I will die without you. I need your peaceful support and harmonious attention to my friends in Nigeria,' I continued.

Tracey looked bemused, and I can't say I blamed her. If my family were to think these were my own words they would think dementia had set in on the flight over, or I'd taken leave of my senses and joined a religious cult experimenting with personality transplants.

'These people are worthy of all you can give them. Sell my house and car if you need to, but give them what they ask as it goes to good men, women and children who have been subjected to terrible wrong.'

I couldn't read the next sentence but made it up as I went along, hoping Chike wouldn't notice my illicit editing.

'I just want to be back home safely. If you need to find help please do so.'

I hoped the last sentence would indicate I thought it highly appropriate to call in authorities, who knew what they were doing. That was if anyone ever got the recording. Fasina seemed to be unsure about the lens he was using, and I'm sure he'd left the cap on while filming. Not being a photographer it was difficult to tell.

He called to Tracey to sit in front of the camera, on the seat I'd vacated.

'You – read the same,' he shouted to her. 'And put that cigarette out, no one said you could smoke.'

I questioned Fasina's stability. It was he who'd given her the cigarette in the first place.

Tracey read her way through the script, faltering through most of it and sounding about as convincing as a double glazing salesman telling his prospective customer he had a one-off discount just for them. I wondered who the kidnappers would contact on Tracey's behalf. It was clear they'd found a number of connections for me and were aware of my social standing, but who would fork out for her? I hoped my release wasn't dependent on her ransom being paid.

'Go back now,' said Chike, as Fasina gave the thumbs up to indicate recording was finished. He picked up his needlepoint by way of bringing our discussions to an end and I noticed he was using the brown yarn to outline all the sheep.

Fasina grabbed us both by the arms and frog-marched us back into our shack where we found breakfast waiting: more eggs, some cake and two tubs of American ice cream, which had melted.

'That was a bit weird, weren't it?' said Tracey once he'd gone, picking up the ice cream and sniffing it.

I thought much the same. Even if my family were to get the message they would think it peculiar and probably hand it to the police. Between them they could raise a fair bit of cash but I doubted that would be considered the sensible route. Even taking into account the fact I suggested selling my house and car, there'd be a number of practical considerations about that – not least me not being there to sign the paperwork. Jonjo would need to consider the implications regarding the best use of his inheritance, while Paddy would want to wait it out in the hope things got sorted without requiring any of his input. It was sobering to consider what lengths my family would need to go to in order to save my life.

'I'm not sure what they are planning on doing with the tape but let's hope it resolves our predicament,' I said. 'I can only assume they will be sending it to any contacts of ours they can find in the hope that someone stumps up the cash.'

Tracey replied: 'Can't see how it will help. Either people know where we are or they don't. If they do we might get out of here, although I can't see Posh Git paying to get me out of here if that's the case. He's the only one with any dosh, but he won't even buy me a birthday card, so I guess a ransom demand is out of the question.'

Feeling somewhat stunned by the morning's experience, we sat down to eat our food, which was very welcome, not for its taste but for its fairly substantial quantity. I'm not one to overeat, but even the church mouse's poverty-stricken maiden aunt wouldn't be full on what we were normally given, so every morsel was valued. I'll never criticise the portion sizes of Marks & Spencer's 'Feel Fuller Longer' range ever again.

While enjoying the flavour of the cake, which I dipped in the melted ice cream, I started to leaf through the various newspapers Gowon had brought us the night before. I noted various stories on local farmers fighting for government subsidy, political intrigue and officials talking about their points of view on a number of subjects. I was about to turn to a newer edition of a Nigerian supplement to do a sudoku puzzle when I spotted a picture of a woman who looked very familiar. Small, petite features, hair loosely gathered in a bun, with tendrils dropping to the side of her ears and excellent bone structure. It was me.

I didn't say anything to Tracey, who was trying to devise a new game of 'Guess the Celebrity Partner' by tearing various faces out of the magazines she wanted me to match up at a later stage, on the basis they were sleeping with each other. As I didn't recognise anyone but Bill Clinton, who could have been bonking any or all of the women she had decided to decapitate, I thought it was a bit of a tricky game.

I looked again at my photo and, checking it definitely was me, read the story. It was basically a plea for anyone who had seen me to get in touch with a company called Forensix Inc. That was the name of the company where Darius worked. I remembered the name from the business card, although he wasn't mentioned in the article. A man called James Grant had been quoted as saying he was keen to know my whereabouts as I hadn't been seen since boarding a flight from London to Lagos over a week ago. It went on to add that my family had received email messages to suggest I'd been kidnapped, and that a ransom demand had been issued.

'Oh my goodness me,' I said, still not really registering what the story meant, although a small bird was flying around in my chest. Or that's what it felt like.

At least the family have realised I'm missing, I thought.

'Whassup?' said Tracey, placing Carol Vorderman's face on top of a pile of other faces. I briefly wondered who the ex-queen of *Countdown* was sleeping with before I pulled myself up sharply, as I was being dragged into the vacuous world of media-ocrity.

'There's a picture of me in the paper. Look,' I said, as I placed the folded paper on top of her celebrity pile.

'The authorities are looking for me and it quotes my son, grandson and people from my bridge club saying they are worried about me. They've held a fund-raiser and everything.'

'Why doesn't it say anything about me?' said Tracey, in the same girly voice she used for getting a cigarette from Fasina.

'Maybe they haven't tracked your family and friends, yet,' I said in as comforting manner I could muster, still reeling from the thrill of being mentioned in despatches. 'But if they are looking for me they will find you, too.'

'I suppose. But you'd think my daughter and even Posh Git might think it would be decent to try and find me, not to mention Baz. Just wait until I get hold of him.'

I read the article again and was surprised at Mavis voicing her concern for me publicly. She gave the impression we were very best friends, which is certainly not the impression I got when in her company. How people can change when there's a chance of a good dinner party story.

There was only so much confidence the article could inspire. We couldn't be sure who would have seen us on our journey from the airport to the settlement, and whether or not Chike and Fasina were known for taking hostages and therefore might have been watched coming and going into the camp. We hadn't heard any sounds of anyone else since being in the shack and guessed we were the only hostages. It explained the video; they needed to prove I was still alive. It also explained their celebrations; they believed I was of sufficient wealth and popularity to guarantee a pay-out.

'What we need to do,' I said to Tracey, 'is to assume people are looking and will soon find us. We also need to keep our bodies supple and minds alert so when we have a chance to get away we can do so without any impediment.'

She didn't seem to understand what I meant but was happy to trade half an hour of Pilates for my time playing her new celebrity matching game, and the rest of my melted ice cream, which even in such deprived circumstances was too sickly for me to finish.

Exercise wasn't a natural occupation for Tracey, who said she thought sitting in the sauna at the gym twice a month and drinking two bottles of red wine a week (even though she prefers white) was more than enough to keep her heart healthy.

'Whaddya wanna get all hot and sweaty in a class when you can do that with a fella!' she said. 'I went to a Zumba class with one of me mates in the summer but every time I jumped up and down a bit of wee came out. It's not a good look, I can tell you!'

She coped with the Pilates, particularly after I told her it was good for her pelvic floor muscles. That was after I explained what her pelvic floor muscles were and the impact they can have on bladder control. It gave her an entirely new perspective on the lessons I was offering.

'Right, I've had enough of that for one day,' she said after twenty minutes. 'I've pulled something here,' she added, rubbing the side of her waist.

'That would be a muscle ,and I doubt you've pulled it, just used it for a change,' I said.

I was pleased we were both focusing on keeping up our strength. The lack of normal exercise during the day could mean we would become weak, and that wouldn't help us should we suddenly have to make a run for it.

'You think of everything, you do,' said Tracey. 'I s'pose it makes sense to keep ourselves in shape. Let's play my game now. It'll keep our brains going and all.'

After pairing someone called Russell Brand with Ann Widdecombe and some elderly-looking male called Keith from with someone from *The X Factor*, Tracey decided I wasn't up to her standards of celebrity know-it-all. She demoted us to another game of 'pin the tail on the donkey', although this time the pin was aimed at Simon Cowell, with far more pleasing results.

'What will you do when you get outta here?' Tracey asked as we were getting ready for bed and willing the herbal drink to come along so we could lose a few more hours of the repetitive boredom that was our daily life.

'Have a damned good wash and find somewhere to eat a good steak.' I answered. 'What about you?'

She prodded her earrings back into her ears and gave the question some thought, which took a bit of time.

'Not sure. I think that what with everything that's happened I don't know who I am any more. I feel different though, as if something has changed.

I was surprised by Tracey's sudden insight, and just as I considered the benefits of imprisonment for those who don't value their freedom sufficiently, she spoke again.

'For example, I don't think I fancy Chinese food any more. I might go for curry instead. 'And why bleach my hair when I can go red, or brunette? What do I wanna be blonde for anyway? Everyone thinks yer thick if yer blonde.'

Tracey was entitled to her own thoughts, although I was glad they were in her head and not mine. In a bid to find something more entertaining I suggested we remembered the words of our favourite songs. I amazed myself by recalling all the words for all verses of 'Morning Has Broken' and 'American Pie', while Tracey sang her way through the first eight bars of about twenty eighties hits, including five of Abba's. 'Knowing Me, Knowing You' was the most tortuous, but the purpose of the game was achieved. I'd never seen her looking so happy.

We'd exhausted our renditions of popular chart songs so went on to television, remembering with fondness programmes like *Blue Peter* and *Crackerjack*. We got on to *Love Thy Neighbour* and wondering how the scriptwriters were allowed to get away with calling a black man 'Sambo' or 'Jungle Bunny'. Any such talk now and the political correctness police would be on you like a shot, although it still seems quite acceptable to call women of a certain age 'Stupid Old Cow', which I think is just as insulting, particularly to someone approaching the autumn of their life.

I'd been thinking how I was going to relish my later years and take full advantage of the knowledge and freedom that comes as a package with middle and older age. If I could keep my wits, flexible limbs and ability to live independently for the next three decades or so, then I could live a full life. It would be a life of continued wonder, challenge and unsupervised trips to the lavatory.

'What colour would you be if you had the choice?' said Tracey. 'Maybe you could go lavender?'

I wondered what on earth she was talking about.

'Yer hair. What colour?' she prompted.

I thought of myself with lavender hair. It would certainly beat the blue rinse brigade and give my children something else to laugh at. Maybe I should do it, just to surprise them.

'I might just do that, Tracey, and get a motorbike as well. If I can't rebel now, when can I?'

'A motorbike? Aren't they dangerous?' Tracey said. 'And those leathers can get very smelly. I know, I used to go out with a bloke what had a Hardly Davies and he loved it more than anything. He was nice and that, but stank and always had helmet hair. I dumped him for a bloke with a Ford Capri. It was old, like, but really classy. A bit like you, Cynthia!'

Our shared imprisonment had created a strange relationship between us. I couldn't imagine knowing anyone like Tracey in my previous existence, one of predictable routines and little uncertainty, let alone talking to her. Now she was talking me into dyeing my hair a strange colour.

'Funny, innit, how we might not have met had it not been for us both being on that flight. Me to get married and you to do your good works,' she said, as she shuffled down the mattress and under a sheet. The weather was often too warm to use the blankets, even at night.

My thoughts were interrupted by her mention of good works. I'd forgotten she was under the impression my only reason for being in Nigeria was to work with young girls who needed education. Had she given it any thought she might have wondered what on earth it was I might be able to teach them.

'Indeed,' I said, as Gowon came in and presented us with our drinks and told us the electricity might go off in the night as their generator had just packed up.

'We had enough to make hot water and then it went off,' he said. 'Good night, Cynthia, and please have some very nice dreams.'

He left the room and, as predicted, the light started to flicker and then finally went out.

'I think he's got it bad,' said Tracey. 'Like a puppy without his mother.'

We drifted into our drug-induced sleep, talking about whether we would be able to escape or whether my family would find us soon. We also wondered what they would think of the video if they ever got it.

I think they only have DVD players now, anyway, I thought.

CHAPTER NINETEEN

'Right, this is what we are going to have to do,' I said, pulling my hair back into the bun I'd effected using strips of material from one of my shredded T-shirts. 'We must distract the guards and then find a way to get as far from here as possible.'

Tracey was lying face down on the mattress, trying to work out the clues on one of the old *OK!* magazine crosswords. She wasn't getting very far.

'Who was Rod Stewart married to before he got old?' she questioned.

I ignored her and continued to plan our escape, one that would involve using elements of my personality yet to come to the fore.

'You aren't listening to me, are you? I said, stamping my foot lightly on the dusty floor of the shack, which had now started to smell of eggs and stale banana. No one could accuse our diet of being varied.

'I am but I can't see how you're gonna get us outta here. We're trapped.' She went back to concentrating on four down.

I let out an exasperated breath as I reminded myself not to lose patience with the woman I'd come to believe had the barest minimum of brain cells – most of which were on timeshare with a sloth. Any headway we'd made previously seemed to have gone, and she was back to pessimistic mode. Maybe that's the difference between those who are successful and those who aren't; the former hang on to every bit of positive thought and drag it through their days regardless of circumstances that could knock it out of them.

'If you think you're trapped, then you will be. We need to have positive mental attitude.'

I sniffed the dregs of last night's herbal drink and looked across the room. The germ of my thoughts had started to take hold and I was nearly ready to share everything with Tracey.

'I need you to listen to me,' I said.

Tracey turned over and lay on her back, a position I was sure she felt most comfortable with.

'We need to save the drinks they bring us at night.'

'Oh no. I love those drinks!' wailed Tracey. 'How can we sleep without them?'

'Just trust me. They may be the means of our escape,' I added, while tearing out a recipe from one of the Sunday supplement magazines. It was for banana cake.

Tracey sat up and started to pick her toes with a piece of acrylic she had bitten off her thumbnail.

'What if we never get out? What will happen to us?'

I sighed and had a waking nightmare where I was appearing in a reality version of *Groundhog Day*.

'Well, we'll probably be egg-bound for a start.'

The door rattled and Gowon made his usual entry. Surprisingly it wasn't eggs for breakfast this time, but just apples and what looked like fruit bread.

'Chike made this,' he said, indicating the bread. 'He loves cooking.'

I hoped it hadn't been laced with anything unexpected, although when I bit into it, the taste and consistency was very good. He'd be a good contender for the WI's annual baking competition.

I tried to get some information out of Gowon, as despite two nights of great celebration and our recent home-made film appearances he still hadn't told us what was going on or why they thought we were the answer to their prayers. I used as many womanly wiles as I could muster, but Gowon remained steadfast in his secrecy.

'You must know what they are planning to do? Have they been told the money is on its way? Will we be released, and if so, when?'

Gowon just smiled broadly, to the point where I thought he looked rather smug.

'What are you so pleased about, then?' I asked. 'You look like the cat that's got the cream.'

Gowon frowned. 'We don't have a cat. Or any cream. Just fruit.'

'It's an English saying,' I added, knowing that learning new English words or phrases was highly desirable to most Nigerians. Darius was always fascinated by our language and its quaint expressions, most of which he'd mastered through years of formal education and watching British films. Gowon had shown a similar interest, although usually only in naming body parts in as many different ways as possible. So far he'd mastered 'tits', 'boobs', 'puppies' and 'knockers', all explained to him by Tracey.

'It means you look very pleased with yourself,' I added.

'We'll soon be pleased. We will soon be rich and be able to live a good and proper life. For this we respect you,' he answered. 'But now it is time for the bathroom.'

'Oh, pants,' said Tracey. 'Tell that bloody sadist to watch out for my arms,' she groaned as she rubbed the red marks left by her guard, who since being walloped by her had been behaving in a way I could only describe as terrified. The slightest movement and he'd flinch, holding his spare hand across his face and pleading for mercy. I considered his disposition to be a good thing bearing in mind my plans for Tracey's part in the great escape.

I'd already taken the opportunity to explain to her the first part of the plan. It involved her trying to be nice to her guard which I thought could be something of a challenge.

'What I need you to do is start to talk him,' I explained. 'Ask his name for a start so we can start getting personal. Make him think you want to be his friend. Show interest in his family, his hobbies. Anything that comes to mind.'

Tracey looked at me as if I'd just walked off a spaceship and given her the meaning of life. Eventually she closed her mouth.

'You are joking? I wouldn't want to be friends with that tosser if he was the last bloke on earth.'

I suspected the feeling was mutual, but needed to get Tracey to understand it was all an act.

'I didn't say you actually had to be his friend. Just pretend to be. We need to get them onside so we can get out of here.'

Tracey scratched her head along the dark line of her parting that was splitting the peroxide blonde into two totally separate entities.

'They're never going to let us out. They think we'll give them their fortune, which is silly cos I've got nuffin. Not now I've given it all to Baz.'

I knew this was going to be a difficult plan to execute but had to persevere, even though I felt I was bashing my head against a brick wall, double-sealed with concrete and iron filings and plastered for good measure.

'They won't know they are going to let us out. We're just going to have to get them to let down their guard a bit. Pardon the pun.'

'OK. You're the boss. Tell me what to do,' said Tracey in a bored voice, suggesting she wasn't whole-heartedly confident I knew what I was doing. If the truth be known, I wasn't totally convinced myself, but one idea was better than none at all. We'd been in the shack for ten days with no sign of release or indication of what our captors wanted to do with us. And I really needed a hot shower and a haircut, not to mention a pedicure. The lack of decent flooring had played havoc with my feet.

In fairness they'd treated us reasonably well, under the circumstances. The food was limited, but as they ate the same as us, I could see an opportunity to use my skills to improve things all round.

'Just work with me on this, please,' I said to Tracey. 'I'm not sure exactly how we are going to get out of here but I have the start of a plan and just need to think it through. If we can get these men to think we are friendly we are halfway to where we need to be.'

Gowon let the other guard into the shack, and he moved towards Tracey with his handcuffs. I saw she tried her best to give him a friendly smile, looking at me for assurance she was doing the right thing.

He looked startled, partly because the gap in her teeth seemed to be increasing on a daily basis, but also because, still sporting the yellowing remnants of his bloody nose, he probably didn't know what to expect next. He stepped cautiously towards her.

'You know what? I don't even know your name,' she said to him. 'Seeing as you see me knockers every day I should know it. It's only polite.'

Her smile was quite scary. Just a few warts and the effect could be witch-like in combination with the lack of tooth and a furry tongue. At least she was trying to follow my instructions, and the knowledge made my heart feel lighter. Maybe we could work this all to our advantage and make our getaway. It might take a few days, but just the glimmer of light at the end of what had been a very dark tunnel was enough to lift my mood. It seemed Tracey's attempts at friendliness, although not breaking the ice, were cracking the surface.

'I call myself Chiddy,' he said hesitantly, while placing the handcuff over Tracey's wrist.

'Weird name. Sounds like Chiddy Chiddy Bang Bang,' she laughed.

The guard looked hurt.

'It's Chiddy Bang. After the Nigerian rapper. He's very famous.'

'Never heard of him, mate. Not exactly Eminem, is it?'

I shot a glare at Tracey. It was important to boost his ego, not alienate him even further than she already had with her boxing skills.

'I think that's a lovely name, Chiddy. Can we call you Chiddy now?' I asked.

He nodded and smiled a bit.

'It's not the name my mother gave me. But my friends call me Chiddy, because he's my hero.'

Now that's a start, I thought to myself.

Gowon put the handcuff over my arm but didn't lock it. He'd learned there was nothing for him in our bathroom ritual if my hands were tied, so to speak. I'd gained his confidence and I think he was falling a little bit in love with me. I didn't mind, although he wasn't a patch on Darius so the feeling was unlikely to be requited.

He made for a passing distraction, however.

On the short walk to the washing area I could hear Tracey making small talk with Chiddy. He was initially reluctant to respond but when she asked about rap music in Nigeria he lit up like a sparkler at a bonfire party.

'Chiddy is da best. He made mix tape called *The Swelly Express*. He broke da Guinness Record for da Longest Freestyle Rap and da Longest Marathon Record for rappin' for more than nine hours, man,' I heard him tell her.

He then went into more detail, which I could see was lost on Tracey, whose eyes had glazed over. She occupied herself with her washing ritual and the occasional nod to express continued interest in the information she was being given.

'*The Swelly Express* is about Chiddy's rise in the music business. He struggled but he works with Kate Nash, Tinie Tempah. He's a legend!'

Tracey was washing her hair as best she could with cold water and washing-up liquid but still managed to raise her head as if in awe of Chiddy's knowledge. For a woman with little going on in the intelligence department she was playing this game quite well.

'Yeah, sounds it. Can you play his music to us?'

Good girl, I thought. I was proud of her. She was doing and saying all the right things to get his trust.

Meanwhile, I was as certain as I could be that Gowon was in my thrall. He clutched my buttock while pressing his body into mine. I'd not taken my clothes off yet and thought maybe I should give him something to wait for.

'You know, Gowon. I'm sure there is a way we can do something far better for you.'

He looked blank and pulled back from his position, allowing a gap between us big enough for me to place my hand down his trousers. His manhood swelled beneath it as I tightened my grip, so I moved it along his shaft until it was stretched to its fullest extent.

'You just need to find us somewhere we can go. Then you can have the benefit of all my experience,' I added, loosening my hold to ensure a level of frustration.

He grunted and pushed himself into me, grinding his hips into my pelvis. I pretended I didn't know what he wanted me to do and started to undress, slowly. His face looked pained but then relaxed as his thoughts unfolded.

'You mean, all your experience?'

'Oh yes, Gowon. Is that what you would like?'

I took off my bra, leaving me just in my smallest underpants, and poured the water from the can over my shoulders, letting it drip over my breasts and onto the floor. It would seem my seduction techniques were popular. I could almost smell his brain burning as he tried to work out what could be done.

'I have an idea. Leave it with me,' he said, not pushing himself against me, allowing me to carry on washing. I kept myself very much to myself to keep the suspense going. He needed to be distracted while I thought what the next part of the plan might be.

Meanwhile Chiddy was in some kind of monologue about the music he could play for Tracey and it seemed she had him locked in enthusiastic discussion. It's amazing how you can suddenly connect with someone just by finding their passion, and she'd certainly found his. Hopefully I'd done the same with Gowon.

We were led back to the shack and both the men left us with smiles on their faces. They were animated and excited; certainly Gowon was, judging by the lump in his trousers. Everything was working very well.

'Did you hear him? Like a bleedin' dictionary of rap music. God knows I likes me music but not that much,' said Tracey.

'You did brilliantly. It couldn't have gone better,' I told her, and went over to squeeze her arm.

She looked at me quizzically.

'Really? I only asked his name.'

'Well it seems that was enough. He is totally onside now, you wait and see,' I said.

Tracey beamed. I suspected she'd had very little praise in her life and was openly thrilled at being useful for something.

'So, what's the plan, boss?' she said.

I was wary of telling her I hadn't really got one and was hoping that some ideas would come to me soon. She'd need something positive to focus on if she was going to retain her commitment to befriending Chiddy, so I gave her the barest details of my thought process: that if we got the guards onside we could somehow get them to help us escape. I wasn't sure quite how, but if they saw us as people and recognised we needed to get out alive to see our families, we might be able to appeal to their better nature. Airing the briefest outline of my thoughts helped give them power and transformed Tracey's demeanour immediately. From being forlorn and passive she was positive and encouraging. Maybe we could do this between us. I felt more exhilarated than I'd been about anything for a long time.

We passed the afternoon chatting about what we'd been missing most in captivity, apart from people. Shampoo seemed pretty high on the list, alongside hot water, a good mattress, white crusty bread and a proper cup of tea. We also both missed *Coronation Street*, while Tracey said she missed *The Jeremy Kyle Show*, claiming she was asked to go on it once but couldn't make it as she was away. I'd never heard of it and it sounded thoroughly ghastly, revolving around the lives of unemployed drug addicts from council estates. I wondered what they'd make a programme about next – the multitude of illnesses you can get from a toilet seat?

Tracey told me about her background, growing up in a south London estate with an alcoholic mother and older brother who abused her on a regular basis. She didn't see it as abuse at the time, as it was all very normal being molested. She thought it happened to everyone.

I told her a bit about my life with Colin and she said it sounded very boring. She was probably right. She asked lots of questions about my family, like what they did, what they liked, what clothes they wore. I couldn't answer many of them. Maybe I should take more notice in future.

When the door opened early that evening we were surprised to see both Gowon and Chiddy bringing the trays of food. Usually it was Gowon on his own, and he'd place the tray down and leave.

However, Tracey's feigned interest in rap music had worked wonders. Chiddy had brought a CD cover to show her, while Gowon's face was one of a child waiting for Christmas Day so he could open his presents. He even tried to wink at me, which made me want to laugh, as both eyes closed, making him look a bit like a koala on sleeping pills. We were getting somewhere.

'I'm getting a bit fed up with eggs and bananas,' I said to Gowon.

'This is all we have,' he replied apologetically. 'We've the same. It's boring but keeps us alive. Sometimes Chike will cook. He said he will make some cupcakes but never gets round to it. He's got to finish 'Baa, Baa, Black Sheep' by the end of the week, so won't hear of doing anything else.'

An idea started to formulate and my heart raced as I thought of it. Where I couldn't see a tunnel, let alone any light at the end of it, a faint glimmer was starting to lead me down a path that could be the one to freedom.

'Can you get flour and maybe some oil? Or maybe some lard or butter?' I asked. As I spoke I showed him the recipe for banana bread I'd torn out of the magazine. 'Chike made us something like this the other day so there must be. If you can get the ingredients I'll make this. Look.'

Gowon looked at the picture of the deliciously succulent-looking banana bread and nodded his head.

'I'll find it. For tomorrow.'

He and Chiddy left the room, and as they did I turned to Tracey and offered her the 'high five' or whatever it's called.

'We've got 'em eating out our hands,' she said, and I momentarily had to agree with her, while also smiling at her use of language. She could be more right than she knew.

'There's some way to go yet but we're on the right track,' I added.

When Chiddy came back later that night with the herbal night cap I told Tracey we had to hide it. We took a couple of sips but poured the rest into the bowl we had used on our first day for our toilet needs. That was enough to ensure we wouldn't be tempted to drink it, even though the bowl had been scrubbed clean.

Getting to sleep was troublesome, as we were excited at the possibility we could persuade the men to help us escape. We passed time talking of our favourite restaurants. Tracey had never heard of the Wolseley and I wasn't too sure about Charlie's Chicken.

It was rather pleasant to experience such extremes of emotion, now we had high hopes of getting out of this place. My life had mainly been on the straight and narrow. Mostly narrow, in hindsight.

We didn't need to be woken up, as the light from the dawn had already prepared us for the morning. The usual ritual of breakfast – more eggs – and the trip to the bathroom was charged with a new energy. The men were preoccupied with their own anticipation and we were gently hopeful we were finally in charge of our destiny.

After bringing us clean clothes, Gowon took me to another shack in the settlement, one I hadn't seen before when we were taken to see Chike. It was away from the road and towards the edge of the water where a rocky path ran alongside. There were tyre tracks that showed a car had come up close to the building, which was far more substantial than ours.

'Why do people travel by boat when there are cars available?' I asked Gowon, thinking back to our canoe trip when we arrived.

'Petrol is hard to get and very expensive, so cars are only used to go out of the town. The people of this village prefer the boats. They get us where we need to be and only big cars can manage the bad roads here.'

Gowon said he was preparing the shack for our promised tryst. It was the penthouse version of our minus-star accommodation with its large bed, furniture, TV, music system and a fridge. There was a dark green shirt hanging on the back of the wardrobe door and I recognised it as the one Chike was wearing the day we were brought in, so suspected it might be his quarters. My thoughts were confirmed when I saw a collection of needlepoint magazines and a pile of wool.

'This is a lovely room, Gowon. Are you sure we will be alone?' I quizzed as I looked around the room for anything that could help our escape. There was a bulge in the pocket of the shirt and I hoped it contained something of use.

'I will bring you here tomorrow. We will be alone,' he said.

'What about the others, your bosses?'

'They won't be here again until we have news,' he told me, with a look that suggested there was more to be said.

'What kind of news, Gowon? Please tell me what we need to do.'

He shifted on his feet, moving his weight from one leg to the other. He was looking at the ground.

'I'm not supposed to say.'

'But we are friends, aren't we? I think we are special friends?' I said.

When he looked up his eyes were watery. He reminded me of a cocker spaniel we had with cataracts.

'If I tell you, please don't say anything. Your family has said they've transferred money. The boss man waits for it to come through.'

How they'd found so much information was beyond my understanding until Gowon told me the bosses had gone through my diary. I'd written all my important telephone numbers and email addresses down in the back. There was also a letter I'd written to college about Tom, a personal reference about his IT ability and how he had helped me get online.

'And have you had any communication from anyone about us?'

I'd rather hoped they had and that my family had secured my release without question.

'No. The bosses have given them five days to get the money but we've been told it will arrive sooner.'

'And then what?'

'I don't know,' Gowon said apologetically. 'I have never done this before.'

Well that puts us both in the same boat, I thought.

CHAPTER TWENTY

It was some hours later when Gowon opened the door and gestured to me, suggesting I follow him. Tracey looked up but pretended not to have noticed what was going on.

'Come with me,' he said. 'I have what you asked.'

I was led back into the main shack. Behind where the camera had been there was a small electric oven, wired up to a generator – the same one powering the light in our shack.

'Look what I've got.'

The table in the middle of the room held a bunch of bananas, two boxes of eggs, a bottle of cooking oil, a cloth bag containing sugar and a jar of molasses. Gowon was looking pleased with himself.

'But there's no flour,' I said, noticing the absence of a key ingredient.

He looked crestfallen.

'I thought I had everything. I'm sorry,' Gowon said, lowering his eyes.

'It isn't a problem. If you can get some flour for me then perhaps I can make the cake then,' I said, wondering if he was going to cry. His mouth had dropped at both corners and his chest sank. 'Bring everything to our shack. I can make the bread there and give it to you to put in the oven for later.'

Gowon took me back to our quarters, where Tracey was pulling at her eyelashes one by one.

'Bloody falsies have all fallen out, apart from three on each side. I bet I look like Ermintrude,' she said.

I hadn't the faintest idea who Ermintrude was – probably some lower-class porn star from one of those *Celebrity Jungle Brother* programmes. I nodded in pretence of caring and went over to inspect the bowl, which contained a good amount of herbal drink. We'd each gone without our sedation, but it should be worth it.

'Gowon has gone to get flour, and then he'll be bringing the ingredients for the banana bread over here. After that we will just have to hope we can figure out how we are going to make our escape.'

'Total faith in yer, Cynth. If you can't get us outta here, I don't know who could.'

I wish she wouldn't call me that. Tom has a habit of calling me Nanny Cynth, and it sounds so common. Like one of those women who go to the Gala Bingo down Pit Shaw Lane on a Wednesday afternoon. I could visualise 'Cynth and Doris' taking time out from their daily routine of domestic abuse and habitual smoking to stick holes in a piece of paper according to the random selection of numbers. Cynthia isn't a great name at full length, but decidedly downmarket when shortened.

'Good. Well when he comes back you know what you have to do. We need to make sure both of them are occupied.'

I thought of the arrangement I'd made with Gowon to explore our relationship further in Chike's room, and so was confident Chike and Fasina wouldn't be around. The idea appealed to me to some extent, but not as much as the thought of escaping this somewhat challenging imprisonment. I needed to get out and also to get some intellectual stimulation. Tracey's conversation, combined with the banality of *OK!* magazine's celebrity interviews had mixed into a toxic broth that had started to dull my senses.

Later that afternoon Gowon tumbled through our door clutching a large bag of flour and all the other ingredients I told him I would need for cooking, as well as some utensils. I asked him to go and get a tin for baking the bread and, while he was gone, put a good measure of flour and sugar into the bowl containing our saved herbal drinks. I made sure the liquid was totally absorbed, even though this meant compromising my judgement as a cook.

'Peel those bananas, Tracey,' I instructed as I stirred the

molasses and eggs into a mixture that was beginning to look like a science experiment rather than a cake. I made sure to put in plenty of sugar to hide the taste of the distinctive herb.

Tracey had finished mashing the fruit when Gowon returned with a rusty-looking tin he said Chike used for making the cake we'd eaten previously. It wasn't ideal, but it would do the trick.

'It looks good,' he said, eyeing up the mixture, and I was grateful for his obvious lack of culinary expertise.

'I hope you'll enjoy it,' I said to Gowon, giving him my best flirtatious look in the hope it would ensure total commitment to eating what I was preparing for him.

Tracey was keeping to her part of the deal well, and remembered what came next without any prompting from me.

'Let's have a party!' she said. 'One everyone can join in,' she added, giving Gowon a flash of a grin that made him look a bit awkward. I think she was trying to be alluring, but had exposed her spiky gap and he started to fidget with his shirt sleeve.

'Tell Chiddy to bring his music and we can eat and dance,' I offered, by way of distraction. We didn't want him getting too nervous to join in.

We knew there was no reason for them not to take up the offer as they had been left in charge for the night. Gowon had said so when planning our night of physical exploration in Chike's shack.

'Here,' I said, mashing the bread mix into the tatty old tin with the back of an oversized fork. 'Put this in the oven for an hour on a low heat. When it's ready, we can start our party.'

Gowon gleamed with anticipation. Being in charge for the night, coupled with expectations of carnal pleasure had gone to his head, or more likely his pants, which was a good thing because his distraction made my job so much easier.

'I will tell Chiddy and be back later,' he said, as he left us in pursuit of a hot oven. 'We will have fun!'

Once the door had been padlocked, Tracey started to cry.

'What in heaven's name is the matter now?' I asked her, trying very hard not to lose my patience. We'd been getting on so well and had been emotionally and physically enlivened by the prospect of at least trying to get out of the camp.

'What if we can't do it? What if it all goes horribly wrong and we make them cross? They might torture us,' she sobbed.

I went over and gave her a hug. I actually wanted to slap her in the face but didn't think that would produce the desired effect. What is the matter with these wishy-washy women? No wonder she's never found a husband.

'We'll be fine. Just wait and see,' I said, wishing I was as confident as I thought I sounded.

Tracey had calmed down by the time the men came back, complete with the banana bread that had gone a decidedly green colour. Thankfully no one seemed to notice and it was placed very ceremoniously on the chair in the middle of the room. Gowon produced a pocket knife from his combat trousers and cut the cake into sixteen squares.

'You have some,' he said to us, picking up the tin and then, finding it was still hot, nearly dropping it before placing it back on the chair.

Tracey was just about to take a piece so I stamped on her foot, pretending I'd lost balance.

'Don't forget about your diabetes,' I said to her in clipped tones, raising my eyebrows to alert her to the fact she must not touch the cake under any circumstances.

Thankfully she twigged.

'Oh, yeah. Keep forgetting about that.'

'We want you to enjoy it all. It's our way of saying thank you for looking after us so well,' I said to the men. They looked proud of themselves, as if they'd been keen for us to enjoy our stay and were pleased to be recognised for the effort they'd put into their hospitality.

They both took their first pieces and devoured them quickly. The sugar and molasses mix seemed to be a welcome taste for the men as they congratulated me on my cooking and relaxed into the idea of sitting around with their prisoners, eating hot cake.

I made some small talk about Nigeria generally, picking bits of information I'd gleaned from my evenings with Darius, while Tracey sat cross-legged on the floor staring directly across at both men, looking rather too intently for signs of impending weakness.

Chiddy stood up purposefully. He had certainly developed a different personality since our discovery of his love of rap.

'I go and get da music,' he said, and as he went to walk out of the shack he looked a little unsteady. My hopes started to rise and I looked over at Tracey and winked. She was already looking more confident about our plan.

Gowon leaned over for another piece of bread.

'Will you not have some?' he asked us. 'It is very good.'

'No, thank you,' I replied. 'I'm a little tired of bananas and Tracey can't eat anything sweet because of her problem with sugar.'

Gowon looked concerned, not realising that had she actually been a diabetic the chances are she would've been dead, kept in captivity with nothing but eggs and bananas to eat twice a day.

Chiddy charged through the door with a large music system. So big it defied the description of 'portable'. He pulled a socket on a wire through from outside and plugged in the CD player. Within a few minutes a tune called 'Rescue Me' was pounding through the walls of the shack, which I thought entirely appropriate under the circumstances.

The music was soporific through repetition, and for a moment I thought both the men were going to go to sleep as they were lying down with their hands behind their heads, tapping their feet but moving very little else.

Then Gowon sat up, looking quizzical.

'What was in that bread? I feel strange,' he said, looking over at Chiddy who was nodding his head backwards and forwards too fast to be anything to do with the music.

The heavy bass was giving me a headache and had a rhythm slightly out of sync with my heartbeat, which was disconcerting to say the least. But I knew I had to concentrate, so eradicated all thoughts of disorientation and focused on the task ahead.

'It's probably the sugar,' I said to Gowon, who seemed happy enough with the answer. We needed a distraction.

'Dance,' I hissed to Tracey.

'Wha'?' she said, unable to hear me over the thudding sounds of Nigerian rap.

I waved my arms about and twisted around in what I thought approximated to a kind of dance movement. I probably looked like I'd been electrocuted, but she stood up and started to move to the beat with ease. Her years of clubbing had at last come in useful, and she stamped around, waving her arms above her head in full theatrical style. Chiddy was fascinated, but then he'd also been fascinated by a spider walking over his foot a few minutes previously.

The men sat up, leaning their weight on their hands, and watched Tracey for a while before Chiddy got up and joined her. It seemed Gowon had forgotten about feeling strange and was entranced by what was going on. Chiddy could barely stand, let alone dance, which I noted with some satisfaction. It was time to act.

'So, when will we be alone?' I asked Gowon. He looked puzzled. Partly because his brain wasn't functioning but also because he couldn't hear, so I repeated the question loudly.

Tracey heard me and so looked over and smiled. She knew what was planned next and gave me a thumbs-up. Under normal circumstances I would've chided her lack of subtlety, but as both Chiddy and Gowon had lost control of most of their faculties, thanks to an overdose of herbs meant to keep their captives compliant, it was unlikely they'd have made anything of her gesture. Even if they had they wouldn't be able to do much about it.

Gowon, spurred on by Chiddy's attempts at dancing, struggled to get to his feet and lurched over in my direction, holding his hand out to pull me up. It didn't work, as he could barely hold himself in one position, and so I put my arm round his waist and led him to the door, turning back to give Tracey a wink which, thankfully, she acknowledged. It was our good fortune that Chiddy had forgotten to lock the door in all his excitement.

He stumbled along, humming the tune of 'Rescue Me' in a decidedly tuneless way. I was thankful he wasn't in the church choir as he's the type of person who would sing hymns very loudly without understanding the annoyance he could generate. I always seem to get one of them behind me on the few occasions I do attend, adding further to the discomfort of being there in the first place.

We made it to Chike's shack, which Gowon had decorated with a carpet of pink petals and a freshly washed bedcover. There was a bottle not unlike the one we'd seen them all drinking from the other night, and two earthenware glasses, placed on the desk. He managed to pour some of the drink out for us both, swaying as he did so but amazingly not spilling a drop.

'This is for you,' he said, his eyelids drooping to the point of shutting, handing me mine. 'It is our special drink, for special occasions.'

'What sort of special occasions?' I asked him, remembering that the men had been celebrating something. I wanted to know what had brought out such levity in them all.

'Just like now,' he said.

He smiled as I sniffed. It wasn't unlike cider so I took a swig, for courage as much as anything. He drained his glass, then unsteadily walked me across the room, having closed the door behind him. I noted it had a lock swinging from a bolt but he did nothing to imprison me.

'So, anything to report to me of interest? I asked him. 'About the money?' He looked blank, and then a flicker of awareness spread across his face.

'Ah. The money,' he replied, grinning slightly inanely. 'The bosses say it's on its way. Lots of it.'

I questioned what he meant by a lot of money. Hundreds? Thousands? Millions? If it was either of the latter two, then my family would be hard pushed to find that amount of cash, unless they'd won the lottery in my absence or had an extremely successful PPI or no-fee accident or injury claim.

Gowon took my drink from my hand, leaving it free for him to hold, which he did before falling back on the bed, pulling me on top of him. He kissed me with his full, pink lips in a sloppy and undemanding way, pulling at my clothing, murmuring that he loved me and wanted me. And then fell asleep.

I waited for a few minutes to make sure I could make a getaway without him noticing. I saw Chike's shirt again and looked in the pocket with the bulge. I found keys and a lighter which I tucked into my knickers for safe keeping. We were certainly safe, to judge by the state of Gowon who was out like a light, dribble running down the side of his mouth with every snore that came from the back of his throat. I went over and gave him a peck on the cheek before taking the key to our shack out of his pocket.

After scouring the drawers of Chike's desk I found over five thousand US dollars in a variety of bills, which also made their way to my underwear along with a selection of Nigerian nairas. I didn't know their value, but thought it would be useful to have local currency so I stuffed them in my bra. I shut the door and padlocked it securely, even though I was certain Gowon wouldn't be awake for some time. Just one helping of the herbal drink would send us off to sleep for at least eight hours. They'd had a bit more than that.

I went back to our shack and the sounds of Chiddy Bang were still emanating at full volume from the sound machine. I peered through a gap in the door and was thrilled to see Tracey tucking Chiddy up in our bed. He'd also gone into a state of coma, so much so that he was unaware that she'd tied his feet together with her leggings and his hands together with his own belt – tightly.

'Good girl,' I mouthed, motioning for her to leave. She looked a sorry sight in just her pants and T-shirt, but she didn't seem to care. If anything she looked totally elated, having completed her mission.

Tracey and I made our way out of our shack which I locked using Gowon's key. Although we probably had hours before they would wake up we were both keen to get as far away as possible, as quickly as possible. It was getting dark and the roads looked treacherous enough.

Our bags were still in the first shack and so we packed up what we could into our hand luggage and got dressed. Tracey was delighted to find most of her cigarettes and her phone were still intact.

'Funny thing is, I don't even fancy a fag now,' she said while sliding into a pair of cut-off jeans. 'But I'll take them just in case,' she added, throwing them into her bag before picking up her phone to check it. The battery had gone dead.

I fished the cash and the car keys I'd found out from my underwear, much to Tracey's amusement. I was hoping the keys were for what I thought they were

'You ready?' I said to Tracey as I picked up my bag. 'Follow me.'

Tracey traipsed behind me obediently, tottering along in yet another pair of totally unsuitable shoes, which she had fished out of her luggage. I suspected all her footwear was of a similar type so said nothing. If she wanted to break her leg then so be it, as long as she didn't expect me to carry her anywhere if she did.

When we reached the car, a black Audi, I could hardly contain myself when the key immediately unlocked it. I have to say it was a daunting vehicle. What people might call a Chelsea Tractor, I think. Too big for most women to drive but they insist on doing so anyway, usually blocking every available parking space at the supermarket, or running over small children because they can't see over the bonnet. It was our only sensible means of getting out.

'Can you drive?' I asked Tracey hopefully.

She shook her head.

'No, I had lessons once but the instructor had just broken up with his girl so spent most of the time crying in cul-de-sacs. I took seven tests and failed 'em all.'

We'd no time to lose, so I hauled myself up into the seat, which wasn't easy – like climbing Mount Everest without the aid of Sherpas. Being small made it worse, and so I hopped repeatedly on one leg to get enough momentum to leap up.

It was difficult reaching the pedals, but after some adjustment to the seat I got into a driving position, which required sitting so near the steering wheel it dug into my knees. We had over two thirds of a tank of petrol, so I started the car and put it into gear – or thought I had. I'd never driven an automatic before, and it took some getting used to, so we lurched backwards, ramming into a selection of bicycles and a large metal container that appeared to hold some kind of sticky, foul-smelling liquid.

'Blimey, Cynth. You sure you're OK to drive this thing?'

Not one to be beaten by a piece of machinery, I persevered and finally found a way of moving forward rather than in reverse, which was a relief for all concerned, not least Tracey who was gripping the sides of her seat so her knuckles had gone white.

'Hurrah. Here we go,' I cheered to myself as we bounded over the bumpy lane.

I thought we were on our way to freedom, before shouts could be heard behind us. I looked in the rear-view mirror and saw Chike and Fasina running through the camp behind us, dressed in black suits and carrying what I could only assume were pistols.

'What was that noise?' said Tracey, as gunshots rattled off the back of the car.

My heart pounded and my legs turned to jelly. I tried to accelerate but couldn't get the automatic gearing to get into place quickly enough. The car stalled as it bumped over a pile of rubble.

'Damn,' I said, as I watched the men advancing on us quickly, Fasina running and Chike lumbering along about five metres behind him. I turned the ignition and nothing happened. Tracey looked out the back window and saw the men, who were catching up with us.

'Get the bloody car started,' she said. 'They've got guns.'

As she turned back around she knocked the gear lever with her knee, pushing it back to drive position. I turned the ignition again and the car jumped into life, bounding over the lane and on its way. The shouting continued, and beads of sweat formed on my eyebrows, one waiting tantalisingly to drop down onto my face.

'Where are you going, you stupid women?' I heard Fasina shout as the gunshots continued. Every now and then a sharp metallic noise could be heard as their bullets bounced back from the thankfully tough exterior of the car.

There was a loud crack and splintering. The back window smashed and pieces of glass fell onto the back seat. We could hear Fasina shouting incomprehensibly at us, and Chike coughing. I looked back in the mirror and I could see him bent over double, trying to catch his breath – while Fasina was just a few yards from us, pointing his gun straight at the back of our heads.

I pressed my right foot as hard as I could on the accelerator and we lurched forward at a faster speed. I found it hard to keep a straight line on the path as I drove blindly along in the hope we wouldn't meet any more obstacles that would prevent our swift escape.

'He's going to shoot us, for Christ's sake. Get a move on!' screamed Tracey, clearly not aware I was doing everything in my power to do just that.

We heard the noise of a gun and waited for a bullet to hit the car, but nothing happened. The only other noise we heard was Fasina shouting at Chike to pass over his gun. Tracey had ducked down and was looking around her seat and through the broken back window, reporting what she could see.

'Chike has thrown his gun to Fasina,' she commentated. 'Christ, he's coming after us again. Quick, get going – he can't half run!'

The car moved smoothly and we made our way swiftly along the lane. I didn't look back until Fasina's voice faded and I thought we were far enough away to feel safe. I saw him standing with his hands on his hips, looking defeated. Chike, meanwhile, was on his knees. He didn't seem used to physical activity, which was a blessing for us.

'Thank heaven for that,' I said, as we drove off the lane and out onto the unmade roads of the village on stilts. I could see why the locals preferred to use boats.

'I thought they were supposed to be somewhere else,' I added, thinking it was a good job Chike didn't find me in his shack with Gowon.

'So much for not showing any signs of aggressive behaviour,' said Tracey. 'I think shooting at us is pretty unfriendly.'

Tracey was shaking. I didn't feel too calm myself. The one bead of sweat developed into a torrent, and they made their way down my face to drip off my chin.

'Well,' I said, 'we've got away unhurt, so let's be thankful for small mercies.'

'I can't say I'm sorry to see the back of that place,' said Tracey, after we'd both calmed down a bit. She was using the mirror in her sun visor to put on some make-up and inspect her hair. 'I really need sorting out.'

I looked over and agreed. Maybe when we found somewhere to settle for a few days I could do just that. A few elocution lessons, some decent clothes and a proper haircut and she could pass for a proper person.

We drove along the road out of the village for about half an hour, when the realisation of what we'd done hit us. The morning sun had risen but the air was still damp. I shivered at the thought of our freedom. We'd been close to poverty and poor housing but as I drove the roads became wider, better made. There were houses with nice gardens and shiny cars. A feeling of liberation manifested as a rising sense of joy.

'I can't believe we did it,' said Tracey. 'We bloody did it. High five!' she added, throwing her hand high in the air to meet mine, which was strangely redundant having no need for gear changing. I made a mental note to look at automatic cars when I got back to England.

'Well, where to, partner?' I said, wondering which direction would be the most appropriate, although anywhere was fine as long as we were heading away from where we'd been.

'Anywhere that sells some decent food. I'm bloody starving,' said Tracey, just as the car hit a huge pothole and veered off the road, finally landing on its side in a ditch.

'Shit,' I said.

CHAPTER TWENTY-ONE

Tracey limped along the road, having lost one of her unsuitable shoes but clinging on to the fact that one shoe was better than none. I'd offered her a pair of my pumps but she flatly refused to borrow them, claiming they made her legs look dumpy.

'That was a close shave, Cynth,' said Tracey, dragging along the bags we'd taken from the car. We couldn't manage all our luggage, so left a fair bit behind, knowing we had plenty of cash from Chike's haul to get new supplies if we needed them.

I was a bit stunned by the accident and glad we weren't hurt. My left foot had banged down on the brake thinking it to be the non-existent clutch and we went leaping along the road. I lost control, and the next thing I knew we were tumbling into the ditch. I'd been in many minor car accidents before but nothing involving the entire vehicle rolling at speed. To say I'd been scared would be an understatement, but I kept my composure, certainly in comparison to Tracey who was screaming obscenities until we came to rest, sideways on.

'I thought we'd be well mashed after that little spin,' she added. 'All I could see was the world going round and round. It was like being in a washing machine, only without the water.'

I ignored her. Had she been able to drive maybe she could've got us a bit further down the road. She's got longer legs for a start and might have been able to reach the pedals. Regardless, there was no point crying over spilled milk. Or spilled mascara, in Tracey's case.

'We're OK and we're away from that place. Be thankful for small mercies,' I said.

I looked around and couldn't see any signposts or any indication of where we could be heading. All we could do was keep walking and hope for something to come along and guide us.

I'm not one normally prone to daydreams but I couldn't help fantasising that Darius would appear from nowhere and save us. Hardly a white knight, but the principle would be the same.

'Where are we going now, then?' asked Tracey. 'Do you reckon we'll meet anyone on this road?'

I thought for a bit. There hadn't been another car for the hour or so we'd been driving, and the further we went the windier and narrower it got. Surely it had to lead to somewhere?

'If only my phone worked. I could see if I could get hold of Baz.' Tracey said. 'He'd come and get us.'

I felt a bit sorry for her, although I had to admire her ability to believe the best of a man who had taken her money and failed to turn up at the airport to meet her, particularly as they were supposed to be getting married. It wasn't like my situation with Darius, who had a genuine family problem and needed my help. She'd been completely taken in and still believed she'd be marrying her 'bit of black'.

'Maybe someone will know my friend. He works for a big IT company and is very successful, which I suspect is a rarity in this country,' I said, thinking that surely everybody would know Darius for his charm, ability and downright good looks. I couldn't imagine anyone ever meeting him and overlooking his many qualities.

'Shall we sing some of those songs again?' asked Tracey, as she launched into her peculiarly individual version of 'Waterloo'. 'Or we could play I-spy?' she added.

For the sake of keeping us occupied we got through two verses of 'I Will Survive' before deciding singing wasn't going to do it for us. The game faltered after neither of us could think of anything but 'mud', 'road' and 'tree' to spy.

'Let's play Snog, Marry, Avoid,' said Tracey, who had to explain the rules. I thought it a foolish idea at first but found it quite captivating once I got into the swing of it. Nigel Havers was definitely a 'Marry', although I'd settle for a 'Snog' any day. Tracey said she'd marry someone called Ozzy Osbourne, who I'd never heard of. When she explained who he was, it confirmed my opinion that she was totally out of her mind.

We went through some other lists, and I only hesitated when she asked about Gowon, who I admitted privately to myself I would snog, but told Tracey he was best avoided. She didn't question any further as she'd thought of a number of other males to consider including Prince William and that bald chap from *EastEnders*. I passed on our future king on the basis he is already married and therefore not a prospect, which I suspected wasn't a consideration for Tracey, and shouted an emphatic 'Avoid' for the balding beast of the east, who reminded me of a newly born rat with a slightly less attractive personality.

Bored after twenty minutes of trying to entertain ourselves, silence kept us company until we approached the next bend in the road. Before I thought my insanity would set in permanently, a car drove up behind us. It was a red VW estate with an English number plate.

A white man about my age sporting a long, grey ponytail stuck his head out of the driver's window and shouted over to us, in an English accent.

'Hello, ladies. Do you know there's nothing here for miles? Can I offer you a lift?'

Tracey didn't answer, but made her way straight over to the car and got in the back seat, pulling off her one shoe as she did so and rubbing her foot.

'You must be some kind of angel,' she said. 'The thought of walking one more step was about enough to get me right weepy.'

The man got out of his car and took the two small bags Tracey had abandoned in the road and placed them in the boot. He opened the passenger door and gestured for me to sit in the front. I was most definitely relieved, and at that point couldn't care less about the dangers of getting into strange men's cars. After our experience it wasn't likely to worry either of us, and anyway, he was English.

'Thank you,' I said, feeling very grateful in a way I didn't think I had before. 'You're very kind.'

'The name is John. Very boring name, but it's the only one I've got,' he said, pressing the button to open the windows.

'The air conditioning has broken, so I hope you don't mind the manual version,' he quipped, looking over in my direction with a welcoming smile. His face looked familiar, but his ponytail didn't. I've never been keen on men with hair that grows beyond the collar. Makes them look creepy.

'I'm Cynthia, and this is Tracey,' I responded. I didn't refer to her as my friend, as I didn't want to give him the impression she was the type of person I'd normally spend time with.

'We think we might be a bit lost,' I added, thinking it better we didn't give too much away about our recent whereabouts in case John was a sympathiser of people who abducted middle-aged women to fund their lifestyles.

'I would say you are, but then, aren't we all? Where were you thinking of heading?'

'We're looking for some people we know. My friend is called Osezua and he works for Forensix Inc. Would you know him, by any chance?'

John laughed. 'There are an awful lot of people called Osezua in this country, and probably a fair few who also happen to be working for Forensix. You might need to be more specific.'

I thought at that point how little I knew about Darius other than his job – to do with using technology to detect fraud – and the fact he was Nigerian. We'd had many conversations about his country but they hadn't conjured any pictures for me. I didn't know where Nigeria was on the map, let alone its capital city or commercial centres. To be honest, I was more interested in other things. He'd told me about tribal differences and corruption but he might just as well have been telling me about the internal workings of a steam engine for all the understanding it gave me. I'd never been to Africa and hadn't, at the time, any intention of going. I would nod occasionally to give the impression I'd taken in every detail, and now wish I had.

What I'd learned from Darius was not much to go on when

searching such a large country for one man.

Tracey was quiet, seemingly happy to allow fate to take its course. No doubt she'd have been quite happy driving around with John all day as long as it meant she didn't have to hobble along like Jake the Peg.

She coughed and said: 'I don't suppose you know Lady Buke Osolase, do you? She's my future mother-in-law.'

I wracked my brains to think where I'd heard that name before.

'My, oh my, you are marrying into royalty,' I heard John say, as I nearly choked with the realisation – that the woman I'd bumped into on the plane was Baz's mother.

'She's one feisty lady. Buke is very well known in Nigeria. She's based at the university, about twenty miles from here,' he said.

Lady Buke Osolase was the large African woman I'd had the run-in with on the flight over. Tracey had probably mentioned her before, but I suppose I wasn't listening. I also wasn't too certain she was someone I wanted to meet again, but fate had intervened and was suggesting she could help us out.

I looked round at Tracey, who was trying to pull a comb through her hair but it had got stuck.

'Lady Osolase was on our flight. I fell into her lap and the hostess told me who she was,' I said.

Tracey looked stunned, and then the penny dropped.

'Oh yeah. Baz said something about her coming back from England. She'd been working somewhere. Cambridge, I think. Talking about clever women, or summin' like that. She's got a degree.'

John was looking in the rear-view mirror at his other passenger and seemed to be slightly amused. Possibly by the comb poking out from where it had become lodged or maybe the general state of her face. Either way, he was friendly enough to us both and showed an interest in Tracey's forthcoming marriage. He asked lots of questions about how she knew Baz and where she planned on living. He certainly showed an interest in her which, along with his ponytail, made me think he might be some kind of liberal.

'Well I can take you to the university and you can catch up with her there, unless you have her address?'

Tracey immediately responded: 'Oh no, I've never met her. She was on our plane, but I didn't know it was her. Probably a good thing, as she seems a bit scary.'

As we had few options I suggested going to the university might not be a bad idea. Even if Lady Osolase wasn't there we could ask for some directions to Darius's company. I considered whether we should go to the British embassy and tell them about our plight, but was feeling nervous about admitting all the facts of our imprisonment and also our escape. I didn't want to be charged for drugging guards, tying them up and leaving them locked in shacks without food or water. And I didn't particularly want anyone to hear their side of the story.

We'd travelled for some miles before John turned very quiet. He'd stopped asking us questions and a frown had started to knit between his brows. Tracey had fallen asleep, and I'd been trying to keep a level of conversation going but had found it increasingly difficult.

'So how far away are we?' I asked.

John sighed deeply and held his breath before answering.

'You'll get there when you get there. Don't be impatient.'

I heard the sound of the doors locking. I looked round, and by that point Tracey had woken up. Her hair was wilder than ever and spread out at right angles from her scalp, with the comb still embedded somewhere above her right ear.

He put the radio on but it made a lot of noise without connecting either to words or music. I got a little frightened and could tell that Tracey's breathing was heavy, which could have been down to cigarettes or the same thought I was having: that this was all getting very scary. I was surprised she didn't say anything.

To hide our concern, I asked a few more questions of John, who was staring straight ahead and had started to lean forward, his head vertically above the steering wheel and his back a good distance from the comfort of his seat. He didn't answer anything I'd asked, but suddenly burst into a description of his life.

We heard he'd gone out to the country in the 1960s to work on a cotton farm. He'd met his wife, an African, and had three children who went to live in the USA, having received a good education that enabled them to get good jobs in finance. She'd died four years ago, and since then he'd been working for an agricultural forum that was aiming to increase investment in their industry.

'Farmers struggle in this country. Not like in the UK where they get EU support for throwing milk away and growing rape seed which no one wants to buy,' John said.

He leant across and I thought he was going to touch me, but instead he pulled open the glove box and took out a packet of Opal Fruits. They are called something else at home now, so either they were very old or Nigeria has different brand names to us.

'Have a sweet,' he said, shoving the packet under my nose.

'No thanks,' I replied. 'My fillings and jaw aren't up to the demands such a chew would make of them.'

He spoke very slowly and deliberately this time, raising his voice.

'Have. A. Sweet.'

'I'll have one,' said Tracey in the back, still tugging at the comb.

'Both of you; have a sweet,' he said, and as he did so he whipped his head round to me. His eyes looked peculiar, as if he'd just sat on something very sharp and uncomfortable.

I took a green-wrapped sweet only to be told it was John's favourite, so I picked a yellow one for me and a red one for Tracey.

'Yum,' she said, as she ripped the wrapper off and threw the Opal Fruit in her mouth.

I didn't find it so easy. The paper had stuck to mine so I shoved the whole lot in rather than encourage further wrath for fiddling while John fumed. As my saliva took on board its task, the paper started to slide off as I chewed. I had a mix of what I could only describe as envelope and rubber mixed with cheap cake flavouring. The only reason I recognised the flavour was because I remembered one of Titch's school home economics sessions where she found the food processor more fascinating than the process of making food. Anything she could lay her hands on was included in the so-called cake mixture, including her school report and a broken HB pencil.

I was hungry and didn't feel things were going quite our way. Tracey was leaning forward in her seat to look through the front window, no doubt wondering herself where we were headed. I gave her a 'look' to suggest she kept her mouth shut.

We were heading down a narrow road when suddenly John swerved the car into an opening no more than the width of his car. We bumped down into a wooded area surrounded by dark, overhanging trees. Everything felt dank and dark and the temperature dropped. He sped up and we were weaving our way through trees like skiers on the downhill slalom. Both Tracey and I were too scared to say anything.

He brought the car to a grinding halt on a platform above what looked like a lake. There were bits of wood, clothing and various unidentifiable matter floating on the surface. The doors unlocked and locked again. John was playing nervously with his keys, and I started to think about my life and how I didn't want it to end just yet. Although I don't want to see too much of my children and grandchildren, I would like to see them now and again. They are grown-ups with their own lives, but I take it for granted they are there and I hope they think the same about me. I could feel a tear well up in my eye.

Is this your home, John?' I asked. I could feel Tracey's nerves jangling behind me and hoped she wouldn't do anything silly.

'Of course it bloody isn't, you stupid cow,' he shouted, and then wound down the electronic windows partially before getting out of the car and slamming the door behind him. He locked the car using his key, which he placed in his pocket.

'What the frig is he doing?' hissed Tracey from the back. I turned round and she reminded me of a frightened llama I'd once seen at Chester Zoo.

'Shhh. I don't know, but I don't think we should upset him in case he does something silly,' I whispered to her.

John turned back to us and stood, looking through the car rather than at us. He took a roll-up cigarette from a tin in his back pocket and lit it, shielding his lighter from an imaginary wind with his cupped hands. He took a deep drag and held the smoke in with his breath. Then he pulled a mobile phone out of his pocket and jabbed at the numbers on the screen.

'I've got them. Where do you want them?' I heard him say to the person on the other end of his phone. 'Yep, OK. Be there soon.'

Rising panic, fast becoming a familiar feeling, escalated its way to my throat. I sensed the tension, and when I looked at Tracey I saw she was nervous. Who was this man and what did he want with us? What on earth was going to happen?

Tracey and I waited silently for what he might do next. He continued to smoke until the cigarette end nearly reached the tips of his fingers, and then he threw it to the floor, grinding it to its death with the soles of his Caterpillar walking boots.

Getting back in the car he seemed more relaxed. He didn't speak to us while he turned on the engine and started manoeuvring. Turning in the few feet that was available looked impossible, and both Tracey and I squealed when the offside front wheel went over the ledge.

'Don't worry, girls,' John finally said. 'Rear-wheel drive – we'll get off here OK.'

After much roaring of the engine he sped back up the lane he'd brought us down and we thought for a moment he might be on his way to the university at last.

'Time for you to see the real Nigeria,' he said to us, still staring forward through the windscreen and not looking at either of us.

'That would be lovely, John, but we would really like to get to the university first, if that's OK. Maybe we could meet up tomorrow,' I said in the hope it would put him off whatever trail he'd decided we should all be on.

'There might not be a tomorrow,' he said. 'So best I show you now.'

What is it about this place? I thought as I looked round at Tracey, who had slumped into the back seat like a grumpy teenager.

I thought we'd got away from kidnappers.

CHAPTER TWENTY-TWO

We drove for what seemed like hours, but what was probably only twenty minutes, through different shanty towns with groups of farmers tending goats and areas of vast landscapes littered with huts, old cars, occasional buildings and dead animals. I was surprised not to see the odd body along the road, left out for the vultures by a country that didn't readily look after its most vulnerable citizens.

John was in a world of his own, grunting in response to any questions we asked and filling any silent gaps with frequent attempts to get his radio to stick to one channel.

'What do you think you're doing? Who are you and where are you taking us?' I asked, and got no reply.

'I'm talking to you,' I added, getting angrier at the thought that this man had snatched the freedom we'd only just secured.

Tracey tapped him on the shoulder.

'Look, mate. You might think we're desperate to see whatever it is you've got to show us, but I need to get married.'

He looked at her through the rear-view mirror and sniffed before looking away again. After a couple of seconds he pulled the car to a sudden halt and forced on the handbrake before it had stopped.

'No one, and I mean no one, needs to get married.'

He looked at us both in turn, settled back into his seat and started up again, veering back into the road in front of a tractor, which was thankfully going sufficiently slowly to stop in its tracks.

'Madman!' shouted our driver to the young African farmworker. Strangely enough, it was exactly what I was thinking about John.

Just as I'd given up hope of knowing where we were going, the road began to look familiar. When I spotted the upturned car in a ditch I knew we'd come back full circle. It was surrounded by a number of official-looking people, some in uniforms taking notes, and what looked like police officers.

John sped past the group and, as he did so, I spotted the back of a man wearing a tight blue suit across a large chest. He was bent towards the car and so his face couldn't be seen. But I'd seen that suit somewhere before and, as we veered round the bend and nearly out of sight, I could swear I saw Darius looking back. The moment passed too quickly to be sure, but I prayed to a God I wasn't sure about, promising everlasting faith and devotion, if it could only be him. Then I'd know I'd be safe.

'Where exactly are you taking us?' I asked again, glancing back at the black Audi and the group, but they were gone completely from view. I wanted to ask him to stop, but guessed it would be pointless. The man was on a mission. Disappointment weighted my shoulders.

'Have you no manners at all? We need to know what is happening.'

I could barely contain myself and wanted to do something drastic to stop this man taking us somewhere we didn't want to be. I thought about grabbing the steering wheel to crash the car, but considered the possibly dire consequences. A vein pulsed in my wrist, a sure sign my blood pressure was above its normally healthy level.

John stopped his car at what we soon saw was the back of the settlement. I recognised the narrow road up to Chike's shack with all its lumps, bumps and metal bins. It was incredibly rough and so close to the water I was surprised we made it past.

He parked in the gap left by the absence of Chike's vehicle, and John told us to get out, which we did – not having much of a choice.

His eyes looked like they were being poked out of their sockets from behind and his face had taken on a purple flush. He squinted and pulled his mouth in a tight line.

'We don't like people taking off without saying goodbye,' he said.

'We find it very rude.'

'Who are you?' I asked, feeling my skin tingling with nerves. 'We deserve to know what you are doing and why you are doing it!' I was getting more and more frightened at what was happening and also very annoyed. John wasn't the kind Englishman I'd taken him for. As a fellow Brit, I thought he'd steer us to our safety, not betray his country and its citizens by leading us to a pit of horror and possible death. I wanted to punch him in the face.

'You are a disgrace to your country. We demand to know what you think you're doing. You should be helping us, not siding with a bunch of dangerous criminals.' I shook with rage and indignation. John ignored me, unmoved by my references to his nationality and integrity.

'What do you want with me, anyway?' said Tracey, who was stumbling about on her one shoe with a lit cigarette hanging out of her mouth. 'I've already been told I'm no use to anyone.'

She seemed remarkably calm, and I wondered whether I should take up smoking.

'You can make me feel better, that's what,' he said, and nodded his head towards the settlement. 'You escaped and I found you. I have to say it didn't take very long.'

There wasn't much else to do but follow him into the main shack, seeing as we had nowhere else to go. And more importantly, nothing to take us anywhere. I glanced at Tracey, who was negotiating her way down the path, head down and with arms splayed out for balance. As soon as I could, I would tell her about seeing Darius. If it was him it would only be a matter of time before we were rescued.

We could hear whimpering. We were pushed through the door by John and could then see that Gowon and Chiddy had been strapped to chairs. They were being whipped by Chike with a bundle of twigs tied together with coloured yarns from his needlepoint set.

'You stupid, stupid boys,' he was shouting at them. 'You incompetent fools with fish food for brains. You are so stupid I want to cut you in half to see if you have anything inside you other than marshmallow and fluffiness.'

He marched around the chairs, choosing different strands of the wool so he could colour co-ordinate his corporal punishment. He stopped briefly to plait three colours together to fashion a rope.

'I have very low expectations, but you fail to achieve them all,' he shouted. 'You turn my life and our business into shit!'

Chike moved towards John, pointing back at the guards as he did so.

'Whatever I do, it's pooh,' he said, as he finally sat down. 'That's a poem,' he added, and I had vague recollections of a small boy and a childhood bear. He'd got it wrong.

'So, you're back,' added Chike as he picked up his 'Groovy Frog' tapestry and unpicked a few bits of green yarn that were out of place. He placed it back on the table and stared at Tracey and me for what seemed like an eternity. His facial muscles moved independently of each other, colouring from blue to pink with various shades between. I was reminded of a film I'd seen about the Northern Lights.

'You mustn't ever leave Chike again. That is very bad.'

'Why won't you just let us go?' I asked. 'We are no use to you.'

Fasina sat in the corner of the shack, behind the table, humming the Nelson Mandela song repeatedly. He rocked backwards and forwards, clutching a crucifix and occasionally crossing his chest. It was the first time I thought he might be a Catholic, and I immediately felt sorry for him. He'll suffer terribly from guilt when he acknowledges what he's been doing.

'Oh, but you are very useful,' he said. 'You are the key to our desires, the summit of our mountain climb, the jam on our toast, and the fingers on our gloves!'

Chike looked over at Gowon and Chiddy, who were still whimpering, possibly more from the indignity of being tied up tightly on chairs in their underwear than any actual pain. They'd also been gagged, and I could see fear in Gowon's eyes when he finally lifted his head to look at us.

'I'm just thinking of what kind of punishment I should give you, and also our very stupid, idiotic and brain-dead guards. Maybe I should tickle them to death? Cover their bodies with honey and feed them to ants? Send them to England to watch repeats of your terrible daytime television? It is rubbish!' he said as he jumped up and down like a kangaroo with fleas.

I hadn't seen Chike like this before and remembered he and Fasina had guns. They'd had plenty of time to reload and find whatever instruments of torture they desired.

'Please don't hurt us,' said Tracey, in a voice that came from somewhere deep inside. 'We're trying very hard to get you what you want, but we can't do nothing while we're here,' she added, though her voice was barely audible.

Chike snorted, and his eyes closed up tightly so you could just see his pupils staring out at us. Fasina increased the volume of his humming and started to tap the table in time with the tune, all the while looking across at Tracey and me with glassy eyes. We'd upset them, and it looked like we were going to pay. I felt sick and very light-headed. Adrenalin coursed through my system, and my heart pounded like a double bass in a jazz band.

Tracey breathed heavily and suppressed sobs that every now and then manifested as soundless shudders through her entire body. I hoped we could think of something to get us out of this situation before Chike chopped us up and left us to rot alongside the animal carcasses and waste – or used our innards to finish off his tapestry.

'Get out,' he suddenly shouted and waved his hands up and down to move us out of the shack. 'All this standing about won't do. We shall have some tea. A very English tea to suit my very English guests,' he added, saluting as he stood up.

Tracey looked over at me with a confused expression. We didn't have a lot of choice but to go along with what was happening. I tried to look nonchalant in a bid to keep us both calm.

John turned round and bowed to us one by one, picked up a hat that was sitting on the table in front of him and put it on backwards.

I wondered if he was on medication, and whether or not it was running out. He could be a potentially dangerous man. One who might eat your liver with a fine Chianti.

'Tea it shall be, so follow me,' he said, turning in military style and marching out of the shack. 'So it's knock out your pipes an' follow me. Oh, 'ark to the big drum callin',' he tried to sing, but his smoking habit prevented any tuneful emission. 'Kipling,' he added, perhaps making a point that his knowledge of poetry beat his colleague's knowledge of A.A. Milne.

'Didn't he make quite good cakes?' said Tracey.

'Exceedingly,' I corrected her automatically, before turning to John. 'Tell us who you are. Why are you involved with these men?' I demanded.

He ignored me and gestured that we should follow him. There didn't seem to be much alternative.

'What do you get out of all this?' I snapped at him, taking hold of Tracey's arm. Her legs were giving way, and I thought she might collapse with sheer terror. Mine weren't holding out much better, so the act of helping someone else distracted me marginally from my own concerns.

'None of your business,' he finally replied, as he herded us back to our original shack. I breathed in deeply to calm my nerves. It was a move I soon regretted, as the smell of stale banana and eggs was now joined by something else. Everything was as it was before, apart from the very strong whiff of fear.

John followed us with the keys. He seemed to have taken over from Gowon and Chiddy, although I suspected his position in the gang to be higher. Chike had treated him like an equal, and he walked with the assurance of someone who knew he was in charge. I thought briefly that my bathroom experiences weren't going to be anything like they were with my young African friend.

'Now, you behave or things will get very nasty,' said John. 'Do you understand me? We can be very nice people but don't like being upset.'

I started to hate the man in front of me, possibly even more than our Nigerian kidnappers – who I suspected had a strong motivation to capture foreigners. But John was one of us, or should be.

'I'm cold,' I said. 'I want my cardigan out of my bag?' I knew I sounded like a petulant child, but all my efforts at keeping calm were outweighed by panic. If I was going to die, I was going to do so shouting.

'What bag?' said John.

'It's in your boot. If you had any decency you would get it for me,' I said, hoping I could find some way to prick his conscience. It didn't work, as he just glared at me.

We're back where we started because of you,' said Tracey to John 'Why are you being such a tosser? Aren't you one of us?' she said, echoing my thoughts.

I shot Tracey a scowl to suggest that winding John up might not be the best thing we could do. He might be unstable, but so far had shown no sign of violence. I hoped we could keep it that way.

I was feeling quite cold, no doubt a reaction to the situation, as the African sun was doing its usual thing of producing sweat on everyone else. In typical British fashion I hoped tea would be on its way to solve all ills. I also hoped it would warm me up. My arms looked like a recently plucked turkey, thanks to goose bumps.

'How are we going to get out of this one?' Tracey said, after John had locked us into the shack we thought we'd left for ever. 'There's no getting away from the fact, we're either going to be here for ever or will be killed. I can't stand it any more,' she said, as she threw herself down on the mattress and beat it repeatedly with clenched fists.

I couldn't think of another way to escape, which was frustrating having got away from the camp on the first occasion relatively successfully. John didn't seem to be the type we could lure with sexual favours, and I don't think either of us could have faced up to that challenge even if he was.

However on this occasion the thinking wasn't down to me. I thought Tracey had finally slumped down in resignation, but she suddenly got up and I could see she'd picked up the needle I'd left behind on the chest from Chike's needlepoint crisis. She moved over to the door and started working the thin shard of metal into the locking mechanism of the padlock, which was just accessible through the gap between the door and the wall. It was hanging on a chain, which she'd managed to pull through inside to get access.

'What are you doing?' I hissed at her, keeping my voice as low as possible so as not to alert anyone to our discussion.

'I've seen this done on the telly. If I wiggle it about it might move the lock,' she said.

By the time John returned with our tea, she'd got nowhere.

'Chike made these,' said John, as he offered a plate of biscuits round. 'He's quite a cook. He loves *The Great British Bake Off.*'

I couldn't understand why he was being so casual. He'd brought us back to this prison and must have had some idea of the danger in which he'd placed us.

'Who are you?' Tracey asked. 'Why won't you let us go? You're a Brit. You should be one of us, after all.'

John scowled. 'That's where you're wrong, my dear. I'm not one of you at all. I came to Nigeria so many years ago I have lived here longer than I did in the UK. I've seen the poverty, the corruption and the lack of justice. I consider myself to be African.'

'Are you part of the gang?' I asked.

He laughed and then stopped suddenly.

'We are not a gang. We have a viable business,' he said. 'We don't harm anyone. Or at least we haven't yet.'

His attitude chilled me. John was clear that he considered his part in the kidnap to be legitimate and that he had every right to conduct himself accordingly. He had no empathy with our fear and didn't seem to care that innocent people's lives were being put in danger.

He wouldn't speak any more of who he was or his part in the operation, and so we made small talk in a bid to keep him happy, until he finally left, telling us we would have visitors later that evening.

We distracted ourselves from increasing levels of fear by playing the games that had kept us occupied before our escape. But the appeal of piercing celebrities' bodies with sharp implements had gone, so we talked about what we thought had happened to the guards when the bosses found out we'd escaped.

'I don't envy them,' I said. 'They could be in even more danger than we are. At least we have a value all the time that they think they will get a ransom. They don't have any value if they can't be trusted.'

Tracey said she thought the guards might have been killed but was relieved to know they were still alive.

'Maybe the gang isn't as nasty as we think. They're just trying to frighten us.'

And doing a good job, I thought.

We weren't too surprised when Gowon and Chiddy where both thrown into our shack, almost unconscious and wearing only pink pyjama bottoms and blindfolds. Their hands and feet were both bound so they were unable to move.

'Do not touch them or help them in any way,' shouted Chike as he closed the door behind them and fixed the padlock. 'They are stupid scum with the intelligence of fish in a fryer, toads in your holes and peanuts in your butter. Brains mushed to mash.'

We were sorry to see them in such a state, not least because we'd probably given them more drugs than we needed to, but also because pink didn't suit either of them. They looked very scared. Chiddy was crying and Gowon was biting his bottom lip repeatedly. Every now and then their heads would drop with the effort of staying awake.

The guards probably knew more than we did about the lengths the gang would go to. I thought about helping them, but it wasn't worth the risk, although we did steer them over to an area where they could sleep. Neither Tracey nor I were keen on giving up the mattress that had been our bed.

'What happened to you?' I asked Gowon. 'Chike doesn't look too pleased.'

He spoke quietly when he answered. He was obviously scared

of doing anything else that would upset his masters.

'We were asleep when they came back and found you'd gone. You got us into very bad trouble, Cynthia. We will be punished for doing nothing wrong.'

'Now you know how we feel, locked up here for no reason,' said Tracey. 'You deserve to be punished for getting involved with them in the first place.'

'You don't know how bad these men are,' said Chiddy. 'They just want money and will do what they have to do to get it. Even keeping old ladies locked up.'

I hoped the reference to old ladies didn't include me, and asked him who John was. Neither of them really knew, other than they'd been told an Englishman was one of the big bosses who'd set up many of the scams by getting hold of British people's bank details. He'd also supplied the technology used to send emails and set up false bank accounts. Chiddy said we were part of a major scam targeting the south of England, where the kidnappers thought the most money would be.

'English are the ones who give us the most money. The English and the Americans, particularly women,' he added.

'What do you get out of it, though?' I asked.

'We get money for our families. The children can go to school and our parents can eat. We get enough for cars, and one day maybe enough for our own home,' said Gowon. 'We can't get that any other way,' he added, sounding apologetic.

It wasn't difficult to understand their position, even if the morality was a little dubious. They were motivated by poverty and hunger and a desire for education; to be part of a competitive and savage world. Compared to the greed-driven bankers we have in our so-called 'civilised' Western culture, they are icons of integrity.

'We're in grave danger,' said Gowon. 'We have displeased our bosses, and if we live, it will be to regret it.'

Tracey showed no interest in their plight. We both probably thought the same thing, that our own escape was paramount and what happened to them was irrelevant in the grand scheme of things. She walked over to the door to work on the padlock again, squeezing her fingers through the gap to get hold of it and just managing to do so, using one of her last remaining false nails to keep the lock in place.

'I reckon I could do this, given enough time,' she said.

'What are you doing?' asked Gowon. 'Don't get us into any more trouble or we could be badly hurt. Please be careful if you think anything of me, Cynthia.'

Tracey looked round at me and shrugged, suggesting that whatever we thought of our guards we were much more interested in our own fate.

'We won't implicate you in anything,' I said.

'I don't want to be implicated,' said Chiddy, through intermittent sobs. 'It sounds unpleasant.'

We weren't given any more of the herbal drink. No doubt we could no longer be trusted, having used it as a weapon to ensure our escape. This meant I found it difficult to sleep, and it must have been the same for Tracey as she spent hours fiddling with her needle, probing the padlock with varying degrees of patience, but without any let-up.

Gowon and Chiddy snored throughout the night, having finally found a comfortable position on top of a pile of newspapers. Once Gowon had gone to sleep I lay down next to him. The proximity of his body offered warmth and some human comfort – a surprising element of solace in what had become nothing short of a nightmare.

My life didn't so much flash before me, as we are told it does when facing death, but sauntered past at a leisurely pace. I'd been thinking about Colin, family life and how easy we'd had it. How slow, calm and calculated everything was. We could afford to have integrity as we had all the opportunity we needed to keep body and soul together. We didn't struggle for food or schooling for our children. Our problems centred around whether the beef needed to be pink or brown, or whether the children should be watching television rather than doing their homework.

There were always jobs when we were first married, although I chose to stay at home after one unsuccessful attempt at full-time employment. We took in a Bulgarian au pair to look after the children, but after she mistook my instruction to feed the children and do the ironing for 'please invite all your friends round and eat the contents of our freezer', I decided it wasn't going to work. I was disciplined by the boss I was working for at the time - on three occasions I was late - after having to rush Annika to the doctor for the morning-after pill, and on another two because she hadn't returned from her boyfriend's house by the time I needed to leave. She pleaded that she had to stay in England as she was in love with her tattooed father of three, a man known locally as 'Slasher', who was 'such a nice man he helps everybody in the community'. After explaining community service was his punishment for stealing cars and attacking a petrol station attendant with a plastic hammer, we packed her off with a one-way plane ticket back to Sofia and the promise we would keep in touch. We didn't.

I was just about to drop off when Tracey crept over and shook my arm.

'I think I've done it,' she said. 'The lock's open.'

Incredulous, I went to check, and she was right. It hadn't completely unlocked, but with a bit of brute force the bottom fell from the heavy, arched pin holding it in place.

'Now what do we do?' she said.

'Get the bloody hell out of here,' I answered.

CHAPTER TWENTY-THREE

We crept out of the shack, safe in the knowledge Gowon and Chiddy were asleep. Their snoring had covered any noise we made pulling the lock apart and opening the door. We could hear faint mutterings coming from the main shack and guessed John, Chike and Fasina were discussing what to do with their errant guards.

'We need to get out of here quick, before they realise we've gone,' I said, as I secured the padlock back into position so they wouldn't immediately know anything was wrong.

'I could hot-wire John's car. It's not an automatic, so I'd know how to do that,' said Tracey.

I was taken aback. First she'd managed to pick her way out of our shack without any real difficulty and now was telling me she had skills with cars I didn't even understand.

'Don't look at me like that,' she said. 'I know people think I'm really stupid, but a few turns in the nick soon show yer a few things, yer know. I could have done computers, but did mechanics instead.'

'Prison? What for?' I asked, reeling from this information. I'd been held hostage with a criminal.

'This and that,' she replied. 'Mostly minor charges, theft and that when I was a kid, and once for pissing in a public place, but that was because I was on a suspended so anything would put me down.'

My knowledge of the justice system was sufficient to know her offences would be more than minor to justify a prison sentence, but I was hugely grateful she'd picked up something worthwhile during her time at Her Majesty's pleasure.

'We could give it a go, I suppose,' I said, wondering if Tracey had been hiding, if not a light under a bushel, certainly a flickering flame.

We walked past the main shack very quietly, listening at all times to make sure the men were still talking, and made our way towards the pathway next to the water. We passed Chike's shack on our way and saw our bags had been left open on his bed. We also saw the guns they'd used during our previous escape, so we went in and I got them quickly while Tracey picked up our bags. We took it in turns to keep watch, and ran out as quickly as possible for fear of being caught. I could hardly breathe with anxiety and hoped my palpitations wouldn't turn into a full-blown panic attack. When we got to the water's edge, John's car had been left unlocked and we were surprised but thrilled to see he'd left the keys in the ignition. I threw the guns into an oil drum propped up at the back of the shack.

'I s'pose he wouldn't expect anyone to nick his car from here!' Tracey said, as she chucked her bag on the back seat before grabbing mine and placing it on her lap.

I jumped into the driver's seat and turned the key. Nothing. I tried again and it revved over a couple of times but stuttered to a halt. I looked at the petrol gauge and could see it was empty.

'No fuel,' I said. 'It looks like we're going to have to think of something else.'

We got out and had a look around, as much as we could in the darkness. It would be at least three or four hours before it got light so we had to make do with the moon's illumination and a faint glow from the poor levels of lighting over the settlement. Once my eyes had adjusted I could see what looked like a small boat bobbing around on the water's edge, tied close to our pathway. It might even have been the one used to bring us from the airport.

'What are you like at rowing?' I asked Tracey as I formed an idea. She shrugged, and I guessed she'd never done it before. Come to think of it, neither had I.

We clambered into the boat with our bags and untied it from the mooring. The rope was heavy and difficult to unknot with shaking hands and the knowledge we had to get away as quickly as we could. We didn't know how long it would be before our absence would be noticed. I picked up the oars and managed to get us from the edge of the water, pushing and pulling on the oars until we were in the middle of the stream.

As much as I attempted to get us to go in a straight line, we kept going round in circles. I tried using one paddle and that made things worse, and then tried going forward, then backwards and both directions using both paddles, but I just rocked us about until I thought we were going to capsize.

I was exhausted, and wished I'd gone on that team-building weekend with the magistrates three years ago. They'd all learned to canoe, apart from Caroline Sharp who had to be airlifted to hospital after capsizing and getting her hair caught in some weeds. She was under the water for over three minutes before the rest of them worked out she wasn't showing off.

'Where are you going, you bloody women?!' we heard from the settlement. It was Chike and John, running down the pathway. I supposed they must have been alerted to our escape when I'd tried the car engine. I froze. I had no energy left to do anything, and felt as helpless as a rabbit in a trap. My life was going to come to an end without any chance to choose my funeral song.

'Give the bloody things to me,' shouted Tracey. 'We won't get far with you faffing about like a blue-arsed fly.'

She grabbed the oars and set off at a good pace, and soon we were heading down the water, which I could only assume would take us back towards the roads we came down on our first day.

Chike and John ran along the bank, shouting things we couldn't make out but guessed weren't too polite. I thought I heard the word 'guns', and was pleased we'd managed to get rid of them. I wasn't sure we'd escape so easily a second time.

Tracey's bat wings flapped vigorously with the effort, and her bust heaved up and down as her pectoral muscles worked tirelessly to move us along. I admitted privately to being impressed.

'I wish you'd told me you had such skills,' I said. 'It would have made me feel so much better.'

'Wha?' said Tracey, as she puffed heavily. 'I really must give up fags, for good this time. I can hardly breathe.'

Another shout came from the waterside and I could see John cycling along on a bike they must have picked up from along the way. I saw the outline of Chike sitting on the handlebars, thankfully hindering progress, particularly as the path was bumpy and his attention to his body mass index was somewhat slack.

'Keep going, Tracey, you're doing brilliantly,' I said, encouraging her as best I could. 'I think they're losing us'.

There wasn't much light – only that coming from the few settlements along the way – so it was easy to keep to the shadows. The water stretched for some distance but we could see a shoreline with lights and buildings in front of us. Every time we thought we would be able to see where we were going the darkness came over us, but we could still keep tabs on the men, who were struggling to keep up. Judging by the coughing I heard, John's lungs were in a worse state than Tracey's.

Tracey was flagging, but I could just make out the bike, which was further away than before. John's legs were at right angles to the bike, which was bumping along what was obviously very rocky ground. Next we heard a thud, followed by a loud splash, a shout, then some moans followed by swearing and more shouting. The bike had hit something, and Chike had flown off the handlebars and into the water. John was lying on the ground clutching his leg.

'Come here, you bloody English whores!' John shouted, while getting up into a crouching position. 'We'll find you, you'll see.'

The shouting diminished in volume as Tracey sped us further away from the camp and towards the light. She certainly put some power behind her efforts, and it was only a few minutes before I looked back and could see the opposite edge of the lake and a jetty. Chike and Fasina's outlines could be seen, and I imagined them scratching their heads in frustration as they saw us making our getaway. I thought I saw Chike smack Fasina round the head, and could swear I heard him whimper.

I resisted the urge to breathe a sigh of relief until I knew we were far enough away not to be caught again. Even if they got in a car to follow us it would take them some time.

Tracey relaxed and let the oars drop for a while, as she rubbed her upper arms and stretched out her back. 'I wonder what they would do if they caught up with us?' she said, pulling her hair about in an attempt to get the sweaty bits out of her eyes.

'I dread to think, but I don't suppose either of us would like it very much,' I answered.

It took just over half an hour to reach the main road where we'd first come from the day we were picked up by Fasina, and I was relieved there was an obvious mooring place and signs of activity, despite it being the early hours of the morning.

'Let's park up,' said Tracey, and I didn't bother to correct her. I couldn't care less about her vocabulary, as I'd decided she was something of a heroine. Left to me, we'd be spinning ourselves back into the hands of our captors.

We climbed out of the boat, through a small and overgrown pathway and onto the concrete square that doubled as a mooring and a car park. We could see a number of vehicles and instinctively tried them all until we found a very old Vauxhall Chevette that had been left unlocked.

'Well, it ain't automatic,' said Tracey, smiling. She bent down into the driver's footwell and found a handle, which she pulled firmly. The bonnet flew open and she made her way to the engine. Within a couple of minutes the car was running and we were clambering in.

'It won't have a steering lock, being so old,' Tracey added. 'Otherwise we'd have to go in a straight line everywhere!'

The car was easy to drive and had over half a tank of petrol. I wondered how far that would get us. We'd decided to try and find our way to the University of Nigeria.

'I'm not sure which way to go,' I said to Tracey, who was busy rifling through the glove box.

'Look what I've found,' she said. 'It's a satnav.'

I didn't know what she was talking about.

'A what?' I asked.

'A satnav. It shows you where to go'

I could have done with that for Mr Gamble and that policeman, I thought.

'Let's fire it up and see if it works,' she said.

Tracey found the cigarette lighter socket and plugged in a series of leads. She seemed to know what she was doing, which I suspected was down to some kind of misspent middle age. What else she was capable of, this dark horse of a woman who I'd completely under-estimated?

'Posh Git's got one of these. It takes you all over, without needing to know where yer going,' she said. 'Just hope it's got the university on it.'

As Tracey pressed different pictures on the front of the machine that looked like a small telly, the thing spoke to us in English.

'You have reached your destination,' it said in a voice sounding remarkably like John Cleese.

'Well it obviously isn't much use, otherwise it would know this is the last place I want to be,' I said to her.

'Hang on, hun. We need to programme it first.'

She investigated the screen and found the university.

'According to this, we are eighteen miles away, which should only take thirty minutes. We need to go to the end of this road and take a right, and it is almost straight all the way there.'

I was stunned by Tracey's competence with the funny map thing, although I worried about driving a car that didn't have the ignition key in it. I surprised myself that I was more concerned about that than the fact it was stolen.

'That's a marvellous invention. Why didn't I ever know about it?' I asked her.

'Expect that husband of yours didn't want you knowing the way anywhere. You know what men are like with women and maps,' she said.

We drove for forty-five minutes. The map machine had taken us to a derelict farmhouse, down three dead ends and to a closed petrol station. When it told us to get out of the car and walk, I decided it didn't know what it was doing.

'I think we are going to need to get some help,' I said. 'We could be driving around for ever if we take any notice of this thing.'

We drove round a bend and saw a bright orange light with a picture of a bed on it, claiming to offer twenty-four-hour bed and breakfast facilities.

'Why don't we stop there for a bit,' I suggested. 'Even if we find the university, no one is going to be there at this time of the morning.'

I looked around and Tracey was asleep, with bits of twig, bracken and leaves poking out of her hair, probably from when we got out of the boat and had to clamber through the hedges on the shore.

I followed the signs to the bed and breakfast, and after about three miles came across a roadside café with a number of men sitting around tables, playing Scrabble, despite the fact it was still only just past breakfast time. They looked up as our car kangarooed into the car park, where it stalled. Not having a key, I decided to leave it where it was. I didn't want to go in alone to ask about accommodation, so I woke Tracey up to come with me.

'We could just sleep in the car,' she said, as she took in the puzzled faces of the seven men of varying ages, all looking in our direction.

A reception area in the corner looked like one of the booths you get in fairgrounds, to change notes into coins. A big woman with bulging eyes and huge hooped earrings sucked her teeth at us and lifted her jaw slightly as if to ask us what we wanted. The men were silent, other than the occasional sound of sucking on their rolled up cigarettes.

'Urm, I'm just wondering if it would be possible, maybe, somehow, to have a room for the night?' I said, offering up some of the nairas I'd taken from Chike's room in our first attempt to escape. Strangely, he hadn't noticed their disappearance.

The woman registered no emotion as she scanned Tracey and me before finally handing us a key.

'One room only. First floor,' she said, as she grabbed all the cash

I offered and shoved it down her cleavage.

'And could we have access to a telephone?' I asked, aware that I should contact my family to tell them I was safe.

'I'll see what I can do,' the woman replied, looking Tracey up and down with what appeared to be some amusement.

'Ta, mate,' said Tracey, seemingly oblivious to the atmosphere. 'Any chance of anything to eat?'

The woman behind the counter nodded over to the other corner, where a very small man was seated. He might have been a dwarf or midget, as he could barely be seen above the serving area. When he stood up you could only see his hat.

'Ladies, what would be your pleasure?' he said in a very posh English accent. It took us by surprise because although we knew he'd gone behind the counter we didn't expect him to speak to us with so much authority. We couldn't quite see where the voice was coming from until he clambered up on a stool, rendering him almost man-sized.

'I suppose a bacon sandwich is out of the question?' said Tracey. The man rubbed his eyes and looked a bit puzzled. He offered us a choice of a meat kebab with a selection of dips or fries. We decided on both, my normal concerns about saturated fats being thrown to the wind. When he took just one of the naira notes and offered us change, I realised how much the big woman had taken for our room. It had better be worth it.

It tasted delicious, and I asked the small man what he'd flavoured the meat with. He told me it was Suya spice, a Nigerian mix of peanuts, ginger and other ingredients he failed to name. I made a mental note to pick some up before going home, now that going home seemed like a possibility.

Once we'd eaten we took our bags up to our room. We walked through a long corridor past a kitchen and then up some rickety old stairs, almost too narrow to pass when carrying a bag. It was so narrow Tracey could use both her elbows at once to help her up the steepest bits. The key was redundant, as we pushed the door open to reveal a double sofa bed that had seen better days, a few blankets and a sink in one corner featuring a dripping tap. A bare light bulb hung from a ceiling that was occupied by a number of cockroaches, dangling menacingly as if waiting for some occupants they could terrorise and possibly eat.

'Not the best place I've ever stayed,' said Tracey, as she looked around the room. 'Yuck. Have you seen those bastards,' she added, pointing to the insects above the bed.

She got out one of her large shoes and started beating them into submission, so they ran into dark corners where they could no longer be seen.

'I hate them things. What's the point of them? I'm all for nature and that, but cockroaches and wasps are totally pointless. Try telling me they ain't.'

I wasn't going to try and tell her anything, although I suspect there is a use for them. David Attenborough would probably say so, anyway.

We were both tired, and thankfully used to sharing bed space and blankets, so made the best of what was on offer, pledging to get away as soon as we'd had some sleep. When we couldn't nod off for fear of attack, we took it in turns to keep an eye out for insects and anything else marauding about our room.

After about three hours or so we must have been tired enough to drop off because we were both woken at the same time by the woman from reception sitting on our bed.

'Who are you?' she said, when we stopped panicking. 'There are people looking for you.'

It took a while for us to register what was going on. We'd been in a deep sleep, despite our surroundings, and neither of us could immediately recall where we were.

'You need to get out of here, and quickly. There are two men here, saying you must go back with them. I know about them and they are not nice to foreign people,' she added.

'What do they look like?' I asked the woman, who had adopted a far nicer attitude to us than she did when we first came in.

'One is English, and limps. The other is Nigerian. I don't know their names, but they are part of a gang who kidnap people for money. They have camps around here with very many hostages, although they don't usually take women.'

'Tits and bollocks,' said Tracey, jumping up and rubbing her face. 'Are we never going to get away from those bastards?'

'Don't worry, I have sent them away. Someone saw you coming in here but I said you wanted a taxi to the airport. They think you are on the way there now and have sent their men in that direction. If you go the other way, you'll be fine.'

We explained briefly what had happened, and how we'd been taken hostage but had managed to escape. We also told her we wanted to get to the university so we could get in touch with the authorities.

'Ah, now I think I remember. Your story was in the papers. I recognise you now, although you look younger in the photos,' said the woman.

Well, we were, I thought.

'They don't like it when people get away, it upsets their egos. They said you escaped twice, so I'm in deep admiration of you both. However, the men have all their contacts on watch for two Englishwomen.'

I asked again about using the phone to call home and was told it wasn't advised.

'We don't want these people to trace you or your family through your calls. We must get you away from them and into the hands of professionals. You must be very careful. You're money to them and nothing else, so they'll stop at nothing if they think they can profit.'

Tracey and I looked at each other and my heart pounded. I'd used as much strength as I could getting away the last time, so didn't want to have to do it again. Thank goodness for British stoicism. It was going to come in very handy.

Tracey's bottom lip quivered and she looked like she was going to cry. Her hormones had been quite manageable in the last day or two, and I hoped they weren't going to let us down now. She'd also been buoyed by her feats at breaking into the padlock and car, not to mention her impressive rowing technique. I thought about nicknaming her Katherine Grainger, but wasn't sure Tracey would get the connection with the Olympic athlete – it didn't seem quite her thing. I hoped her unexpected displays of competence weren't going to desert her now.

'I'm so pissed off with this. I just wanna get married and stop all this running about,' she said. It was a sentiment I agreed with, even though I might have expressed it differently, and without the marriage bit.

'Please stay here,' the woman said. 'I will sort something out for you. Don't go back to the car. You stole it from one of the men's brothers, and he is very cross.'

She swayed out of our room and we could hear the stairs creak as she made her way down to the bottom. I tried to work out in my mind's eye how someone with such wide hips could get down the narrow steps without getting stuck.

Tracey's head was in her hands and she was sniffing, wiping her hand across her nose as she did so.

'Please don't cry,' I said, placing my hand on her shoulder, although I wanted to cry too.

'I ain't crying,' she answered. 'I'm allergic to animal fur, so reckon there's something lurking about. I haven't been like this since me neighbour's hamster escaped and got in under my floorboards.'

On cue, a large rat made its way from behind the sink, ran across the room and dropped down into a very small space between the door frame and the door.

When the woman came back into our room to tell us she'd managed to sort out transport to get us away in safety, she found Tracey and me with our arms wrapped round each other and standing on tiptoe on the bed.

If Tracey and I wanted to find any common denominator other than the fact we'd both been kidnapped, we'd found it in that room.

We both hated rats.

CHAPTER TWENTY-FOUR

Once we'd recovered our composure, we picked up our bags and made our way down to the kitchen, where the woman told us to wait. She'd shut the premises while she made a number of phone calls, and I didn't feel so bad about the amount of money she'd taken from me when I saw how many customers she turned away.

'I've found you a driver and he is reliable and trustworthy. Maybe you'd like to go to the airport or to the British embassy?'

'I do really need to sort everything out,' I said. 'My family will want to know I'm safe.'

Tracey wailed that she wanted to see Baz as soon as possible, and I had to admit to being keen on tracing Darius. He'd infiltrated my being, and since thinking I'd seen him I was convinced it was only a matter of time before he found me.

But I thought the embassy was the proper place to go first. I was imaging my children all pitching in to get the ransom money together, selling everything they owned to ensure my return; or at least I hoped they would be doing something along those lines rather than resorting to Bobbie's general apathy and unfounded belief that everything would always be all right.

Apart from that, our captors should be brought to justice. We needed to report what had happened and get them all punished. I did think of Gowon and Chiddy, though. They were only following orders so they could earn a living in a world that didn't provide one very easily. As for Chike, he was clearly a sandwich short of a picnic, and in our legal system would be treated for insanity rather than given any type of sentence. John struck me as the type of person who would be able to wipe his hands clean of any criminal involvement. I thought that was probably the case for a lot of white people in Africa.

'Can't we just go to the university and do the embassy stuff when we're there?' said Tracey. 'If Baz's mum is there we can get her to sort everything out.'

I thought that was a fairly good compromise, and that maybe the university would be a better place to find a man who worked in technology. We'd been missing for a while, so another hour or two wasn't going to make much difference, and maybe it would be better to have someone help us find our way around the Nigerian authorities as I hadn't a clue where to start.

'OK, let's go to the university, but if Lady Osolase won't or can't help us then we must go to the authorities as the next priority. We need to make sure people know what has happened to us.'

The woman nodded her head and picked up her phone. After a number of conversations of varying degrees of loudness she'd got things sorted for us.

'My brother will take you. He is a professional driver and will chauffeur you for one hundred American dollars, if that amount is OK,' she said, her eyes twinkling as if to suggest it had to be, or we'd be stuck washing dishes until we gave in.

It occurred to me that if this woman hadn't gone through my case she wouldn't know I had any American dollars. Thankfully, Chike's stash was going to play a further part in our release. A fact I found most satisfying.

Her brother was well dressed, wearing a suit, white shirt and tie. His shoes were highly polished and he spoke with a refined accent, as if he's spent his life in the colonies with a nanny and a butler.

'I'm very pleased to meet you, ladies,' he said when he arrived, nodding slightly with deference. 'My name is Luter.'

I went to shake his hand but he turned away. After all our recent adventures I wasn't sure we could trust him, but I felt we had no choice. I just hoped he wasn't taking us straight back to the camp and the oh-so-familiar shack.

'My car is waiting for you,' he said, indicating our way out of the building through the back door. 'Please, come with me. We can't be too careful.'

'Good luck with everything,' said the woman. 'Watch everyone and stay safe.'

She rubbed her fingers together, suggesting I needed to make a payment. I found one hundred dollars of Chike's cash and went to pass it to our driver, but the woman grabbed it and shoved it in her jacket pocket.

'That is fine, now go,' she said, being friendly but firm about the transaction. She could give Alan Sugar a good run for his money, that's for sure.

Tracey and I clambered into the Volvo estate. I'd gone to sit in the front seat but Luter shook his head and opened the door behind his.

'Thank you, kind sir,' I said, hoping the friendly recognition of his helpfulness would keep us in good stead.

We explained where we wanted to go and he nodded, claiming he knew exactly where the university was and that it would only take twenty or thirty minutes to get there.

A very expensive taxi ride, I thought.

Tracey asked him if he had a girlfriend and he said he didn't. I asked him if he lived round here and he said he did. He wasn't overly talkative. I also noticed he was changing gear with the wrong hand. I screwed my nose up and conveyed my thoughts to Tracey, not wishing to alert him to any concerns.

'Bleedin' hell, Cynth. He's only got one arm. Look!' she whispered.

I looked over to the driving seat on the pretext of addressing a clothing issue and she was right. A plastic arm stayed inanimate on his knee while his other did the work of two. Apart from the occasional judder, it would have been difficult to tell his driving was compromised in any way.

'Have you been driving for long?' I asked, nervous about the answer.

Luter looked straight ahead, checking the rear-view occasionally and with concentration.

'Ten years, on and off. I took a break for a while, after the accident.'

I was about to ask him about his accident and if it had been responsible for the loss of his limb, but he became distracted, checking the mirror more frequently and driving erratically – not because of any disability, but through a deliberate effort.

He drove along the road at a speed I considered to be far too high given his missing limb, although he coped with every bend and turn well.

'We're being followed. Don't panic, I will get rid of him,' said Luter.

We'd only been on the road for five minutes, so I couldn't understand why he thought someone was following us.

'Are you sure it isn't just someone going the same way?' I asked, as the ride got bumpier. Tracey was trying to put on some mascara and was poking most of it in her eye.

'He's been on my tail since we left. It doesn't smell right' he added.

Someone's been watching too many American films, I thought, as he looked again in his mirror before accelerating hard around a bend and then taking an off-road route across sandy, deserted terrain that led to a road running below the one we were on. Tracey's mascara wand had left a trail of black across her cheek and into her hair. As she tried to rub it off it spread over her face, making her look like an extra in the *Black and White Minstrel Show*.

I looked behind me and saw a silver Ford Mondeo driving parallel to us on the road we'd just left. It kept with us as we travelled along, slowing down when we did and speeding up to match our pace.

'We'll need to change cars,' Luter said, picking up his phone with the only hand he had, thereby letting go of the steering wheel temporarily. Tracey screamed and made him jump. 'Don't worry, ladies. I will get you where you need to be in complete safety.'

He spoke to someone in a dialect I couldn't understand and then called another number, using his knees to balance the steering wheel as he did so. It didn't fill Tracey or me with confidence, although he seemed adept at dealing with his disability.

'Bill, it's Marcia's brother. She told you the problem.'

There was a brief pause, followed by Luter's response, and then he threw the phone across into the passenger seat, taking hold of the wheel again with his hand. I breathed a sigh of relief.

The car above disappeared from view. Luter looked at the road we'd been travelling a few times before speeding up, telling us to hold tight. As we got to a junction, we could see the other vehicle coming towards us from the left. Our car was reaching a queue of traffic, which he overtook before spinning round in a U-turn to come back on ourselves, much to the annoyance of other drivers, who took to hooting, swearing and spitting.

'Dirty bastard,' said Tracey, as she spat back at an older man who'd managed to aim his spittle directly through the gap in her window, hitting her on her forehead.

It was like a scene from *The Italian Job* as Luter took us through overgrown paths, down hills, up rocks and across fields containing a variety of livestock including disgruntled chickens and hundreds of nonchalant goats, all of which continued to slide their jaws about in the business of chewing whatever they could get into their mouths.

'Jesus wept,' said Tracey. She'd been clinging to the strap above the back door, until a particularly bouncy bit of the ride made it come away in her hand. 'This is some bloody joy ride.'

I thought all my bones were going to break, then Luter screeched to a halt in front of a small, makeshift office building. Checking all around before he let us out, he ushered us around the side and up some steps into a reception area with a desk.

'Stay here. Don't move,' he said, as he tried to get into an office at the back, but it was locked. Another door opened into a small room piled with filing boxes.

'Come in here. My friend isn't here yet, but is on his way and will give us another car.'

I asked him if he still thought we were being followed and, if so, why?

'You've escaped from a big gang. They think you're worth a lot of money to them so will put word out to get you. Dead or alive.'

Tracey wailed.

'Not dead! Why dead? We've done nothing wrong, and I'm getting married!'

We heard a noise. It sounded like someone running up a metal staircase. Luter got hold of Tracey's arm and guided her into the storeroom, pushing her down under a table, gesturing that I should follow them. He was about to leave us so he could investigate when we heard a man's voice.

'Two girls, bound and gagged. Knickers only and no funny business,' the voice said.

We all kept still. I suspected Tracey was thinking the same as me – that our fate was sealed and we'd be back in the shack, only this time our captors wouldn't be so nice. *Damn and blast.*

Luter crouched down low, listening for more sounds. We all heard a phone ring and the same male voice.

'Two girls, bound and gagged. Two hours,' said the voice, which coughed and then burped loudly. Tracey looked at me with a wrinkled nose to express her disgust.

We sat in silence, although I could swear my heart could be heard beating across the entire country. Tracey clutched hold of my arm with both hands and was so petrified she was barely breathing.

The noise of the phone could be heard again, along with another cough.

'I'm coming, I'm coming,' said the voice in a husky, almost inaudible, way. 'Two girls, bound and gagged.'

It was getting a bit repetitive. We knew what he had planned, but did he have to keep going on about it?

A car could be heard parking outside and Tracey's eyes widened. She must have thought, as I did, that the stalker in the car had found us. I hoped neither of us would pass out as we heard footsteps make their way up to the cabin. The door opened.

'Luter, Luter, are you here?' shouted an English voice, as we heard keys being jangled.

Luter slid along the floor of the storeroom and poked his head out round the bottom of the door.

'Bill, it's me. I'm here,' he whispered. 'There's someone in your office. He's been following us.'

A loud laugh could be heard, and then the sound of keys in a door.

'Don't go in there, Bill, it could be dangerous,' said Luter to the sound of further laughing.

'There's nothing dangerous about Pussy,' said Bill, still chuckling as he spoke.

Luter stood up gingerly, and I didn't blame him. I wouldn't believe someone asking for bound and gagged girls could be considered nothing to worry about.

Bill, a round man with a soft, pillowy face and a vast moustache, marched over and peered through to where Tracey and I were suffering from an adrenalin rush and were shaking like leaves in a wind tunnel.

'Come, see. There's nothing to worry about,' he added.

We got up and shook ourselves down before being led into the back office, where we were greeted by one of the biggest macaws I'd ever seen. Blue and yellow, it was perched on top of a large cabinet, tethered by a long chain it was holding with its beak and one claw.

'It's a bloody parrot!' said Tracey, incredulous at the sight of this huge bird eyeing her up with big beady eyes.

'Suck my cock,' it screeched in her direction. 'Tickle my arse,' it added for good measure.

Bill went over and tapped the bird on its nose, which hissed at him before making the sound of a telephone ringing.

'I'm so sorry about Pussy's behaviour,' said Bill. 'I rescued her from a brothel in Lagos and haven't quite managed full rehabilitation. Her language can be terrible!'

'Get yer tits out,' Pussy continued, enjoying having an audience. She ran up and down her perch sideways before imitating a phone again. 'Two girls, bound and gagged.'

Bill gave Pussy a grape and it occupied her sufficiently to keep her quiet while Luter discussed the need for another car.

'If you could keep mine until I've delivered the ladies safely, it should act as a decoy,' he said, proving himself to be our saviour.

We were offered tea and some toast, which we accepted after Luter checked there was no sign of our pursuer. Bill was very attentive and wanted to take care of us, it seemed, although I found his constant staring at me a little off-putting. However, it was delightful to have real butter and marmalade, home treats I'd stopped giving myself on the grounds they weren't healthy.

Sod health, let's live a little, I thought, making a mental Post-it note to do more delicious things in my life.

Bill told us he came from Brighton, and I guessed his age at around fifty-five, although he may have aged badly. His large round gut and lack of hair gave him the badge of middle age, although it could easily be the result of the privileges of living an ex-pat life as an oil worker; hotel meals, expense-account lunches and numerous invitations to parties held by other British people living away from home. Bill had been working for a large corporate organisation which had made him redundant four years ago, but he'd decided to stay and set up a car hire business. I suspected it wasn't very profitable, judging by its location and the state of the vehicles parked outside.

'The wife ran off with a young black man. He was only about thirty-five,' he said, and I felt myself blush.

'She took him back to England to show him off to all her friends. Some menopausal desire to prove someone found her attractive, in my opinion,' he added.

I flinched at the scenario and made a mental note to never mention Darius, particularly his age and colour, to anyone in Surrey.

'He's welcome to her. The novelty will have worn off now, and instead of home-cooked meals and clean sheets for romantic nights, she'll be moaning he never does anything round the house and making him sleep in the spare room,' said Bill, topping up our tea.

'The only peace he'll get is when she goes out on her Chardonnay and tapas nights with her friends from the gym, which is easily eradicated on her return, as she'll be so pissed she'll demand an argument, ending up with her telling him to fuck off and get out of her life. Then she'll cry and everything wrong in her life will be his fault. I'm best out of it!'

'Fuck off,' Pussy could be heard saying from the back office.

'On that note, let's get you a car sorted out. We don't have much to offer, but as you haven't got far to go I'm sure we can get you to your destination in one piece.'

He showed us to a rusty old Morris Minor Traveller with one tyre considerably flatter than the others and the windows taped up with old bin bags. Looking at the bird droppings on its roof I assumed it hadn't been driven for a while.

'I love them cars,' said Tracey. 'You can lie down in the back of 'em!'

I didn't comment, and went over to pull the driver's door handle to look inside, half expecting a family of wild animals to appear. The handle fell off as I tugged it, and Bill came rushing over to help me, noticing my embarrassment.

'Don't worry, that's always happening. I'll sort that out,' he said, pulling a Swiss Army knife from his pocket and screwing the handle back into place.

'It's a good runner. We'll pump up the tyre and get you going soon enough.'

Bill handed Luter the keys and went back for our luggage.

'As the windows are covered up, you can't be seen. Stay in the back, and if we get followed again they won't know you're in here,' said Luter, as he pumped the tyres with considerable effort.

It was a good plan so we settled in, making ourselves comfy on the various blankets and cushions that were scattered around. Bill opened up the back doors and placed our bags to one side.

'My old dog, Blackie, used to love it in here, rest her soul,' he said, adding that he wished us good luck and hoped to hear of us again soon. Tracey started to sniff, and this time I put it down to dog fur rather than dropping levels of oestrogen.

Bill banged on the roof and went back inside to answer a phone call. How he knew the difference between a real one and Pussy's impression was a mystery.

Luter turned the engine over but it wouldn't catch. The Morris would rattle into some kind of life and give up, like an arthritic pensioner making her way up the stairs.

On the seventh go the car fired into life and juddered its way out onto the road, which was eerily quiet. Luter was tense throughout the drive, finding the absence of one arm a major hindrance with a steering wheel that had a life of its own. He hung on marvellously throughout the rest of the journey, which was only fifteen or twenty minutes – and from our viewpoint far more relaxed than the drive to get here.

Tracey was contemplative as we drove along, and then sat up with a start, leaning in to the driver's seat.

'You're a good bloke, you are. We could have met another bastard, couldn't we, Cynth?' Her eyes were glinting and I wondered what she was up to.

'But Luter here, he's 'armless!' she added, laughing loudly at the brilliance of her joke.

CHAPTER TWENTY-FIVE

It was the start of the working day and there were hundreds of students milling about, carrying bags and books and looking like any undergraduates might in any city. The University of Nigeria was a huge campus made up of many orange-coloured buildings, each reached by long, inviting driveways. I'd expected it would be more dusty shacks and young people squatting around camp fires with scrappy notebooks.

Luter dropped us off near the main entrance and we walked to the door, not sure whether to go straight in or not. We didn't look like typical university visitors. Tracey lit up one of her cigarettes, having retrieved them from her luggage, and started to cough. She leaned forward and clutched her chest as she did so, as if to hold in her lungs before they were violently expelled.

'Ugh. This is horrible,' she added, once she'd regained some composure. 'Reckon I've actually given up. That'll save a packet.'

Quite a few packets, I thought, as I watched her break the lit end off and flick it into an area of bushes beside us.

'Well, I think we'd better go and see who we can find,' I said to Tracey, who was stamping out a small fire she had created in the undergrowth.

Once inside the building we were greeted by a row of female receptionists, all of whom looked the same to me. Big, wide grins full of white teeth, round cheeks perched on high bones, pink lips accentuated with bright red lipstick, and straight, shiny hair. I wondered how long it took them to get it like that or whether they needed some kind of reverse perm.

All looked welcoming, and so we went straight to the first desk.

'We are looking for Lady Buke Osolase. We understand she

works here?' I said in as an informed voice as I could. I'd become aware we didn't look too smart, having survived imprisonment and a minor road accident. Thankfully Tracey kept her mouth shut, which helped on a number of levels.

If they'd noticed our dishevelment they didn't give any indication, and our receptionist immediately rang through to an extension number.

'Who shall I say is calling?' she asked.

'We're friends from England,' I said.

Then Tracey added: 'And she's my prospective mother-in-law.'

The receptionist didn't bat an eyelid, and within a few seconds that seemed like an eternity to me, she told us to take a seat and that Lady Osolase's secretary would be down for us.

When the lift came down to our floor a while later I was surprised to see she'd come to meet us herself, and got rather scared. Our last meeting hadn't gone well, and the fact Tracey was likely to offer herself up as daughter material wasn't very promising.

'Hello, ladies. So lovely to see you,' she said, as she glided along the tiled floor, swishing her coloured robes behind her as she moved.

She wore a bright orange, yellow and red turban that set off her features, making the spectacle of her advance rather magical.

I stood up, and as I did so could see the flash of recognition creep across her face. I thought about running away, but said hello back and hoped I'd be able to bluff my way through my fear.

'We met on the plane,' I blustered.

She smiled in a professional manner, with lots of teeth but the smile did not meet her eyes.

'I know dat,' she replied.

Tracey jumped up alongside me and held out her hand.

'I'm Tracey – or Trace – and I'm engaged to be married to your son, Baz.'

Lady Osolase grimaced. Her head whipped round to meet Tracey's gaze and she said nothing, other than to turn to the receptionist and ask for tea to be brought to the meeting room.

'Follow me,' she finally said to us, and we dutifully lagged behind as she swept her way through the corridors and into a small back room. It was decked with literally hundreds of photographs of her with different people from across the world, including faces I could recognise such as David Cameron and, strangely, Tom Jones. The abiding sense was one of colour, making everyone around her look grey. I began to feel the same.

She pointed to some leather chairs grouped around a beautifully ornate wooden coffee table engraved with various African animals, and told us to sit. We did exactly as we were told. For the first time in my relatively long life I thought I'd lost my voice.

'So, me son's bin up to his old tricks, den,' she finally said to Tracey, with no apparent disdain but just a faint look of sorrow.

The tea arrived and she poured it out, saying nothing more. The silence was solid. It felt like you could physically shift it around the room.

'Where did ya meet me son?' she said, handing around china cups and saucers and offering sugar once we had taken them.

'On PlentyOfFish,' said Tracey.

'What d'yous say?' asked our hostess, looking puzzled.

'It's a website, for dating. Then we went on holiday and he asked me to marry him. That's why I'm here.'

Lady Osolase breathed heavily through her teeth and sat up very straight. She took another breath.

'I'm very sorry to say dis a familiar story. I s'pose he asked yous for money, too?'

Tracey was looking to the floor, and I wondered if she'd finally realised what was going on.

'Yeah, five grand.'

'Oh my dear girl. I'll make sure yous git it back.'

She stood up and asked to be excused as she needed to contact someone urgently. She also asked us if we would like to freshen up, which we said we would. It was pointless trying to pretend we didn't, as both of us looked like we'd been to a 'Dragged Through Hedges Backwards' competition – and won.

In her absence a younger woman came into the meeting room and led us to a shower room within Lady Osolase's office suite. She also gave us soap, shampoo and conditioner and clean towels, telling us she'd return in half an hour.

It was a delight to get properly clean again, and even Tracey looked vaguely human after so many days of using washing-up liquid as shampoo in the camp. The towels were a delight, smelling of fresh roses and having enough thickness to absorb the water left on our skin. We were like schoolgirls, dancing around in front of the mirror and spraying ourselves with the perfume left for us on the shelf. I suspect I was suffering from some kind of demob dementia, but didn't care what people might think if they saw me. I even agreed to allow Tracey to apply a small amount of make-up to cheer up my otherwise pale skin. I wiped most of it off while she wasn't looking, but was glad of the bit of lipstick that remained. After all, I was hoping that our new friend was eventually going to help me find Darius.

Within the hour we were back in the meeting room enjoying some interesting sandwiches –filled with what I could only describe as chickpea and mustard paste – and cakes.

Once I thought we could trust our hostess I told her of our kidnap, how we got away and how I needed to contact my family.

'Dat is why I recognise yous,' she said. 'Der has bin much press coverage about da English 'ostages. Yous must haf bin through hell and high waters. Yous is a fine example of womanhood, and I honour you for dat.'

She immediately organised for messages to be sent to the embassy, and their advice in response was that we should make no direct contact with family until we were told the coast was clear. One of the staff came in soon after Lady Osolase had issued her instructions and told us my daughter had been contacted and the family were over the moon to hear I was safe. They'd been trying to call my mobile phone and hadn't got through, leaving many messages that went unanswered – although the truth is I wouldn't have known how to use it anyway. We were also told to be careful, as it was likely that the kidnappers would be angry at losing us as bargaining tools, and might not be prepared to give us up too easily.

It was the first time I'd thought of my phone for a very long time. That Blackberry thing I didn'tunderstand. Tom had tried very patiently to explain how to work all the various bits, but I just wanted something to make calls on. My fingers are too stiff for that texting lark and the screen far too small for me to see the letters anyway. I'd packed it with me to keep him happy but had completely forgotten about it until now. I suspected Chike or Fasina had whipped it anyway.

'They don't want ya family put in any danger by da kidnappers. If dem are frustrated they may take it out on dem,' she added. 'Please wait to be advised and be assured we will mek sure da rest of your family know you are safe and well.'

Having got my priorities sorted out, and gaining trust in Lady Osolase, I mentioned my connection with Darius, remembering to call him Osezua and mentioning where he worked. Rather than laugh, as John had, she said if she didn't know him, she would know someone who did.

'Forensix Inc. is a very big company. Dem haf 'undreds of people working for dem in many countries as well as in Nigeria. I know many people from my work and will hope to find who yous looking for,' she said.

Lady Osolase went on to tell us that Darius's company had sponsored many outreach programmes which helped young women across Africa gain education and health advice.

'Maybe dis is something yous would be interested in?' she added, before the phone on a desk in the corner rang loudly. 'Please, excuse me.'

She floated over to the phone and could be heard telling the person on the other end to show someone in. For a brief moment I hoped it would be Darius, but accepted it was unlikely anyone would have traced him that quickly. I wondered what the outreach programmes involved and whether he'd been directly involved. He'd often talked about the need for education in his country, and maybe I should have listened to him more. It might be a way of keeping in touch. I wanted to dig deeper, but Lady Osolase seemed distracted so I decided to drop the subject for a while.

There was a knock on the door and a young Nigerian man walked sheepishly into the room.

'You wanted to see me,' he said.

Tracey screamed.

'Where were you, you bastard? You were supposed to meet me at Lagos airport! Now we've been kidnapped and everything.'

I made the assumption this was 'Baz'.

His mother got up from her chair and moved slowly over to him. She lifted her right hand and I thought she was going to shake hands with her son, which seemed a little formal. But she didn't. She took a wide swing and whacked him round the face so hard the sound of the slap could be heard resonating around the room.

'Yous stupid boy. What haf you done to dis poor woman? You take her money and make promises yous don't keep.'

Baz looked over at Tracey with some horror. I suppose he never guessed she'd end up in Nigeria, much less in his mother's office.

'Well, you will pay for your sins dis time,' Lady Osolase said. 'Yous will be married to Tracey next week and yous will pay her back da five tousand pounds yous stole from her. How dare yous dishonour our family name.'

Tracey went into a delirium of emotion, jumping around like a hyperactive child on a diet of Coca-Cola and E-numbers. So much so, she couldn't hear Baz's protestations or his mother saying if he didn't do as he was told he'd be disinherited and sent to live in a leper colony.

'Right,' said Lady Osolase as she pressed Baz into the remaining available chair. 'Let's start mekking da arrangements.'

Baz's head hung low as his mother again informed her audience the wedding would be booked for the following week, and in the meantime he'd be confined to his mother's quarters, with an armed guard to prevent him making any escape.

There seemed to be no question of me going home before the

formalities were over. She organised that Tracey and I would have the use of a small bungalow in the grounds of her home while the arrangements were made. Despite being a formidable type of woman, she was certainly kind and fair when she thought someone had been wronged. I admired her stamina and determination, and her ability to insist her son did exactly what she required. Perhaps I should have been the same with Jonjo and Paddy? Perhaps they would have had better career prospects.

Tracey didn't seem to mind Baz's house arrest, claiming it would be bad luck to see her man before her big day. His look suggested he thought it would be bad luck to see Tracey ever again.

'Hold ya chin up, boy,' said Lady Osolase. 'Yous getting married, and yous will be proud. This is wat yous aksed for!' She glowered as she spoke, although the sentiment was lost on Tracey, who was babbling on about dresses, shoes, bridesmaids, guests and what could she do about her tooth.

'I've got to look perfect. I've been dreaming of it since I got "Engaged Barbie" and planned everything to the last detail.'

She slumped down a little in her chair as she asked if she'd be able to invite any of her friends and family from England. Although Tracey was informed that she could have whatever she required, I had a sneaking suspicion that those who hadn't acknowledged her disappearance were unlikely to attend a wedding in the middle of a Nigerian suburb.

We said our goodbyes and thanks to Lady Osolase, who asked one of her staff to show us to the bungalow so we could settle in and unpack. It was only a short drive away from the university, which backed on to the big house and its gardens.

'She ain't got far to go to work,' said Tracey, as she eyed up the pathway that led from the big house into the back of the campus. 'Lucky cow.'

I didn't think luck came into it, more a force to be reckoned with. I liked Lady O, though. She didn't take any prisoners – unlike her compatriots who we'd had the misfortune to meet. I looked across the grounds which stretched for what seemed to be miles into the distance and noticed bright lights aimed in our direction.

'I wonder what that is,' I said to Tracey, trying to blink away the blindness that the strong beam had caused.

'Just one of the staff, I expect,' she answered, not interested in anything but making her way into our new accommodation.

The bungalow had an open-plan lounge area with sparse but tasteful furnishing: a couple of low settees made from leather and dark wood, a table and a selection of floor rugs. The kitchen was tucked away around a corner, opposite a corridor leading to a bathroom with a shower, and two double bedrooms. I chose my room and threw myself onto the bed, delighted to experience the bouncy mattress and clean sheets. I thought of my bed at home and the unexpected delights it had brought. *How I've taken so much for granted*, I thought as I drifted off into a deep sleep that lasted until I heard a shriek from Tracey.

Imagining horror tantamount to severed heads, murderous thieves or the resurrection of Michael Winner, I was relieved to note her dismay was at the smallest of spiders in the shower room.

'Get it out, get it out,' she was screaming, oblivious to the fact that she was completely naked and hopping from one foot to the other as if on hot coals.

I looked around the bathroom and picked up the glass sitting by the side of the sink and placed it over the offending creature. It moved, and Tracey screamed some more. I noted it had the shape of a violin on its back, where its legs met. Only then did it occur to me it could be poisonous.

'Get me some paper or cardboard,' I said, as I stepped back from the spider, which had decided to wiggle about in its unexpected conservatory setting.

Tracey was only too pleased to oblige and returned with the back of a flour packet from the kitchen. I slid it under the glass and thankfully the rather mobile beast sat happily on top of the McDougalls logo while I took it out to release in the gardens. When I returned, Tracey was sat naked on one of the settees, drinking brandy she'd found in one of the kitchen cupboards.

'Bloody hate spiders,' she said, and then wobbled her way to the bathroom where I heard the shower going full blast and the sounds of Tracey's attempts at singing.

I had a sudden feeling of freedom, which lasted until Tracey returned in a dressing gown, to start what amounted to a monologue about what she wanted to happen at her wedding. The plans for marriage, even to someone who clearly had no feelings for her, became her sole topic of interest – and one that nearly drove me to her murder. I even thought about getting the spider back as an experiment.

It was a shame, because I had begun to like her.

CHAPTER TWENTY-SIX

The plans for the wedding were coming along nicely and things seemed to have settled down. The embassy had made further contact and also passed on messages from my family, who it seemed were content to know I was safe and sound. Tom had been helping the authorities in the UK by going through my computer and was apparently thrilled to be part of an international crime investigation. No one had asked if I was coming home, which was something of a relief as I wasn't sure I was ready to face my family just yet.

As for Tracey's wedding, she spent every waking hour talking of nothing else. I had no choice but to listen, as she had awarded me what she thought was the great privilege of being her matron of honour, which it turned out involved doing absolutely nothing.

It was a role I wouldn't have volunteered for at the best of times, but it gave me an opportunity to find out more about Lady Osolase. There was no doubt she was a very well-known and influential woman. Just the sort I'd like as a friend, as I was sure she could be trusted with her promises to help me find Darius, among other things I could just see myself taking her to bridge club so she could sort out Mavis!

It was difficult to know what to do with Tracey, so I asked Lady Osolase what a matron of honour might do for the bride when in Nigeria.

'Well now, dat is not the question, Cynthia. What we need to tink is what we can do for Tracey,' she said as she winked at me, explaining that under 'normal circumstances' there could be three types of wedding.

'Da families would meet and talk and price decided for the bride.

I don't tink dat going to 'appen'!' She roared with laughter. 'Best we keep it simple.'

Seeing my desire to have some kind of a role to play, she suggested visiting Lekki market at Victoria Island, adding it was where all the British visitors went to buy bags and shoes and 'to escalate the extinction of da African elephant', thanks to the various goods made from ivory.

Lady Osolase offered to lend me her car, and so I made plans to take Tracey the next day, hoping it would take her mind off the wedding itself, if only for a few hours.

The news of a market where shoes might be bought was well received. So much so I think her shrieks nearly burst one of my ear drums.

'You are a bloody star, Cynth,' said Tracey, as she pulled on a pair of boots over some dubiously thin-looking pink leggings. I wasn't sure whether to tell her the heart-shaped patterns on her G-string looked like nasty bruises where they showed through and was relieved when she pulled on a long green top which covered everything up.

Lady Osolase had only just bought her brand new Mini convertible and I was a little nervous about driving it, particularly as Tracey insisted on having the roof down. The dust and flies didn't seem to bother her as much as they did me, but then she was wearing sunglasses as big as saucepan lids. I also wondered about our safety, bearing in mind the warnings we'd been given about going out and about unsupervised.

'You just be careful and call me if you need me,' said Lady Osolase, making sure Tracey had taken a note of her number for such a purpose. 'Lekki is a tourist area so I am sure you will be fine if you stick to the main roads and don't get side-tracked.'

'An adventure!' shouted Tracey, standing up in the seat with her head through the roof as I drove out onto the side road and headed towards what the Nigerians call a motorway but what I would call a very wide path. It was difficult not to bump along, and after one particularly nasty pothole, and a real bruise to show through the pink leggings where Tracey had fallen against the gear stick, she decided to sit down.

After a few miles we saw the sign to the market and headed off down an even bumpier track. I couldn't see any further signs and started to panic a little until at last we saw a couple of traffic officials standing in the road.

'They'll know where we have to go,' I told Tracey as I pulled up in front of them and we both got out of the car.

'Is this yours, madam?' said one of the officers in a voice that might suggest he'd been to a rather posh English school.

'Er, no, it is a friend of mine's,' I said. 'I'm hoping you might be able to tell me how to get to Lekki market.'

The man walked around the car and gave one of the tyres a kick. I wondered if he'd do that if Lady Osolase had been driving.

'You got the MOT certificate?' he added, getting out a notebook and pen from his top pocket. Meanwhile the other man was standing some distance away and talking into a phone.

'I told you, it isn't my car,' I said, feeling a surge of indignation. He reminded me of that silly police constable outside the bank.

'Come on, mate,' said Tracey. 'Just tell us where to go. It's not our car and I'm getting married tomorrow.'

The officer looked up from where he was writing in his notebook and raised his eyebrows.

'Really?' he said, adding, 'How wonderful for you,' in what could only be described as a very patronising tone. 'So. No MOT. That will be fifteen thousand naira fine. Payable now.'

'You 'avin' a bleedin' laugh,' said Tracey, more affronted by the officer's lack of interest in her wedding than by the fine. 'Ain't you got anything better to do?'

She flung herself back into the car, leaving me to negotiate.

'That's rather a lot of money, isn't it? I'm sure the car has an MOT. The owner only bought it a while ago and I am sure it is new.'

'If you don't have the certificate then you have to pay. Now.'

I went back to the car where Tracey had been going through the glove compartment looking for paperwork and found nothing. She had also tried to call Lady Osolase in the hope she could help.

'Bugger, no signal,' she said.

It just so happened I had fifteen thousand naira in my purse and so I handed it over, vowing to sort the matter out when we got back to the bungalow.

'Don't I get a receipt?' I shouted out after the officer as he marched back to his car, an unmarked and quite old Nissan which didn't look much like an official vehicle. The two men jumped into their seats and were soon making dusty tracks as they disappeared into the distance.

'You thinking what I'm thinking?' said Tracey, picking a bit of apricot skin from between her teeth with an old match she'd found in her handbag.

I hope not, I thought, suspecting Tracey's mind to be occupied with wedding nonsense and underwear designs.

However her thoughts were quite valid on this occasion.

'I think we've been had,' she said, prising out the bit of fruit between her finger and thumb before taking a look at it and wiping it on her car seat.

I felt I had to agree, but dismissed the fact we'd been subjected to a further con and drove on to the market, which turned out to be only a few more miles down the road. I suspected we had been stopped at the ideal place for unsuspecting tourists who believed there was an on-the-spot fine for not have an MOT on a brand new car.

But what was I to do? Had I not coughed up, anything could have happened and, quite frankly, I'd had enough of being held to ransom. It was a shame they had taken every bit of my cash, though.

We struggled a bit to get the roof back on the car once we had parked up, but Tracey found the right buttons and, using a bit of brute force, managed to close it, with only a slight gap above the driver's door which she stuffed with some used tissues. Not necessarily very logical, but I did have to agree that passing thieves might think twice about dealing with snot-filled handkerchiefs.

'Wow, look at all this,' said Tracey, as she came across an entire street dedicated to shoes and fashion accessories. She tried fourteen pairs of shoes, six hair extension pieces of varying colours and a large hat – which we soon found out belonged to the stall owner – before finally moving on.

Small children flocked around us, touching us for luck and, on one occasion, jumping up to touch Tracey's voluminous breasts.

'Cheeky little shitbag,' she shouted after him, before his friends came back with him, also wanting a feel.

'Get stuffed,' she said as she swung her bag at them and they finally fled, only to be replaced with some more determined young men, aged about twelve, who insisted on showing us round.

'We show you all the lovely things of the market,' said the leader, who also spoke exceptionally clear English. 'Stay with us and we find you many bargains.'

Stall holders called after us, 'Please come and look, looking is free', and so it was until you got hauled into areas behind curtains and fed a sales pitch intended to make you buy something you didn't want.

'Lucky lady, take this beautiful gift,' said one elderly man who took pride in carving up bits of elephant tusk to resemble other animals such as giraffes and snakes. The irony seemed to be lost on him.

Three of our young hosts decided to take us through some back streets which led into a meat market, where whole sides of beef were being axed inefficiently into unrecognisable lumps for sale.

'Aagh, that's gross,' said Tracey, as blood spurted out from one shop, hitting her in the legs.

'Wish I'd kept those tissues now,' she said, taking the offer of a grubby rag from one of the boys and spitting on it before rubbing the blood even further around her clothes. 'I want shoes, not bits of cow.'

I didn't bother telling her that the leather shoes she'd been trying on were also bits of cow and let her weave her way through the colourful bangles and cloth that lined the stalls.

'Here, lovely ladies,' said a man in a loosely fitting suit as he came out from a hidden alley. 'Come with me, special discounts. Looking is free.'

His teeth moved up and down as he spoke, and I wondered if Nigeria had a second-hand denture trade, as his certainly didn't seem to fit.

I wanted to walk past this man but he pulled Tracey by the arm and into a narrow passageway which led, after many turns and twists, to a workshop where a number of young girls were busy making carpets by hand.

'Very, very good quality,' said the man as he invited us into his office at the back of the shop, which I noticed looked out onto water. I also noticed that our young guides had disappeared, which I found disappointing, as they might have helped us at this point.

'I don't want a bleedin' carpet,' said Tracey, pulling back her top where it had been man-handled out of position. 'I want shoes.'

'You, lovely lady,' he said, looking at me for rather too long. 'You have good taste; lovely hand-made, beautiful carpets – any size or colour. You are rich lady. You can buy, no?'

I had to admit they looked good and engaged in some conversation, keen to get out of the place. I was aware of the fact he kept staring at me. One of the girls brought us mint tea, which Tracey spat out on the first sip.

'That tastes like toothpaste. Haven't you got any builder's tea?' she asked, and was ignored by the man who sucked his teeth before turning his back on her. I thought he was very rude.

'Anyway, we must be going now,' I said to him, at which point he stood up and walked around the office until he was in front of the door. 'Could you please just take us back to where you found us?'

He looked at me, again for too long, left the office and locked the door behind us. There were no windows on that side of the office so we had no idea what he was up to.

'I want to go for a pee,' said Tracey. 'That bloke is getting on my tits.'

A bit like everyone else today, I thought.

It was only a few minutes before the door opened and the man, accompanied by another wearing a better-fitting suit, came back into the office. But it was long enough for panic to start rising.

Getting kidnapped was becoming something of a habit.

'See, it is her,' said the first man to the other. 'I know it.'

The second man looked at a piece of paper he had in his hand and then back at my face. He looked over to Tracey, who stuck her tongue out at him.

'I need the loo,' she said, crossing her hands across her chest defiantly. 'When you tossers going to let us out of here?'

'Aha, it is you, too,' said the second man. 'I recognise your English, sickly face.'

'Get lost, rude boy,' said Tracey, pinching her cheeks tightly and producing a red flush. 'Nothing sickly about my face.'

'You are wanted by people,' said the second man. 'We get money to hand you in.'

I groaned.

'For goodness sake, we are worth nothing. Please just let us go.'

The first man stood in front of me. 'Well we could let you go if you match the finders' fee for handing you in. Fifteen thousand naira would do it. We're not greedy people.'

I thought of the MOT fine and how that money might have come in very handy right now.

'Have you any money, Tracey?' I asked, knowing it was unlikely. Any cash she managed to get was usually 'borrowed' from her purse by Baz almost the minute she put it in there.

She opened up her bag and let out the predictable lament about her husband to be and how he was always taking her cash. I thought she had some dollars but, if she did, she was hanging on to them.

'I've got about three hundred naira,' she said, looking up at the two men. Then, in a flash of inspiration that altogether surprised me, Tracey suggested the men take her bank card and her PIN number and go and get the cash themselves.

'That way you'll know you've got it and that we will be here waiting for you.'

I didn't for a minute think they would go for it, but they were soon on their way armed with Tracey's Nectar card and a fictional PIN number of seven digits.

They walked through the door and made sure to lock us into the office.

'Well that's all great, Tracey, but what happens when they come back empty-handed?'

'We won't be here,' she said. 'Look, the window's unlocked. We can get out here.'

The drop the other side wasn't as bad as I thought it might be. There was a narrow pathway around the water's edge, and just as we were making our way round what looked like a makeshift jetty, the boys who'd been showing us around appeared in a small boat.

'Come on board, ladies. We take you to safety.'

There was just enough room for us, and I was delighted that they could row even better than Tracey and get us to the road leading to the car park way before our escape had been noticed.

'Thank you so much,' I said to them, but they refused to leave.

'We need a reward,' said the lead boy.

'I don't have any money,' I explained, but they weren't worried. They wanted a phone.

'Here, have this,' said Tracey. 'It's the only one we've got.'

I thought of the one I had, which Tom had given me before this trip started. I'd have been happy to hand it over.

Once they had gone, happy with their day's takings, Tracey explained that the phone could be locked and even traced back to them.

'It's worth nothing to us, really, but everything to them,' she said. 'For the moment, anyway.'

We got back to our bungalow, pleased with ourselves. We were safe and sound. I didn't tell Lady Osolase about the MOT business, or the attempted kidnap. It just seemed better to keep it to ourselves.

CHAPTER TWENTY-SEVEN

Lady Osolase hadn't wasted any time setting the wedding wheels in motion. Being a churchgoer and having such high standing she had no trouble finding a suitable minister. The speed and efficiency at which she worked was inspiring. She was a woman after my own heart, one who got things done.

'It's all arranged,' she told us only hours after agreeing the date. 'We have da priest and da church. I haf my son ready and he will do da decent ting.'

She'd also booked for Tracey to see a dentist, no doubt thinking of the wedding pictures, and handed over the services of her own dressmaker, Noelle, to make whatever clothing was required for the day.

Tracey was a bundle of nerves on the big day and lit up numerous cigarettes, only to cough violently and put them out again. She was marginally pleased with the dress Noelle had made for her, after much discussion, and although the shoes weren't the Louboutin copies she'd asked for, were sufficiently high-heeled to prevent a major tantrum.

'I wish me dad could be here,' she said, tripping around on the shoes like a kid playing dressing-up games with her mum's clothes.

'We can take photos,' I offered by way of consolation.

'He's been dead ten years, so won't be able to see them,' Tracey said, matter-of-factly.

'I'm sorry,' I offered, wondering whether Baz would be so keen to have family witnesses to his impending marriage.

'Don't be. I hadn't seen him for thirty years before that. Wouldn't recognise him if he came up and punched me on the nose.'

There was a knock on the door and Lady Osolase came in,

bringing with her three glasses of brandy, which she placed on the coffee table.

'Ma goodness. There's a treat for da eyes,' she said kindly to Tracey, looking over in my direction for support in her false praise. 'She clean up well!' she added, holding up her glass. 'Let's have a toast!'

'Oh, I'm too nervous to eat,' said Tracey as she swilled the brandy in one swallow. 'And I don't think we've got any bread.'

Noelle and one of the kitchen maids came in, holding bunches of beautiful pale pink flowers and a larger orange bouquet of lily-like stems wrapped in lemon and red silk. They handed the bouquet to Tracey.

I sneezed seven times, and after recovering, told Tracey she was the perfect bride. She beamed and I was surprised not to swallow my tongue, having had to place it so firmly in my cheek.

As if on some kind of hormonal timer, Tracey started to cry, a habit I was beginning to find somewhat nauseating.

'This is so emotional,' she blubbered. 'And now I've gone really hot and sweaty,' she added, waving her hand in front of her face as its colour increased from a pale pink to an extreme red.

Lady Osolase swiftly took Tracey by the arm and moved her towards the door, gesturing to us all to follow.

'Come. Da car is waiting. It has air conditioning.'

Throughout the drive Tracey was mopping her face and armpits with a cloth handed to her by Noelle. She was sweating profusely, and cried at every available prompt, particularly one suggesting she might have hit the menopause.

'I ain't that bleedin' old,' she said and I kept quiet about her being exactly the average age for such hormonal depletion. I know, as I was the same age when my eggs said goodbye to fertility and started causing havoc with the essence of everything I'd trusted to be my true self. It started with a sense of agoraphobia and general anti-social behaviour, then escalated to bouts of paranoia, extreme aggression and a constant desire to exterminate anyone who was in my way for any reason. I can see why women don't often get jobs as airline pilots. Flying a plane full of moaning passengers on a bad day could have very serious implications.

When we got to the church, Tracey had cooled off physically and emotionally. A last-minute burst of oestrogen must have saved the day, which was a blessing considering there were about two hundred people waiting outside to join in the ceremony. The women, who'd gathered together in one big group, were dressed in bright colours and wore hats with oversized flowers, while the men, skulking in more dispersed bunches depending on whether they were smoking or not, were in sharp but lightweight suits that oozed sophistication and expense. Gospel music was blaring through the church doors, and the atmosphere was buzzing.

'Who are these people?' said Tracey, who was like a rabbit in the headlights at the sight of the crowd. Her thoughts, directed earlier at me, were that there would only be a dozen or so people in attendance. Something she'd worried about, as it didn't fit with the persistent childhood dream of her wedding day.

'I've waited a long time to get married and I'm gonna do it properly,' she'd told Noelle and me as she demanded an off-the-shoulder number in white, with maybe a few bits of colour here and there. Noelle had got on with making the best job she could with the tools she'd been given and Tracey was happy enough being the centre of attention while this progressed. She gave her commands on what she wanted to wear and issued instructions where she could on food, drinks and music, but had little input on who she wanted to attend other than me – and Baz, of course.

'They are your guests, ma dear,' said Lady Osolase as she swept her arm across the vista of faces. 'And some of dem will soon be ya family.'

Tracey had told me the prospect of marriage to such a family was very exciting, adding she was 'totally loved up', which apparently means you have very strong romantic feelings for a partner who feels the same. That didn't seem to apply to Tracey's intended, who appeared to be the complete opposite. I'm not sure if 'loved down' is an expression, but if that is what he was, she hadn't noticed.

Whatever I thought of the arrangement, every dog has its day, and hers was her wedding, however shambolic the circumstances.

I looked more closely at some of the people. They wore expensive clothes and spoke with confidence, as if they had always been told they were important. They had an air of entitlement and status, which was all rather splendid in the circumstances. I was looking forward to meeting some of them.

Cameras flashed around us as Tracey got out of the car. A big cheer went up and three photographers crowded round her, taking picture after picture. I noticed how one of the photographers seemed to be focusing most of his attention on me and I hoped he didn't think I was a relation of the bride. Thankfully he left earlier than the others, which I thought was a bit strange, but maybe he wasn't there so much for the wedding but because it was an event hosted by Lady Osolase.

Lady Osolase asked them to move away to allow the bride to get through. As we approached the church doors a nervous-looking Baz was waiting, wearing a white suit and a pale green shirt with a dark green tie. He looked handsome, but scared as hell.

'Say hello to ya bride, son,' she barked at him.

'Hello,' he said dutifully.

Tracey threw her arms round him and kissed him full on the lips. He didn't respond, but stepped backwards to regain his balance. Cameras continued to go off around us as we and the guests made our way into the church and into pews assigned with various names, including some that were prefaced with titles such as 'Rt Hon.' or 'Minister', suggesting they were from very high places indeed.

The ceremony was over in less than five minutes, and Lady Osolase didn't leave her son's side until he'd signed the register. He and Tracey were officially married, and in front of enough witnesses to ensure he could never deny it.

Caterers must have worked overnight on the massive banquet that had been ordered for the wedding breakfast – held in a marquee at the back of the Osolase home. All of Tracey's requests had been honoured, and she was delighted, particularly with the chicken nuggets and mini cheese burgers she didn't expect to be available.

Lady Osolase was remarkably happy to oblige with all requests, even those for a karaoke machine and tequila shots as welcome drinks. There were various other minor details such as a visiting Elvis impersonator, those nasty mint crisps that everyone had at dinner parties before Hotel Chocolat was invented – and the possibility of a comedian, if one could be found in Nigeria. Certainly a direct woman, Lady Osolase was generous in her dealings with Tracey, explaining to us both she was disgusted by her son's behaviour and would insist he put things right. She added he'd be a good husband, which was something I doubted, given his actions to date and the fact he'd have to tolerate Tracey as a wife. I supposed that children would be out of the question, which was undoubtedly a blessing.

After everyone had eaten, Lady Osolase stood up and gave what might have passed as a best man's speech in any other circumstances. There didn't seem to be any other contenders for the role. If there had have been, I suspect she'd have found something else for them to do, a long way away.

'My son is very lucky to haf met such a nice British girl,' she said, to a silent audience who neither assented nor disagreed. 'Tracey is welcome to our family, and we wish dem a long life together,' she added, without any sign of having crossed her fingers. As she sat down, she added: 'Now ma son would like to speak.'

Baz looked horrified and turned to his mother, his eyes pleading for clemency. There was none.

'Um. Thank you all for being here,' he mumbled. He was about to sit down but his mother coughed loudly and pointed to his pocket, nodding her head in its direction while she did. 'Er. I've a present for my wife.' The last word nearly choked him, and I was sure I could see tears in his eyes that didn't appear to be from joy.

He pulled out a piece of paper from his pocket which he opened up and showed to be a cheque. It was for five thousand pounds. He shoved it in Tracey's direction without looking at her.

'For you,' he added, and quickly sat in his seat, taking a large swig from the drink placed in front of him.

Tracey was speechless, I was pleased to note. Otherwise I suspect she would've stood up and said something entirely incriminating. She shoved the cheque inside the small clutch bag she'd been carrying and smiled weakly around the room, looking at the guests, who were still cheering at her husband's extravagant 'gift'. She looked over at Baz but he was clutching his head in his hands, or at least he was until his mother knocked his arms off the table, bringing him to a near collision between head and plate.

Before anyone had any chance to think about what had just happened, the music started and various guests were up on the dance floor moving in a way only black people can. I remembered dancing with Darius to 'Mrs Robinson' and fantasised about him making a sudden appearance, so he could declare undying love and waltz me around the floor, winning every spectator's admiration. As I watched the crowd sway easily to the music, I wished I possessed that sense of self and oneness with the beat.

I was sitting and watching the spectacle before me when Lady Osolase came over. She sipped her drink and I noticed a twinkle in her eye as she spoke.

'Well, I haf a surprise for you, dear Cynthia. Some of my people haf been doing some investigating.'

'Oh, that's nice. What have they found?' I asked, hoping against hope it was something I wanted to hear.

Someone was talking behind me, greeting a number of people on their way through the crowd. I thought it might be one of Lady Osolase's colleagues from the outreach programmes. She'd been asking repeatedly if I was interesting in helping them.

I'd prepared myself to put on a fixed smile and offer my best polite, diplomatic conversation when I saw a vision I hadn't expected to see again. It was Darius, accompanied by a beautiful young woman I hoped he had nothing to do with.

'Hello, Cynthia. How lovely to see you,' he said, kissing me gently on the cheek.

Time stood still and I couldn't speak. I hadn't been prepared for meeting him this suddenly and he seemed distant, like a stranger. He looked at me with his beautiful, kind eyes with no sense of guilt or shame. Did he not know he'd torn out my pounding heart and crushed it?

'This is Chinaza,' he said, introducing me to the young woman accompanying him.

'Very pleased to meet you,' I said automatically, even though I wanted to axe her into tiny pieces.

'I've been reading about your adventures in the press and heard from Lady Osolase that you were here. It sounds like you have had quite a time,' Darius said, gleaming through his pink-tinged lips and showing the tips of his icy white teeth.

My insides turned with nerves, and I hoped he couldn't hear the gurgling. My left foot started to quiver, so I shuffled slightly in the hope he wouldn't guess my state of anxiety.

I was glad I was dressed well and hoped he'd remember our liaisons with fondness. I wished I was in something a little sexier than my sensible courts. Perhaps I should've asked Tracey for a pair of her 'shag me' shoes.

'Well, it's been interesting,' I said, hiding untethered emotions as deep in my soul as I could. 'Not everyone can say they've been kidnapped and survived,' I said as I smiled at Darius, wondering if this woman might be the object of his attentions.

'We were very pleased to hear from the university you'd arrived there safe and sound,' he said, as he moved forward and touched my arm. A thrill ran through my blood as if I'd touched an electric fence.

'We're also delighted to tell you we've managed to capture your kidnappers,' Darius added, and I felt a wave of relief wash over me. 'Chinaza is on the investigating team with me at Forensix Inc. She led the project to find and arrest them. They will appear in court in a few days,' he added.

Actually, that isn't quite true Mrs Hartworth,' drawled Chinaza in my direction, giving me what I could only describe as a sickly smile. Even her teeth were perfect. 'We believe the main instigator of the scam is still at large. The others are too scared to give his name, although we understand he is known to many as 'just John' '

I couldn't stop looking at this woman, who was at least a foot taller than me yet probably ten pounds lighter. I imagined her breasts being upright and full, untouched by the teeth of mewling infants. She turned away to talk to a guest who was passing by and Darius continued to explain what had happened, but I felt like someone had blown dry ice into my brain to prevent it from functioning.

I still clung on to the hope this young female was not the recipient of Darius's affections. My stomach lifted, and I could have happily tap-danced my way round the house and garden dressed in nothing but a tutu had I been assured of that.

A number of people came up to us, mainly to talk to Darius and Chinaza. They both seemed well known, which didn't surprise me.

Then a stab of pain nearly knocked me off my feet. I'd looked over to see Chinaza pick a piece of fluff from Darius's shirt. Until that point I was prepared to think, hope, that they were just colleagues.

That's far too intimate to be just a work relationship, I thought, as I ran to the ladies to have a good cry. As salty droplets of sadness cascaded down my cheeks it occurred to me that many lovers meet at work. How could I think they were anything but?

When I returned, Lady Osolase's secretary, Idowu, came over and asked if I was OK. 'I understand you've had some bad experience of people in our country' she said. 'For this I must apologise,' she said in a very clipped and precise manner. 'I always feel very sad these people represent our beautiful nation so badly.'

I looked around and couldn't see Darius, or that witch of a woman, anywhere. I wanted to ask where he'd gone, but wasn't sure I wanted the answer. I was glad my red-rimmed eyes could be blamed on a kind of post-traumatic stress disorder and not the consequences of a broken heart.

Idowu was dressed in crisp, coloured clothes that hadn't bent to the movement of her body and remained crease-free and fresh. Her hands were beautifully manicured, especially when compared to my short and unvarnished nails. In her presence I felt very badly maintained.

'It isn't your fault,' I said, thanking her for her concern. She went on to ask how I dealt with being in captivity and how we'd managed to escape.

Before long I was telling her about Darius. I was propelled towards such a conversation, like all those newly immersed in unrequited love. Not all the details, of course, but just the fact he was a friend I'd been looking for. I was economical with the truth, having decided there were some things best left unsaid. We talked about the problems the country had with some of the people who are using technology to fight their way out of poverty. She added that Darius was one of the leaders in his field, and very well respected. He'd apparently left a short while ago, with Chinaza.

'She's a lovely girl. His family know her family,' she added, and that clinched the scenario for me. Arranged marriages are commonplace in Nigeria, although no man was likely to complain about being promised to such a beautiful woman, or no woman to such a beautiful man.

My world was crumbling, but I knew I needed to keep up a good pretence of being unmoved by the news. *Life goes on, dammit.* I hadn't been listening to Idowu's conversation, spending my energy trying not to think about Darius and Chinaza together. I could barely register what was being said, and chastised myself for entertaining any thoughts he might ever have taken me seriously. I made a supreme effort to concentrate.

What she also told me, as we watched Tracey and Baz stumble their way through their first dance to 'I Love You Love' by Gary Glitter, somewhat inappropriately given his offences, was that Baz was a bad boy.

'It isn't just poverty that motivates people,' she said, as her words finally filtered into my distracted brain. 'We have the same issues here as anywhere, with greed, power and envy. I'm so glad Abassi has seen the error of his ways and is settling down,' she added, looking over as Tracey got her heel stuck in the bottom of her dress and was hopping around the dance floor trying to extricate it.

'His mother got so upset by his behaviour. He's been in prison three times, and it would've been more if it wasn't for the efforts she goes to for him.'

This news interested me, and I worried for Tracey. I wanted to protect her from coming up against any more unexpected disaster in her life.

Apart from scamming British women for money, she told me he'd also been arrested for drug trafficking through Morocco and supplying cocaine to his mother's university students.

'It is like he wants to disgrace her. He is just like his father, unfortunately. Not like her other son, Mabu, who is honest and hard-working. He has a good job working as a customs officer in England. She'd like Abassi to be more like him, and is determined to make something of him rather than see him continue his life of crime.'

I personally didn't think marriage to Tracey was the answer, but could see how it served as a suitable punishment from Lady Osolase's point of view. I wondered how long it would be before Tracey thumped him the same way she did Chiddy. I almost felt sorry for him.

As I had a ready source of information, I set to finding out more about our hostess and her life. Maybe I could take up her offer to work in Nigeria, using the few skills I had? I was sure I could find something else to be useful at, now ideas of a future with Darius had come to such a disappointing halt.

Through subtle questioning I discovered Lady Osolase was truly an inspiration to many people. Apart from being the first Nigerian woman from her tribe, one of the poorest in the country, to get a degree, she went on to become a professor in Ethical Studies and a leading expert in the education of women in the Third World. She was also the mother of five children, who she brought up on her own after her husband left, citing the fact he felt emasculated by his wife's success. That and the fact he had a twenty-four-year-old Brazilian lover with a beautifully toned chest and a people-pleasing personality.

This knowledge made me feel a bit inadequate. I'd given up on my own battle for further education at an early age and settled for a life of marriage and domestic support, which challenged nobody, other than me. I kept all disappointment to a minor level, which was easily masked with social nicety and the meeting of middle-class expectations. Whether Colin would ever have left me for a younger woman had I ever been successful in my own right is something I'll never know. I thought it unlikely, given his lack of appetite in the bedroom department for anything other than a good book and clean vests.

Maybe being kidnapped had given me a new perspective on life, but I certainly no longer felt I was the same Cynthia. Something had shifted. I might have spent many years bringing up my family and being a devoted wife, but I'd tasted something else. It was adversity, for the first time, and a feeling that life is very, very short.

I felt sad, and tried also to feel blessed that Darius had been part of it. As the saying goes, 'better to have loved and lost, than never to have loved at all'.

Whoever said that was talking rubbish.

CHAPTER TWENTY-EIGHT

Although the purpose of the party was largely false, it was an impressive affair. These people knew how to entertain, and even the karaoke had a certain class to it. The Nina Simone sound-alike did a rather rousing rendition of 'My Baby Just Cares for Me', which almost brought me to tears.

Lady Osolase came over to me as the party was beginning to slow down, many hours after it had started. The dancing, singing and celebrating seemed to be endless, and my feet throbbed from the sheer effort of it all. I'd enjoyed it despite a heavy heart and a strong sense that nothing would be the same again.

She patted me on the back and introduced me to more people, each individually apologising for what had happened to Tracey and me and telling me of their shame at their fellow countrymen. I couldn't imagine anyone in Britain apologising to foreigners for atrocities we'd visited on them. We'd made our country great on the back of such behaviour, after all.

Once the final stragglers had gone and Tracey was going round the tables mine-sweeping any remaining alcohol, Lady Osolase said: 'Most importantly, Cynthia, are you having a good time?' emphasising the word 'good'.

'I'm having a really lovely time. And your friends are very nice,' I replied, hoping my blatant lie didn't show through my teeth. I didn't want to be churlish to my very generous host.

'Oh, I haf few friends, Cynthia.'

I was surprised. A woman with all her qualifications and influence must have lots of friends, I thought. If she lived in Epsfield, Mavis would want to be her friend. But I'm not sure I'd be happy with that because I would like to keep her to myself. Anyway,

Mavis always shouted at black people – thinking them not only 'foreign' and therefore unable to speak English, but also deaf.

'I'm wealthy. I'm well known. I haf power. Da people want those tings I haf, but not me,' she said in a surprisingly sage tone. 'If I'd nuttin' they would not be here, but I don't mind. I can get tings done dat I want done. I haf worked for everyting I haf, so use it for ma goals. I haf big goals, yous see.'

I couldn't fail to be impressed. Lady Osolase really didn't care about what people thought of her. She wouldn't worry about changing the rota for sandwiches at the bridge club sessions or passing an Advanced Driving course under the watchful eye of the opinionated and judgemental Vera. She was changing the world. My life in comparison seemed futile, one where I filled in the days to get to the next one.

'I would like to take yous to see me programmes. Dat is, if you haf the time,' she said.

I saw a whole new world opening up in front of me. One that didn't revolve around whose turn it was to invite me for Christmas or which child of mine wanted to patronise me about my driving, swimming, bridge and the number of times I say I'm going to move but never actually do it.

Not only that, I could forget Darius, love, passion, sex. It seemed a poor swap, but I needed something to focus on, and the prospect of Mavis and the bridge club plus never-ending family events just didn't cut the mustard.

'I would love to see what you do, Lady Osolase. Thank you.'

'Call me Buke, I'm sure we can be friends,' she said, as she got up and swished along the floor to warmly greet another guest.

And that meant more to me than she could have ever known.

CHAPTER TWENTY-NINE

Buke organised the trip to the outreach programmes for the day after the wedding, which I was very grateful for. They were a good day's drive away, and we spent three days visiting children, teachers, governors and fund-raisers. It gave me time away from the revelation that Darius was otherwise engaged.

Tracey and I were still being advised to keep a low profile while the authorities moved in on the entire kidnapping ring. They didn't want us targeted by the 'big boys', who might want to persuade us not to testify against their gangs. I thought again of John and whether or not I would describe him as one of the 'Big Boys'. His only power was probably the fact he was English and more plausible in his ability to scam white women. I wondered if he could be bothered to come looking for us again.

'You haf done very well,' said Buke, as we made our way to the car due to take us back to the university. Baz and Tracey were due back from their honeymoon, and I was interested to see how they'd got on.

Buke gave no indication she thought the marriage was destined to fail. If I asked her how she felt about her son marrying an Englishwoman old enough to be his mother, she replied that she was very happy they'd found each other, and turned the conversation to her work.

One of the visits had been to a Girls' Power Initiative that had been running in one of the programme's schools for some time, aimed at talking to young women about an 'empowered womanhood' and the threat of HIV. One girl told me she couldn't attend many of the sessions because her parents wouldn't give permission, which surprised me. I constantly packed my kids off to anything going on at school, just for the peace and quiet. Bobbie wasn't too happy with the motorcycle maintenance course running in the summer of her fourth year at secondary school, but I told her she'd never know when it might come in handy. Jonjo benefitted greatly from the advanced sociology programme when it came to applying for jobs in the public sector. He told me his use of the phrase 'socio-demographic' clinched his position in marketing for Croydon Council.

We didn't stay very long, just enough time to say hello and goodbye to a number of people. Buke seemed particularly keen to leave after a young student presented her with a bracelet made of rice.

'Dat is lovely,' she said, sounding sincere as she bent down to the small girl with wide, innocent eyes looking up to her. She threw it in a bin at a petrol station we stopped at on the way back, claiming she didn't want to wear something that might attract insects. I think my cat felt the same about flea collars. He'd never keep one on for longer than a day.

It was good to get back to the bungalow. I enjoyed the trip to the programmes, but Buke's energy exhausted me. She could survive on just a few hours' sleep a night, and was like a Duracell rabbit, permanently on the go. I'd thought of asking her to come and stay with me on her next trip to England, but it would be like having a whirling dervish in the house. That, or one of those hoovers that goes round on its own while you're out.

I'd settled down onto the settee, having agreed to meet Buke later for dinner at her place, when Tracey came bursting through the doors.

'Did you have a good honeymoon?' I asked, looking around for Baz.

'I suppose so. The place was great and I had loads of spa treatments thanks to mummy-in-law. The sex was crap, though. Baz did his back in so couldn't perform,' she said.

I tried not to think of the two of them in bed together, and looked around the room, which I noticed was full of washed and ironed clothes, including mine.

'Someone has done the laundry,' I said.

I walked across the wooden floor towards a pile of T-shirts, tops and trousers which had been neatly folded and placed on a sideboard on the wall facing the corridor to our bedrooms.

'Yeah, I did it,' said Tracey. 'So don't worry, no one's been going through your knickers!'

'Oh and I charged up yer phone 'n' all. I found it in one of the bags you left behind when I was looking for your clothes.'

I'd forgotten about my phone. Not that it would be any use without Tom's notes.

I was stunned by Tracey's domestic proficiency and wondered if it was the novelty of being married that had spurred it all on.

'That's very sweet of you,' I said. 'How did you manage to do all that and go on honeymoon?'

Tracey flicked the kettle on in the small kitchen and set out two mugs to make coffee for us both.

'We've got a washing machine. We only went for two days. Baz had to come home for some kind of business, although I'm not sure what.'

She brought over the coffee and sat down next to me and picked up a phone that Baz had given to her. She'd kept the SIM card after handing over her last one at the market and it seemed to be working.

'Hey, I've got all my numbers,' she said, scrolling through her contacts and then tting the phone down again quickly.

'Nothing. No bugger has bothered to see if I'm alive or dead, not even my daughter, who would know I'm not at home cos I've not been on Facebook for weeks. I bet Posh Git has stopped her contacting me again. There has been some bloke following us about in a car, though. Probably something to do with Baz and his business deals rather than anyone interested in me, though.'

There was a knock on the door, and one of Buke's staff told us dinner would be at eight that evening and she'd expect us both half an hour before for a cocktail.

'Bloody marvellous,' said Tracey. 'I could do with a good stiff one. Ha ha!'

We both got ourselves ready for dinner and I put on my little black dress, the one I wore the first time I allowed Darius entry into my womanhood. I felt nostalgic and rather frustrated. The last thing

I thought I would miss about being with a man was the sex, but my dreams were often punctuated with vivid images of his vast body and healthy blood circulation. Now there was the addition of Chinaza, and as much as I tried to blank her out she was there in all her splendour – satisfying my former lover while I looked on, helpless.

Tracey emerged from her room looking at her phone. She was dressed in an African trouser suit that made her look like she was entering Billy Smart's Clown of the Year competition.

'Baz is going to be late. So looks like you're me date for tonight,' she said.

We checked ourselves out in the small mirror beside the door, both smoothing our hair and rubbing hands down our sides. Me to check out any lumps and bumps in my dress, Tracey to wipe the crumbs off her hands from a packet of nuts she'd been eating.

'Hope we get some decent grub,' she added, as we walked out of the door, arm in arm.

Buke's house was opulent and colourful, with plenty of influence from nature, either in the hue of material thrown casually over various pieces of furniture or through the display of African animals either in pictures or as statues.

'Good evening, ladies,' said Buke as she floated towards us. 'I'm so pleased to see you. Come, let's go to da garden for cocktails.'

We followed her through the rest of the house and to the back of the kitchen, which opened out onto a veranda shaded by a wooden structure draped with a pale blue flowering shrub that dangled its loosely hanging fronds into my hair. It smelled sweet and almost sickly, not unlike candyfloss.

A tall, slim man with a very thin moustache across a wide upper lip offered us an orange and pink-looking drink from a tray he was holding.

'Please, enjoy,' he said and then nodded his head in deference. I noticed there were another eight or so glasses still remaining on a table placed against the kitchen wall.

'How many are you expecting?' I asked Buke as I spotted Tracey helping herself to another drink without being asked.

'Yous wait and see, me dear,' she said, looking at her watch.

'Now, where is dat son of mine? He haf a wife to attend to.'

Buke went back into the house and I could hear her talking loudly in what I assumed to be an African language. There was a noise at the front door and then the sound of voices, male and female. Buke was welcoming them and it was difficult to tell how many people were there until they came through.

The group that was shown in looked similar to that surrounding the Audi I'd crashed. I knew it was him as the smell of his aftershave preceded him. It was Darius again. Just as I was beginning to think I could get over him.

'Hello again,' he said to me, smiling. 'What happened to you at the wedding? You were there one minute, and gone the next. Sorry I didn't wait to say goodbye but I had a car waiting.'

And a beautiful young woman to make love to, I thought.

I took a deep breath to calm my heart rate, and although it didn't work I remembered everything I could about retaining dignity. I might be hurt, feeling used and most of all desperately wanting to feel his excitement again, but I mustn't show it.

'I think it was too much food and wine. We weren't offered much in the camp,' I tried to joke.

I looked around for Chinaza and hoped my wish she'd fallen off the planet had come true. I thought about asking after her but didn't want to look as if I cared.

It seemed the reason Buke had invited Darius to the party was to keep us up to date with the investigations which, we were told, had gathered much momentum in terms of publicity, first when we were reported as missing and then again following the arrest of various gang members including Chike and Fasina. Darius told us there would be a court case and we would be seen as heroines for escaping the kidnappers and helping to bring them to justice.

Baz was still conspicuous by his absence, so I assumed Buke's demands hadn't worked on this occasion.

'Maybe we'll be in *OK!* magazine!' Tracey laughed, as Chinaza opened up a small laptop to reveal page after page of news reports showing pictures of us both. I wondered where they'd got the one of me in my dressing gown. I looked like something from a catalogue about nursing homes.

'I'm not sure what we've been up to would be of sufficient interest,' I replied. 'We would need to have had triplets and then lost all our post-baby weight in two days, or married someone related to royalty and sold the soiled sheets of our honeymoon bed to the editor for that kind of privilege.'

The conversation was lost on Tracey, but thankfully Darius and Lady Osolase chatted enthusiastically on about the investigation, both taking turns to praise Chinaza for her work. I wanted to kick her in the shins, even though I knew it was churlish. Not only was my love rival a beauty, she was clever. No wonder Darius came back to Nigeria.

The evening drained me. Trying to smile when I wanted to spit was challenging. Every time I felt myself glowering I had to give myself an internal talking to. It wouldn't do to look like I was jealous.

When it finally seemed a reasonable time to go, partly because it was getting late but also because Tracey was getting drunk, I was relieved to be able to take our leave.

'Come on, Tracey, you look tired,' I said, hoping that lack of sleep rather than excessive gin punch would explain the drooping eyelids and vague look of palsy her face had taken on.

'Let me get a car to run you round,' said Buke.

'No, no, the walk will do us good,' I replied, wanting to break from the evening as soon as possible.

We said hasty goodbyes and left as soon as we could, to protestations about us walking in the dark.

I thought maybe they were right. I could see and hear a myriad of things in the undergrowth, including something sneezing. There was a rustling in some of the bushes lining the road to our bungalow and I was ready to scream at the top of my voice.

'What the fuck is that?' said Tracey, suddenly coming alive. The warnings about the 'Big Boys' came flooding to my head and I was convinced our time was up.

'We should have got the bloody car,' said Tracey. 'Now we're in for it.'

There was another sneeze, and I nearly passed out with fear until I saw what could only be described as the biggest rat I'd ever encountered, scuttling across our path.

'Jeez, that punch must have been strong, innit?' said Tracey. 'That rat is huge!'

She then screamed and ran, as much as she could, to the front door, wobbling from side to side on her high heels until one of them broke. She kicked them both off in the direction of the rat, which stopped, looked round and sneezed again.

I thought I was going mad.

Tracey started fishing about in her bag for her keys. I pushed the door, which opened immediately, as it hadn't been locked.

She tipped her handbag out onto the table in front of the settees. She distributed the contents using splayed hands, picking up individual items and putting them back.

'I'm sure I had a key,' she said. 'I put it in here earlier.'

She slumped down in a chair and sighed while looking around the room.

'Aha,' she said, coming to life and picking up a phone from the table. 'Look what I have here, Cynthia. It's all fired up. You've got loads of messages.'

Tracey had mentioned charging it but I dismissed the comment, as even if it had worked, I didn't know how to use it. Why I can't just have something that rings and I answer it I don't know. I'd mistakenly managed to take a picture of my shoe and a video of next door's cat when I first got it, but hadn't got to speak to anyone on the damn thing, so in my mind it was fairly redundant.

'I don't know how to get to my messages,' I told Tracey. 'My grandson got it for me and it might as well be a rusty Rubik's cube covered in baby oil for all the skill I have with it.'

Tracey frowned at me and jabbed at the screen.

'I can work it for you. Look, you've got fifty-nine text messages, thirty-six emails and your voicemail is full.'

She showed me what to do. I went through the voicemail messages first, which included one of Tom calling after I'd been gone for three days. The concern deepened as time went on and then the emails were about the money transfer, the ransom demand and what the family were aiming to do to rescue me. I was touched.

Tracey slid down into her seat and appeared to be dribbling, half asleep but trying to keep her eyes open with various shudders and self-administered slaps to the face.

I thought that had we known all the effort and concern there was for us while we were imprisoned, it would have given us so much hope, rather than the worry of whether or not we'd be slaughtered and our bodies put out to rot with the fish and sewage. However, without the uncertainty we might never have found the impetus to plan our escape – one occasion where ignorance is a positive thing.

The messages included a number from Mr Gamble urging me to respond to letters he'd sent about my 'financial circumstances', as he called them. He can be such an irritating little man. When I get home I'm going to tell him I'm investing most of my money in a farm for producing edible worms and the rest on learning to pole dance. *Let's see what he has to say about that*, I thought

Tracey had fallen asleep, and when she tried to turn round she fell off the chair and onto the floor, landing with a thud. She remained there for a while, so I gave her a kick which brought her back to life.

'Ow, that bloody hurt,' she said, rubbing her knee as she unfolded herself in an upward motion. 'What are your messages about, then?'

I told Tracey how the gang had contacted my family by email and text message and that they'd sent a ransom demand giving my family five days to hand over the money.

'I can't work out the dates, but it would appear we escaped before the deadline.'

A chill went down my spine. What would have happened to us if we'd been there at the deadline and the money hadn't come in? Would they have killed us or let us go? The thought of being there at that moment of their disappointment, when they had to decide whether our lives were worth preserving, made me go cold. I took a swig from one of the glasses of brandy left over from earlier, regardless of its sandpaper-and-fire aftertaste, and prayed to my new friend God, in the vague hope he existed. If he did, then I really wanted to thank him for helping us out in our dire need.

'Well, they didn't bother contacting anyone I know,' Tracey said, looking a little forlorn as she picked up her phone. 'Not a single bleeding message other than three texts asking me if I want a payday loan and an email from my catalogue telling me the shoes I ordered only go up to a size six. Nothing from anyone else.'

'Perhaps they couldn't get through,' I suggested, and changed the subject before she noticed.

I read on and found out the bridge club had organised a fund-raiser to get publicity for my plight. 'By all accounts my friends put together a big bridge event and a British Legion collection which raised over fifteen hundred pounds,' I told Tracey, who was making her way to the kitchen to get another brandy. I'd decided I'd had enough to drink for one night.

I could just imagine the men from the bridge club holding forth at the Legion. They would talk a story up about anything if it was sufficiently interesting to encourage an audience and the purchase of a pint or two of fine ale for the storytellers. I laughed out loud when I read a bit saying Mavis had made badges for the event with 'Save Cynthia' on them. I didn't like the news that she'd told everyone at the club I'd been tortured and under threat of murder. Although I'm sure the tale earned her some attention from the others, who would have revelled in what they were being told, however unreliable the messenger might be. But then they hadn't seen anything out of the ordinary since Harry Winslett had mooned at the Girl Guide Remembrance parade three years ago, so any distraction was worthwhile, regardless of its provenance.

'Don't know where the bastard has gone,' said Tracey as she came back into the living room, wearing a dressing gown she'd taken from the back of the bathroom door. 'Do you want a drink? There's some brandy or beer.'

'I think it's about time I went to bed,' I said to Tracey, who could barely keep her eyelids open. The messages had overloaded the inner workings of my brain and needed to be digested. I hadn't taken all the information in and needed some time to piece together the missing bits of our kidnap jigsaw. It seemed a lot of people in a lot of places were taking it all very seriously.

As I stood up to make my way to my room, Baz came through the front door with two men, one looking very shifty and carrying a large, full hessian bag under one arm and a roll of brown paper under another. The second man had a set of old-fashioned scales and a kitchen knife.

'You two still up?' Baz said, ordering his two companions to sit in the spare seats opposite us. 'I thought you'd be asleep by now.'

'Come on, husband of mine, let's go to bed,' Tracey slurred. 'I've got plans for you,' she added, as she pointed her index finger right at his nose.

'You go, I'll follow when I've finished my business,' he said, pushing her arm aside sufficiently hard to knock her slightly off balance.

'All right, Mr Misery Guts. I hope this business is worth neglecting your new bride for,' she said, and then blew a long raspberry while she staggered out of the room.

I took my leave, as I didn't want to be involved in a domestic situation between husband and wife, and I had a lot to think about.

'Goodnight, Baz. See you tomorrow.'

He grunted and huddled down with his companions, making it clear they wouldn't be getting on with anything until we were out of sight and earshot. He watched until I'd left the room, and I could hear low-level mutterings of voices that didn't want to be heard.

I settled down into the large, wicker-framed bed and lay on my back with my eyes open. It was warm, and the sheet felt heavy on my body. Through the window I could see bright stars shining in a clear sky and could hear various animals making sounds of the night.

One of them was Tracey. She was snoring.

CHAPTER THIRTY

Baz had gone by the time Tracey and I emerged for the day. She'd been sleeping off a hangover while I'd been awake until at least five a.m., going over all the messages and information from my phone.

'Eugh. I don't know why I drink, it always makes me feel like someone has stuffed me head with candyfloss and stuck acid down me throat,' said Tracey, still wearing the dressing gown and wiping sleep and mascara from under her eyes. One of the false lashes she'd managed to stick on after finding them in her luggage was dangling to one side of her right eye, causing her to blink rapidly.

One of Buke's staff brought over some breakfast rolls, fresh coffee and yogurts, and gave us a message from Buke that we'd be needed later that day to talk to the prosecution team for the forthcoming court case against our kidnap gang. They would be meeting at the Forensix Inc. offices.

I can't say I was thrilled at the idea, although the thought of seeing Darius made me feel like a drug addict about to get a fix. It would be bad, but seemed worth the consequences just to see him. What I didn't want was the opportunity to see the raven-haired beauty again.

A car came to pick us up at eleven, by which time I'd given some serious thought to what to wear. He may no longer be mine, but I could at least try and get him to remember what he was missing.

Meanwhile Tracey had managed her hangover with copious amounts of the bitter-sweet coffee and a cold shower. She'd asked for some Diet Coke, but had been told it was against Buke's principles to support the Coca-Cola enterprises, a fact that flew over her head.

'I only want a bleedin' drink,' she said, settling for a glass of water and an ibuprofen I'd found in my wash bag, along with an old plaster and an empty tube of haemorrhoid cream. I promised myself I would sort out the bag when I got home, replacing all the tatty remnants of traditional holidays with some more useful items. *Like a gun*, I thought.

During the car journey I thought we were being followed. The same car was behind us even after we'd stopped for petrol, and I just had that feeling you get when someone is staring at you without you knowing. But after everything we'd been through I suppose I was just being over-sensitive. Surely no one else could be out to get us now?

We arrived at Forensix Inc. to a vista of sweeping driveways, sparkling white buildings and manicured gardens. The chauffeur, who was dressed in a light blue suit with white piping and a collarless jacket, making him look like something from *Thunderbirds*, told us the company employed over fourteen hundred people across Nigeria and also the USA, the UK, Japan, China and Brazil. They specialised in technological fraud prevention and were working on a number of projects to track down spammers.

Darius hadn't told me that much detail. I hoped this was because his position in the UK was sensitive, not because he thought I would neither understand nor care.

Once in the noting that his palm was wet. He clearly had an issue with perspiration.

'Call me Cynthia, and this is Tracey.'

We walked into a large, open-plan office with a number of people sitting around a large table. Darius was there and he embraced me, pecking my cheeks with the faintest of kisses, soft as a butterfly's wing. I shuddered and relished the memories of more powerful contact, and was delighted when he shook hands with Tracey, not offering her the benefit of his inviting lips.

'Everybody, this is Cynthia Hartworth and Tracey Burton. I'm pleased to announce they have arrived unscathed, despite some recent adventures, and are willing to help us complete our mission to capture the four-one-nine gang operating around Lagos,' Darius said.

He continued to direct the meeting, during which we learned how the investigation found Chike's car after I'd driven it into the ditch, and how it led them back to the camp where we'd been held. I could barely take in the details as I looked wistfully at Darius's chest moving as he spoke. I wanted to undo his shirt buttons and put my hands inside.

'We traced the car to Chike Buhari, who was already suspected of running a number of ransom plots, including the kidnap of oil workers from Canada. You'd be surprised at how many clues the vehicle gave us.'

The news from home asking the kidnappers to release us were very emotional, with Jonjo telling the world how worried my family were about me. He'd said to a row of microphones: 'Her children and grandchildren miss her.'

I was shocked to see them looking so upset about my plight. They let me go to Croydon unaided and never thought about all the things I have to do alone like use the petrol mower or answer calls from Jehovah's Witnesses. The fact I was kept locked up in a shack for a while was only marginally more intolerable, but evoked emotions I thought were reserved for large Irish families with drinking issues.

'The team gathered a lot of data and then it was a matter of liaising with all the relevant authorities to raid the settlement,' he said.

'Part of the information was tracing money the gang had taken from your account after you'd received one of their scam emails, Cynthia. It all went back to a central suspect who is part of a much larger ring operated partly by Nigerians and partly by Brits who have access to international data through their work with big corporations – all very clever and all very greedy. You'll be pleased to know we have recovered the ten thousand pounds, and it is back in your account.'

Any issues with money became irrelevant compared with everything that had been going on, but anger rose in me. All that time I'd thought I was helping a friend, not funding a group of gangsters.

The reality of being taken for a mug started to sink in, and where before I might have had some kind of sympathy with our kidnappers, I was furious they thought helping themselves to my husband's hard-earned savings was morally acceptable. I thought about Chike's car and just wished I'd done more damage. It had probably been paid for by some young family's inheritance or the remnants of a pensioner's life savings.

Bastards, I thought, using a word usually reserved for the delivery men from Cundy's electrical store, who refused to adjust the legs on my new oven on the grounds I'd served them Earl Grey tea. They said it tasted like Brut aftershave, spat it into my sink and walked off, leaving me with a wobbly hob.

'I wish I'd seen the raid,' I said to Darius, once I'd regained my composure. 'I bet they were shocked,' I added, wishing they'd been shocked even more. I was too embarrassed to admit I thought the money had been taken legitimately, and to help him with his mother.

'Well, we thought we were going to find you there, particularly after we found so many clues to suggest you would be,' he answered. He moved in closer and whispered, 'Like that red bra of yours.'

I'd forgotten we had to leave some of our luggage behind, taking only what we thought would be absolutely necessary. I regretted leaving my underwear, knowing it had an effect.

As I lost concentration on the meeting, the proximity of Darius brought back many feelings, including rising lust, which I'd tamped down in recent days. It was like an unfinished fire in the hearth, glistening with dying embers until a gust of air breathes fresh life into its ability to produce flames.

It wasn't the same with Gowon. He was just there as a memory. *Maybe of my blackest times*, I thought, and nearly laughed.

I was wondering about Gowon and Chiddy and whether they were further punished by the leaders, when Darius said: 'There were two guards, who were only too willing to give us all the information we needed to arrest the big men.'

I hoped they hadn't given too much information.

'By all accounts they'd beaten them for letting you go and were going to mete out their own kind of brutal justice. We let the young guards go with a caution, and I expect they will be in hiding for some time to come, at least until after the trial,' he continued.

A smartly dressed blonde woman of about forty-five, clutching a large briefcase, came into the room and introduced herself as a representative from the British embassy. She was in an immaculate black suit that would look more appropriate in Canary Wharf than a commercial centre on the outskirts of Lagos.

'Virginia Jones,' she said. 'You must be Cynthia Hartworth and Tracey Burton. I recognise you from the press photographs. I hear congratulations are in order,' she added to Tracey, as she opened her case to reveal a number of pictures, including one from Tracey and Baz's wedding.

'Yeah, thanks,' muttered Tracey. She'd been very quiet throughout the proceedings, and I couldn't work out if it was her hangover or whether she didn't have anything to say.

'I am the lawyer working on this case, which as you know has been led by the very capable Chinaza Medoc. She has instructed me to put together the prosecution case against your kidnappers, and I hope you are happy to work with me on this and will also be willing to give evidence.'

The mere mention of Chinaza's name made me want to be a bit sick. If I'd had a bigger breakfast, I might have been.

'Yes, of course,' I said, for both of us.

'We have been dealing with your family, who have shown considerable concern about the kidnap, and so I recommend we put you in touch by Skype before the end of today so they can be assured of your safety.'

What is Skype? I thought to myself. *Sounds like one of the diseases the children got when they first started school.*

'Have you also been in touch with Tracey's family and friends?' I asked Ms Jones.

'We haven't been able to contact anyone as yet,' she replied, flushing red. 'The kidnappers sent one email to someone called Jimmy but he said he didn't know you, I'm afraid, Tracey.'

'Well I suppose he would say that,' she said. 'His wife was probably reading his messages over his shoulder.' Ms Jones coughed and said they'd also tried to make contact with Tracey's daughter but had no reply.

'That'll be down to Posh Git. Don't worry. I'll let them know what's happened when I get back. If I ever go back, that is. Now I'm married and whatnot.'

The room went quiet for a few seconds before we went through the details of the charges for Chike and Fasina.

'We have retrieved at least three hundred thousand dollars from their business bank accounts, not to mention piles of cash and other assets, such as cars. Or car, actually, now that the black Audi has been trashed,' said Darius, smiling in my direction.

He stood up and stretched, revealing an inch or so of his chest through his shirt as he did so. I so wanted to touch the skin I could see revealed between the gaping buttons. Once the information had been exchanged, Ms Jones snapped shut her briefcase, shook hands with us and went to leave, telling us she'd see us in court.

Once she'd left, Darius opened the door to show me out of the office and I brushed against his arm, quite deliberately. If he noticed, he didn't acknowledge it.

'The Skype service is ready for you. I will take you down to the communication room,' he said.

I was put into a cubicle in front of a computer screen, and within a few moments a bad picture flicked into life and I saw it was a group of my family huddled round talking at me. I was initially excited to see them and wanted to tell them all about my adventure.

However, after I'd spent a few minutes being patronised by Bobbie and Jonjo via a screen that stretched their faces in various directions with comedic effect (it reminded me of when I used to take them to the Hall of Mirrors at the fun fair when they were young) I lost momentum. The whole of Nigeria saw me as a heroine who bravely took on a dangerous gang of criminals; my family saw me as a silly old woman who got herself into a mess I was lucky to get out of, and more or less told me so.

After telling them I wouldn't be home for at least a week, probably longer, I pretended I didn't know how to work the computer and 'accidentally' shut it off, thereby shutting them up. I wasn't in the mood for being morphed back into the Cynthia they expected me to be.

CHAPTER THIRTY-ONE

Darius collected me from the communications room and escorted me back to his office, still occupied by people discussing our case. Then he invited me to dinner.

'I would love you to see where I live and get to know more about my home,' he said, and I couldn't help wondering if the invitation was just for me. At first I thought I shouldn't go, but curiosity took over and accepted on my behalf.

I certainly hoped going to his house didn't involve that woman, who I'd seen flitting through Forensix Inc.'s corridors with the air of someone who knows they can catch a man's eye. I didn't want to get to know any more about her. I knew enough about her slender legs, healthy skin and a décolletage without a hint of wear and tear. If anything I wanted her to fall off a cliff and be swept out to an angry sea, never to be found again.

My hands shook as I got ready. Tracey had made arrangements to go out with Baz and his friends, so I at least knew she wouldn't be part of the evening's entertainment. I sat in the bath and did as much maintenance as I could with a rusty razor and yogurt as a face mask.

A car picked me up at seven-thirty, by which time I'd considered cancelling on at least five occasions. Apart from the fact I'd been getting increasingly nervous about going out, constantly feeling I was being watched, Darius hadn't mentioned Chinaza so I wasn't sure if she would be there or not. I hoped she wasn't going to be, but then tried to push ideas of sexual activity as far from my mind as possible. The last thing I wanted was a whole load of disappointment brought about by kind rejection.

I picked at the edges of my clothes, a loose cotton skirt and a sleeveless silk T-shirt, (chosen to deal with any outcome) until I got there.

Darius's house was beautiful. It was square, painted dark pink on all its smooth outer walls, and had a large veranda at the front. All the upstairs rooms had balconies, decorated by nature's own growth of jasmine, miniature roses and other, unfamiliar, shrubs. I couldn't help but think of *Romeo and Juliet*, even though when I tried to remember the quotes from my school days my memory failed me.

He opened the door as soon as the car parked in the crescent driveway. I mentally took a picture of the vision, capturing the moment for my future pleasure. He wore a lemon-coloured shirt and white linen trousers, showing his colour to its richest advantage. His feet were bare, and as I got closer I could see that, as ever, his nails were immaculate.

'So there you are,' he said, turning to one side and gesturing with his arm for me to enter his home.

My feet wobbled on the uneven gravel of the pathway, and it was all my lungs could do to draw breath. He caught my arm and helped me across the threshold.

'I've cooked goat meat stew with Nigerian fried rice, all to be washed down with local palm wine,' he said, as if we'd never been apart.

I looked around nervously for signs of a female – *that* female – and could see no trace of any other guest. As he led me to the kitchen, I could hear music coming from a room to the side of the vast hall, which I guessed was the living room.

The table was laid for two, and I wanted to jump up and down and punch the air. Such displays are not in my nature, so I concluded I'd spent rather too long with Tracey.

'Oh, just the two of us?' I said.

'Who else would I want with me, now I know you are in the country?' Darius said. He looked shy, which I thought was unusual for him.

The palm wine tasted not unlike watered-down port. I was glad of it, as it had a calming effect.

After some polite conversation about the food and Darius's home, which I found out he'd owned for three years and renovated with the help of his brothers-in-law, he took hold of my hand across the table.

'I've missed you, Cynthia,' he said. The way he looked at me suggested he meant every word. His eyes watered and he held on to my hand so tightly I thought he'd break the tiny bones between my wrist and finger joints.

'I've missed you, too,' I said, hardly daring to believe that Darius might still be interested in me. Hope was on standby, ready for a part to play in this unfolding scenario.

He moved his chair to face me and took hold of my other hand. I was glad to note he'd loosened his grip.

'Why are you here? How did you get yourself into so much trouble?' he asked.

The questions seemed separate, even though in his mind he probably considered them connected.

'I came to see you and help you. You didn't expect me to just forget about you, did you? I was worried about your situation, and what with your father and everything . . .' I told him, gulping down the rising expectation of a reunion.

'What situation?' he asked, knotting together his eyebrows quizzically. 'I was waiting for you to contact me. I gave you my card but heard nothing. I assumed you'd lost interest.'

If only he knew how much interest I had in him, I thought.

I explained about the messages and how I had seen them as him wanting my help. As the misunderstanding unfolded, we both cried and laughed at the same time.

'I thought you considered me too young and silly to bother with,' said Darius. 'I can't believe you came out here for me. If only I'd known that,' he said, choking back emotion.

'And I thought you would want to seek out a younger woman and get married, maybe have a family,' I replied. 'Maybe with Chinaza?'

Darius laughed.

'Goodness, no. That's the last thing I want. She's very clever, but far too high maintenance. Daddy's little rich girl. Not my type at all.'

I grinned to myself, and mentally notched up a feeling of superiority over youth.

'So what *is* your type?' I asked, fishing heavily for the compliment I immediately received.

'Surely you know the answer to that, Cynthia?' he said as he fell to his knees and kissed my hands, allowing his lips to trace the edges of my arms and tease them with their generosity. Whatever it is that rises in a woman to make her want a man had hitched a fast ride in the lift to the top of my passion tower.

He stood and pulled my arms to get me to stand, kissing me full on the lips and allowing his tongue to investigate the nerve endings of mine, setting them alight with desire and longing.

I never thought we'd be here again, enjoying each other as lovers. *How did we get it so wrong?*

Darius picked me up as a giant might pick up a small child and carried me upstairs to his bedroom, laying me down gently on the vast bed. He unbuttoned his shirt and dropped it to the floor before pulling off my top and stopping to admire what he saw.

'You've lost weight,' he said. 'I shall have to feed you up.'

I watched him as closely as I could without staring, hoping my mouth wouldn't drop in awe as he removed the linen trousers, revealing the fact he was wearing nothing underneath. His lasting interest in me was apparent as he kneeled down to remove my skirt, in doing so allowing his right hand to explore my breasts. He sat in front of me and pulled me into the sitting position, giving freedom to his hands to remove my bra. He dropped his head to take my nipples into his mouth, rolling them gently with the softness of his tongue. They felt like they were on a string to the pit of my abdomen, pulling more tightly until I was crying for his attention.

'I've been thinking about you every night,' he muttered, as he moved down my body, taking time to reacquaint himself with my flesh, assaulting it with nips and nibbles until he pushed his knees between my legs to part them. I was still wearing my knickers but he pushed them to the side, pulling the material tightly against my clitoris to add another dimension to his ministrations.

We were lost in ourselves. Tearing off what was left of my underwear, the bedcover held us gently in its weave as we moved against it together, riding the waves of physical pleasure and unity.

It had been so long, yet we were pulled together instantly by that moment of ecstasy, as we both leapt over the mountain of desire and into the pool of satisfaction. We were at one.

Darius held me closely, as if he didn't want to let me go. I felt so safe, and as he was stroking my hair, the CD that had been playing earlier jumped back into life.

'So here's to you, Mrs Robinson,' it sang out from downstairs, with Darius following up the next line with; 'And I love you more than you will ever know.'

It was bliss.

CHAPTER THIRTY-TWO

Once we'd exhausted our physical desires for the evening, we opened a bottle of wine Darius had brought back from the airport the day he left England. He said he'd been keeping it for a special occasion, and there could be no better reason than I was in his house.

He told me again how they'd found and arrested Chike and Fasina. They'd traced the camp using a number of bits of information from the messages they'd sent my family, and some sightings. A number of locals had come forward in response to press calls for information, saying they'd seen two white women being driven to the settlement area. It is still sufficiently unusual to see white people in the poorer parts of the city for it to attract attention.

'We're fairly confident they will get a very long sentence,' said Darius, after we dressed and settled ourselves in the front room downstairs, where Darius brought in the food he'd prepared earlier. The extra cooking time meant the meat was particularly tender. I thought it was probably the best meal I'd ever had in my life.

'Have they kidnapped women before?' I asked, sipping the palm wine from an oversized crystal glass.

'We don't think so. But they haven't taken ordinary tourists before either. This gang usually concentrates on business people, working abroad and with the backing of big companies who have to look after their needs. If they don't, no one wants to volunteer to work in Nigeria long-term.'

Darius offered coffee and went into the kitchen, from where I could hear the clanking of cutlery and china. In his absence I looked around the sparsely furnished room and took note of the selection of books, mostly non-fiction, and a number of small, framed photographs of young women and children. I guessed them to be of his sisters and their families. There was also a picture of an elderly black couple I assumed would be his parents – reminding me to ask about their health.

Darius came back into the room and handed me a large blue coffee cup, the type and shape found in the nicer cafeterias in London. I took a sip and immediately made a face when I tasted it.

'I remembered you took coffee white but should've warned you, it's goat's milk,' said Darius, who was drinking his coffee black. 'I can't touch it since I've been back from England. It has a peculiar taste now.'

I followed him into the kitchen where he made another coffee, black this time, and I asked how his mother was. He replied she was stable after being prescribed new drugs.

'My parents are elderly so are bound to get worries,' he said, while I tried to work out how much older than me they could be. Possibly twenty years, although that would make them late parents.

As if reading my thoughts, Darius said: 'I was the youngest of eight. They kept trying until they got a boy! I've been surrounded by older women all my life,' he said, laughing and looking at me with devilish eyes. 'Maybe that is why I'm so comfortable with you,' he added, leaning forward to kiss the end of my nose.

Darius wanted to tell me even more about the rescue mission, particularly now he was fuelled by the fact my predicament was precipitated by my concern for him. I had the impression he wanted to make amends for my experiences and wanted me to be sure every effort was made to find and release us.

'It was all over really quickly,' he explained. One of the officers from the raid team told us they'd got all four of the men they knew to be directly involved in your kidnapping, but there was no sign of any other people in the camp.

However he did say there'd been signs of captivity, such as padlocks and mattresses, along with eggshells and banana skins. They'd also found a bottle of Chanel N°5 perfume. 'We thought that might be relevant as it didn't seem likely it would belong to one of the gang.'

'It's mine,' I said. 'The guards kept most of our luggage in their shacks.'

'Well, it's not the sort of thing you'd expect a Nigerian gangster to have as a bedside accompaniment,' said Darius. 'Anyway, we were pleased to get our men, but worried about the whereabouts of the hostages, namely you two,' said Darius. 'We didn't know at that stage whether you'd been taken somewhere else, hurt or even murdered.'

I flinched at the thought.

'Murdered? What for? Surely they wouldn't have done that to us?'

'Well, they don't normally kill their victims, but as they've never taken tourists before, we weren't sure how they'd react if they couldn't get any money from you,' he said.

I heard it was the guards who revealed we had escaped.

Darius added: 'Two of those we caught refused to say anything, even when they were pistol whipped. They refused to give any information about any hostages. However, they've been fast-tracked into court, where the charges will include fraud, false imprisonment and kidnap, plus anything else we can add to the mix,' said Darius.

I was very impressed by everything he was saying, and felt so very warm in his presence. I felt safe, nurtured and cared-for in a delicate and sedate manner.

I wanted to ask about other women, and whether he'd been with anyone else since me. I pushed my antics with Gowon to the back of my mind but couldn't help thinking Darius must have had lustful thoughts towards someone, if not Chinaza. Just thinking about her and her beauty made me want to will her into a very big hole, or for her to evaporate like a snowman in a heat wave, so he could never look at her again. I called on my angels and made a pact to really, really believe in God if only he'd get rid of her and anyone else who might turn the head of this heavenly man in any direction but mine.

Darius outlined for me how the legal formalities would work in the court, and they sounded very similar to my own experiences on the magistrates' bench. Prosecution followed by defence, although this would be in front of a judge with legal training, not a selection of middle-class wives of bankers.

'I suspect there will be a lot of press there, as they will like to hear how you coped with the scammers. They will want to write stories about how you never know who you are going to meet on the internet.'

'Or on Advanced Driving courses,' I said, looking at him in a way I hoped made him realise I wanted him to make love to me again, right there and then.

CHAPTER THIRTY-THREE

The court was full. Chike and Fasina were handcuffed in the dock, looking solemnly straight ahead. Various officials moved around the rows of sturdy wooden seats, whispering in hushed tones and passing on pieces of information to each other in an important fashion.

A bell sounded, then a clerk stood and told the court to stand. Everyone who wasn't already standing stood up, while a rotund man of about seventy years old, complete with gown and wig, entered the room and told them to sit.

'Not you,' he bellowed at the two defendants, who hadn't acknowledged each other at all.

'Are you Chike Buhari and Fasina Amaechi of Manita Territory? Neither of them responded.

'Speak up,' said the judge. 'I can't hear you,' he went on, impatiently.

'Yes,' muttered Fasina, while Chike set his mouth into a hard line and lifted his chin in defiance. Both were wearing dark green cotton jumpsuits – the uniform of the holding prison they'd been bailed to.

'If you do not answer questions when directed to you, then your punishment is likely to get more severe. Do you understand?'

Again it was Fasina who answered the judge by way of a nod, while Chike stared into the middle distance as if he was posing for a portrait and needed to look enigmatic.

The judge looked at him briefly, shook his head and peered down at his papers, taking his time perusing the contents while unwrapping a chocolate bar and eating it noisily as he read. He whispered to a neighbouring clerk, who had to refer his question on to the prosecution team, one of whom went outside and returned a few minutes later. Once he returned, the Chinese whispers went in reverse, until the judge was given the answer he required.

'I understand you don't have any legal representation,' said the judge, looking at the defendants over half-moon glasses.

Chike whipped his head round and hissed at Fasina, leaning his body into him aggressively enough for his prison guard to pull him back with the handcuffs, as a dog owner might do with a lead.

Fasina coughed and answered the judge: 'We do not have the funds for lawyers.'

'And whose fault is dat?' hissed Chike again, struggling aggressively against the restraint he was under.

The judge banged a gavel on the bench and called for silence in the court.

'Unless you are answering my questions or those of the lawyers, please keep your comments to yourself, Mr Buhari. Can you confirm you wish to go ahead with this committal without any defence in place?' he said, again looking over his glasses, giving him an increased aura of authority.

Fasina nodded, and Chike sucked his teeth loudly and kicked his co-defendant sharply on his shin bone. Fasina yelped. The judge ignored him and called on the prosecution to read out the charges.

A prosecution officer told the court the two men had been found defrauding individuals and companies out of hundreds of thousands of pounds using fake office set-ups. The name of John Baker was mentioned, and I assumed that was our 'rescuer'. He'd gained access to data available to him through one of his business contacts.

'We've been monitoring the entire operation with the help of our specialist technology partners, Forensix Inc., and have traced a number of bank accounts which have been emptied as a result of their victims supplying personal details under false pretences. To our knowledge, they have amassed over three hundred thousand dollars in the last two months alone. They also prey on vulnerable Brits, often oil workers but in this case, for the first time, older women, whom they hold to ransom.

I closed my eyes and shuddered, hoping no one thought of me

as I did then – a silly old cow with stupid ideas of her own attractiveness.

There was another yelp from the witness box. In a moment of relaxation while the prison guard had loosened his grip slightly, Chike had lashed and kicked out at Fasina, this time stamping on his feet and elbowing him in his ribs, hard.

The judge said: 'Please keep your arguments to yourselves.'

He turned to the officer and asked him to continue, adding: 'I believe there may be further charges.'

'We have two female witnesses, one of whom has been a victim of the "Dear Beneficiary" email scam directly linked to this group of criminals. The other was not connected to this particular crime,' added the officer. 'Both were kidnapped and imprisoned soon after their arrival at Lagos airport, on the pretence of being offered help finding friends in our country. Our defendants targeted Mrs Hartworth after accessing her email accounts and tracing a booking from London to Lagos in her name.'

My shame didn't run too deep. Tracey and I were united in being foolish enough to follow our hearts. Better than letting them rot in middle-aged decline until late life incapacity waved goodbye to all passions.

The judge glared at the witness box for long enough to make both Chike and Fasina look uncomfortable. He closed his file and stood up, coughing to indicate that the rest of the court was also expected to stand. I noted that the courtroom protocol wasn't nearly as formal as in my days on the bench, where anyone not respecting the authority of the law would face contempt, not only of the court, but every single magistrate and official in the room.

'In the absence of any legal assistance I suspect the defendants' ability to effectively cross-examine anything is highly dubious,' he said. 'There will be a short recess, and on my return I hope to be able to come to a clear conclusion about this matter,' he added on his way out.

The court buzzed with discussion within the pews and further aggression from Chike towards Fasina. They were both taken down into the cells to the sounds of further yelps and shouts.

'What's going on?' Darius asked the prosecution officer.

'The prison guards told us the defendants had to be separated, as they keep fighting. The shorter, fatter one keeps accusing the taller, thinner one of stealing their cash. He swears he didn't, but it seems they have no funds at all, despite the likelihood they should still have thousands we've not yet traced,' he replied.

Darius looked round at me from his pew in front and winked.

At this point the main doors to the room crashed open, and a small, bespectacled man fell through on top of a police officer who, in turn, fell into the lap of a large woman who'd been watching the court proceedings while simultaneously knitting three pairs of baby bootees in succession.

'Mind the bird,' shouted the small man, getting back on his feet just as a large parrot flew up into the air from under a blanket he'd been carrying, coming to rest on a ledge atop one of the high windows just above us.

'Suck my cock,' shouted the parrot, followed by 'tits out, no knickers', and it was then I recognised it as Pussy. No other bird would be quite as rude.

'What in the good Lord's name is going on here?' asked the judge, as he came back to his bench, wiping crumbs of chocolate from his face.

'Fuck off,' said Pussy, and let loose some droppings which landed on top of Tracey.

'Fuck off yerself,' yelped Tracey, as she tried to wipe the muck off her hair with the sleeve of her blouse. 'Filthy git.'

'Filthy git,' mimicked Pussy, watching from her new perch as the court descended into mayhem.

'I am looking for Cynthia Hartworth,' said the man with the blanket. 'She is the sole beneficiary of the macaw you see above you, left to her in the will of one of her fellow Britons.'

'That will be you, then,' said Tracey. 'Rather you than me.'

It was then that Luter came in and pointed his only arm in my direction.

'There she is!'

The judge called order and asked the two men to explain themselves. They said they knew I'd be in court, from the publicity the case had aroused, and had been looking for me since Bill's death, as it was his express wish that Pussy be given to me.

Luter had tried to trace me to the university, but no one would hand over any information, having all been instructed to say nothing about us in case the kidnappers were trying to find us.

The men explained they had sent private investigators to find me, but they hadn't done their job properly. However once the court date was announced they knew where I would be. At that point the business at the market, the cars following us and various other suspicious activities started to make sense. It turned out there had been a reward put out by the solicitors acting for Bill's estate, and they were given express instructions to find me.

'While he didn't seem to have made it clear, it appeared that he took a liking to Mrs Hartworth,' explained the man to the judge. 'We were told to find her, as he believed she would be the only person who could look after Pussy properly.'

'Oh no,' I thought. 'What on earth am I going to do with a swearing parrot?'

I thought of the brief meeting I'd had with Bill and was flattered he thought so highly of me. He can't have had many friends.

'Take the bloody bird out of here and sort this out when the case is finished,' boomed the judge.

'Fuck off,' said Pussy, and was immediately charged with contempt of court.

After the matter of Pussy was sorted out as best it could be, with some explanations about who was following me and why, Tracey and I took the oath. I swore on the Bible, honouring my new-found connection with God, while Tracey opted for an agnostic version, having realised that swearing-in didn't require blasphemy.

Chike looked angry, and I wondered if he was thinking how I'd managed to steal his car and then wreck it. Fasina looked apologetic.

There was no sign of Gowon and Chiddy, although it was confirmed how they'd supplied evidence about their bosses in exchange for not having to appear in court against their bosses or face any charges. I was relieved for both our sakes.

'Were you given adequate opportunities to use the bathroom?' the prosecution officer asked me when I took the stand, at which point Tracey snorted loudly. I glared over at her, and she pretended to sneeze and cough.

'Yes, indeed. We were well treated in that respect.'

'And was there any physical abuse of any kind?'

'Absolutely none,' I replied, daring Tracey to make any further comment, keeping in mind I could have mentioned her brutal assault on her guard and the use of her clothing to tie up Chiddy before our escape. She kept very quiet.

'However, you were unable to leave the premises until you made your own escape, is that right?'

I said that was the case, and the questions were over. Tracey's interrogation was much the same, and although we were both told the defence had the right of cross-examination, it never came.

'Will the defendants please stand,' the judge said, having allowed the defendants to sit during the proceedings as long as Chike stopped punching Fasina. He almost managed it, although every now and then a squeak or suppressed moan would come from the dock.

'Do you have anything to say?' said the judge.

Chike stood up, dragging his prison guard with him.

'I do, sir!' he shouted.

Fasina looked to the floor and sighed.

'Please, go on,' said the judge.

'This lyin', cheatin', good for nothin' so-called man next to me stole all the money from our business account. There was thousands in there – all gone!'

The prison guards raised their eyes to the heavens and stood back to wait for the monologue they'd heard every night while the men had been behind bars.

'We had a lot of money – all mine and earned from my hard work and investments, but it's gone.' He pointed at Fasina and shook his fist. Fasina sighed and raised his eyes to the ceiling. 'He the only one, the only one, who knew my account numbers, he steal everythin'. That is why we've no defence, me lord and honour. That is why.'

And with that he promptly sat down and adopted his previous pose, crossing his arms for further effect.

The judge looked at Fasina, who shrugged his shoulders and shook his head in denial.

'I think from what we've heard, you are both cheating, lying thieves who have taken advantage of gullible people. You pray on their weaknesses and a lack of understanding of the technology you have clearly mastered. It's a shame you don't put the same energy into putting that understanding into something more positive. I sentence you both to fifteen years imprisonment with no parole. And any money or assets taken from your accounts will be held by suitable authorities for repatriation to your victims.'

Chike shrieked and stamped his foot. Fasina shrieked because Chike had also managed to stamp on his foot at the same time. They were immediately led down to the cells, and this time both of them were whimpering like babies.

'Nice work,' the prosecution officer said to all of us. 'We won't be seeing them for a long time,' he added, shuffling his papers back into his battered briefcase.

'I'd like to make a point of saying well done,' said Darius to the team gathered round. 'To one very brave lady, Cynthia, who took on an entire gang almost single-handedly and won!'

Tracey whooped in agreement, despite her own contribution to the final outcome. And the fact she still had parrot poo in her hair.

CHAPTER THIRTY-FOUR

The publicity surrounding the court case was phenomenal. We were hailed as heroines to have taken on the kidnappers and escaped unscathed. Questions were thrown at both Tracey and me, asking how we dealt with the conditions and how we were treated.

Tracey still snorted when asked if we were physically abused in any way, and I would always throw her a look, suggesting that any disclosure of my activities with Gowon would be met with severe punishment. She would cheerfully wink at me, and tell journalists we'd been treated with utmost respect by our guards at all times.

Darius pulled us away after half an hour of interrogation by reporters from across the world.

'Your faces will be seen by people from countries in every continent,' he beamed, hugging me to him with his engulfing embrace.

I wanted to curl up and die, thinking about Mavis and friends looking at news clips, in which Tracey also told the media we enjoyed the drugs we'd been given and that more of Chiddy Bang Bang's music should be played on British radio.

I know we all get our fifteen minutes of fame, but I didn't want mine for being a dope-swilling granny with a penchant for rap music. Even if it was partly true.

Darius arranged for us to be taken back to the camp by the investigation team to collect any belongings we may have left behind and to provide a first-hand account of where we were kept and what shacks were used by whom. Forensix Inc. had also pledged a substantial sum of investment money to turn the camp into an outreach centre, hoping to create a silver lining from a number of clouds.

We were just about to leave the camp after being emotionally reunited with a place that felt strangely home-like, when Buke arrived in her official car. Sweeping along the pathway to meet us she extended her arms wide to embrace both myself and Tracey.

'My favourite 'ostages,' she said with a laugh. 'So what do yous tink of da new school?'

'Don't look much like a school to me,' said Tracey. 'But what do I know? I hardly never went to one anyway.'

'Oh, it will be. Yous see. Now we haf da funds we will grow and grow,' she said, adding to me: 'We're hoping you'll come over to open da school and maybe yous can stay and set up our programmes for young, feisty women?'

The idea of working with Buke was certainly an attractive one. The thought of telling Mavis and the Magistrates' Association I was a consultant to the Nigerian education authorities gave me a thrill.

'That would be marvellous, but I'm not sure I'm qualified,' I replied.

'Nonsense, Cynthia!' said Buke, as she threw her head back in laughter. 'Yous are da first women kidnapped and dis is where yous were 'eld. So wat is more fitting dan yous coming into a school dat turns girls into strong, independent people? You are da inspiration.'

I thought about it for a few seconds more and came to the conclusion I'd love to come back to the school. There's only so much satisfaction you can get from producing regularly edible soufflés or keeping a neat herbaceous border.

'Well, I shall put my thinking cap on and see what ideas I can come up with – hopefully something better than goat stew!'

The group around us went quiet, and I thought maybe I'd better keep my thoughts about African cuisine and how I could improve it to myself. I was sure there was more I could do with the available ingredients, although I might have to give the eggs a miss for a while.

'So, you might be staying,' said Darius, when we were alone in the car, having arranged for Buke to take Tracey home. So far neither of them had given any indication they knew of our relationship, possibly because it was so unlikely.

'I think I would like to, although the practicalities could be tricky. I don't know the culture and haven't a clue how to get round the country or get anywhere to live. It would be very daunting,' I said.

He looked thoughtful and took my hand, holding it over the gear stick so he had no reason to let it go.

'I'll help you,' Darius responded. And I knew he meant it.

CHAPTER THIRTY-FIVE

I'd decided I needed to go home and tell my children my plans. The Nigerian government, by way of an apology for my plight, offered to reschedule and upgrade my original flight tickets.

I'd discussed working with Buke's outreach projects and agreed to a six-month trial so we could see how things went. I wasn't sure about being based at the camp where I'd been held as a prisoner, but also thought it would be a good way of addressing any issues that might develop as a result of the kidnap.

The decision was mostly driven by my desire to be with Darius, although I wasn't sure how his people would accept us as a couple, or how I might miss my home comforts and my family. Despite his assurances he'd hold my hand, both physically and metaphorically, all the way, I couldn't see how I could fit in. No one yet knew of our feelings for each other, and we'd decided to keep it secret a while longer.

I was booked to land at Heathrow on the following day's flight. When I was back at the bungalow, packing, Tracey looked tearful. She had agreed to look after Pussy who she told me had been particularly offensive that day but I didn't think it was that bothering her. In fact I had my suspicions she'd been teaching her new words as he'd said something about being taken from behind only that morning. As Tracey's eyes became more watery, I made a mental note to mention the benefits of evening primrose oil, but then told her of my plans to return to Nigeria.

'Woah, go girl,' she'd said, clearly pleased that our paths would be entangled for a little while yet. She hugged me so tight I could smell her hair.

'Baz and me have got you a present because we thought you

were leaving. Well, Baz got it actually. It's something very Nigerian. We want you to take it home with you,' said Tracey. 'So you might as well take it now.'

I was touched they thought to get me a present, and my eyes watered. I pretended I'd got an eyelash stuck as I wiped away a tear.

'Bollocks and Bums' said Pussy. I covered her cage with a blanket and she went back to imitating telephones.

'I can't believe you'll be coming back, hun. That's made me so happy,' she said, and I felt genuinely touched by her enthusiasm and warmth. She threw her arms around my neck and hugged me so close I could smell her armpits. Tracey was probably one of the most embarrassingly common people I'd ever met, but when you've both relieved your bowels in the same bowl and used *OK!* magazine instead of toilet paper, it brings you together on a unique level. And you don't mind their smells.

'That is really very nice of you,' I said, as she handed over a small box wrapped in brown paper and sealed with a considerable amount of packing tape. She really didn't want me to open it in a hurry.

'Actually, Baz wants to go to England soon, so if you are still there, we can open it together. I'm not sure what it is, but Baz reckons it's good stuff.'

She skipped around in apparent delight as I took the present to my room and wrapped it in my T-shirts, tucking what was left of my clothing around the sides. It really was very sweet of them to think of me, and I felt mean for thinking so badly of Baz. He was clearly a changed man. *I wonder what it is?* I thought.

Being in Nigeria, while it had certain moments I wouldn't wish to repeat in a hurry, did have its upsides. The people were interesting – and interested in me – and I'd done more with my life than I'd done in a very long while, even taking into account sending Giles McDonald to prison for stealing three packets of bourbons from the Murco garage.

The worst feeling was knowing I'd be leaving Darius behind, if only for a short time – certainly less than we'd already been apart.

He took me to the airport himself, rather than allow Buke's chauffeur to drive me. There was a sadness in the air, as we both knew our lives were going to change. Even being together, as right as it seemed to both of us, would have its problems. We are from different cultures and generations. How could we make a relationship work?

I was tearful and not sure what to say to Darius after I'd checked in. It was two hours before the flight, and I considered buying a cheap novel to entertain me on the journey when Tracey and Buke showed up.

'We couldn't let you go without seeing ya off,' said Tracey, who was wearing what I could only assume was one of Buke's cast-off robes. It might have worked on her if she hadn't added to the ensemble a lime green baseball cap and a pair of pink trainers, not to mention the huge hoop earrings that kept getting caught on the wispy cloth on her shoulders, stopping any sideways movement of her head in its tracks.

'That is wonderful,' I said to them, genuinely moved by their consideration. 'And thank you so much for looking after Pussy. I know she can be a handful,' I said, realising that I was getting quite fond of the old bird.

Tracy and Buke offered their wishes for a good journey and left the airport. I was sorry I couldn't say goodbye to Darius properly, but keen not to openly display our affection in public, he gave me a big hug and left the smell of his aftershave lingering on my scarf, which I sniffed periodically on my way to the departure gate.

I went through the various security checks and finally into the departure area, which was no better than the arrivals shed. It was overheated and claustrophobic. There were insufficient chairs, and those available were dirty and plastic, guaranteed to bring on a sweaty patch.

After what seemed a lifetime the flight was called, and I boarded the plane with a couple of hundred other clammy and impatient passengers. I settled down to try and read the book Buke had given me on the politics of African education. I wasn't looking forward to it, only ever really reading the *Daily Mail*, the occasional Jodi Picoult and not much else. I thought I ought to learn more about my possible role as a school consultant.

The more I read the more I admired Buke and what she'd had to do to achieve her degree and then to build her reputation as one of her country's leaders. It made my attempts at keeping a clean and well-ordered household look less like an achievement and more like drudgery.

After the flight out to Lagos I'd expected something more eventful than the easy landing we had at Heathrow. We'd made it into the airport fifteen minutes early, and the weather looked good – sunny and clear.

It was a stark contrast walking through the arrivals at the airport. It was much cooler than Lagos for a start, but the efficiency was evident. Those in uniform looked like they knew what they were doing and weren't looking for backhanders from isolated tourists. The Nigerians visiting London were treated with much more respect than tourists to their country, although to hear some of them shouting about the validity of their passports when they were being taken into interview rooms you'd think they were being tortured.

There was a lengthy hold-up in the baggage area. Luggage from my flight wasn't coming through and passenger information told me there was an issue with one of the cases. I walked past the customs gate, and looking through saw a number of people gathered waiting for their loved ones to appear, some of them holding banners.

It was a short while before I realised the banners were for me. Various members of my family, the bridge club and some of my magistrate colleagues held banners reading 'Welcome Home, Cynthia' while Mavis and Tom both had T-shirts emblazoned with big 'Free Cynthia' slogans on them. Even Marjory was there, with a placard bearing my picture and the caption 'Cynthia is My Sister', which I found to be something of a revelation.

I even saw my next-door neighbour in the crowd, which was another surprise. He'd only spoken to me once since the incident regarding his raised flower bed. And that was to ask me if I'd considered moving house.

I moved forward to wave to them, but was pushed back by a black customs officer. His name tag was covered with a strip of white paper with the name 'Mabu' taped to it.

'Have you got your luggage, madam?' he asked.

'I'm still waiting for it,' I replied. 'I understand there has been a delay.'

'Which flight were you on?' asked the officer.

'Lagos. We landed about twenty minutes ago, so it should be here by now. Do you come from Nigeria?' I asked, thinking he had a familiar look.

'If I do, it is none of your business, now get back and wait for your luggage inside the collection area, please.'

A cheer went up in the arrivals lounge. Mavis had spotted me and had started up a chant which sounded like 'Cynthia is Free'. It could have been something else, but I settled for that sentiment and told the officer that people outside were cheering for me. I don't know what I'd expected, but it wasn't the answer he gave: 'Good for them, let's see how long they can keep that up for.'

The cheering continued as I made my way back to the baggage area, where still nothing had come through other than a child's pushchair, a set of golf clubs and two pairs of underpants that may well have been going round the carousel for some weeks, to judge by the state of them.

My case was one of the first to arrive, and seemed to be in one piece, but was sporting a huge orange sticker on the front.

As I pulled it along through the 'nothing to declare' channel, I was stopped by the same officer.

'I need to look in your bag,' he said.

'I see. You've a bit of power and you have to use it on a vulnerable woman,' I said, hoping he'd realise he was just wasting his time trying to annoy me.

'Please open the case,' he commanded, pulling my bag up onto the desk.

I opened it up and revealed dirty clothes, my little black dress, some washing items and my present from Tracey and Baz.

The officer handed me a knife and asked me to cut into the package.

'But this is a present. I don't want to open it until I get home,' I told him, remembering what they had said to me about keeping it until their visit.

'In which case I will do it,' he replied, and as he did so, a large amount of brown, floury stuff appeared within the box.

He called on his radio, and within a few minutes he was joined by another customs officer and a police dog handler. The spaniel was all over my case and took particular interest in the present.

'We have reason to believe you have imported illegal drugs and you will be taken by my colleague to be searched fully and charged accordingly, Mrs Hartworth,' he said, as I thought about the effect a full search might have on my irritable bowel, particularly after all it had been through in recent months.

I didn't like being held in a cell. They made me take off all my clothes and get into a paper suit that made me look like a forensic man in a cheap detective TV series.The bed was concrete with a thin mattress – even less comfortable than the one in the settlement. The toilet was open and in the corner of the room. It didn't even have a seat or paper, you had to ask for that.

As for the inspection, the female officer investigated parts that even Darius was banned from.

'So, it seems you're clean, Mrs Hartworth,' she said after extricating her gloved finger from my anus.

'I had a bath this morning,' I told her, affronted that she would expect anything less than total hygiene from me.

'No, I mean you don't show any indications of drugs being secreted about your person.'

I wish I hadn't made the comment about people swallowing illegal substances when they fly, otherwise I might have avoided the unnecessary scans and salt water that certainly made me retch but didn't bring up anything other than a piece of carrot and the remains of that morning's coffee.

I was eventually released without charge and without apology. The powdery stuff turned out to be a very large quantity of the Suya spice I'd often mentioned since eating the kebab at the B & B.

The customs officer explained that they had to be thorough, and hoped I could understand that the spaniel they used for drugs checks was particularly fond of peanuts, hence his interest in the package. They asked if I needed a lift, but I assured them my friends and family were waiting to take me home.

I refrained from telling Mabu I knew his mother.

CHAPTER THIRTY-SIX

The family were surprised at my decision to return to Nigeria, even though I'd kept the gory details of the kidnap to a minimum – and my affection for Darius to myself. Bobbie cried and said she'd miss me. Tom thought it was 'cool', Titch wanted to know if she could visit, and the boys gave the impression they thought I was a very silly old woman indeed.

'So where are you going to live?' asked Jonjo. 'In a mud hut or something?'

If I'd thought he was sneering I would've given him a cuff round the ear, but his belief system suggested he thought all Africans lived in tents with bones through their noses. I held back from describing Darius's coffee-making machine, which not only filtered the beans but the water as well.

Mavis pretended to be interested in the teaching, but I could tell by the flat expression on her face she was unconvinced about the reality of my exciting future. Her lips stick to her teeth when she attempts animated enthusiasm.

'So it's like an extended holiday really?' she said when I announced I planned to stay for six months to see how I got on.

'What qualifications do you need to teach Nigerian children?' asked Mavis. 'Can anyone do it?'

'No,' I replied, as I had an inkling she thought she might be able to come and join me. I didn't think her presence would work too well. She's the last person I'd want to have to entertain in Darius's living room, which featured strongly in my daydreams about how I would spend my evenings. I still had carpet burn on my knees from what we'd decided to call our 'rug of love'.

While I was at home I sorted out a few administrative things such as cancelling my subscription to the gym. I also asked Tom if he'd look after the house while I was away. He agreed with a degree of enthusiasm I doubted had anything to do with a desire for home-making or quiet nights in. I refused to worry about the state the place would be in should I return, or what the neighbours might think about having an eighteen-year-old with a strong interest in loud music and parties, living on their street. I also visited Mr Gamble to arrange my finances and a transfer of funds to my new Nigerian bank account, set up legitimately by Buke for the purposes of paying expenses for my new job.

'Are you sure this is what you should be doing?' he asked. I looked at his dismal appearance and wondered if he'd already given up on a life he'd barely started. We were only a few years apart, but I was embracing the excitement of new ventures, while the pile of Saga Holiday brochures and a choral society pamphlet on his worn, wooden desk suggested he had entirely different views on late middle age.

'No, I'm not,' I answered. 'Which is what makes it so thrilling.'

With my banking sorted, I made my way back to the car, which I'd parked in the Waitrose car park so as to avoid a repeat of any altercations with passing police officers. I vowed to never, ever go on a holiday designed exclusively for the over fifties, for fear of meeting the likes of Mr Gamble and his world-weary wife.

I sorted out insurance on my car so Tom could drive it. The condition was he had to pass his driving test so he could take me to the airport for my return journey to Nigeria. Good to his word, he passed first time and, despite driving like a roadrunner on speed, was relatively responsible behind the wheel. At least he had two arms to hold it.

There were a few more family conferences and a couple of disapproving discussions with Jonjo and Paddy, after which I decided to book my flight as soon as possible. Surrey didn't have the same appeal as Africa, and while I was aware my family attachments would be a pull, my new life and love were pulling me to another place.

When I landed at Lagos on the second occasion, Darius was there to meet me. He arrived on his own, and when he saw me, he ran through arrivals and picked me up in his arms and swung me around until my spasm-stiffened spine clicked delightfully back into place. I made a note to call on his help next time my back was giving me problems.

'There you are,' he said, kissing me all over my face to the point where I asked him to stop.

'You're making me all wet with that slobber,' I said, secretly enjoying every moment of his attention.

He picked up my bags and carried them to his car, placing them carefully in the boot before opening the passenger door. My seat was taken by a huge bunch of red roses, which I knew would not only be a rarity in this country, but very expensive.

'For you, my English rose,' said Darius.

My heart was fluttering in a place of delight, brushing its wings against the gossamer of perfection. *Had I died and gone to heaven?*

Darius got me to his house and I asked him if he had found me any accommodation, as he promised he would before I left.

'Say no if you think it's a silly idea,' he said, as he set my bags down in the hallway. 'But why don't you come and live with me?'

The idea had crossed my mind, but I never thought for a single minute Darius would want to publicly announce his relationship with a white woman of sixty.

'What would everyone think? I'm more than twenty years older than you,' I said, thinking what a marvellous proposition he'd just made.

'I don't care, if you don't,' he said, as a screech came from the kitchen.

'Get yer kit off,' Pussy said.

'Now there's an idea,' said Darius as he swept me up into his arms. Something I'd been looking forward to throughout the journey back to Nigeria.

'So here's to you, my very own Mrs Robinson.'

ACKNOWLEDGEMENTS

Writing a novel, certainly a first one, isn't a job for just one person. As solitary as the occupation has been I cannot overlook the impact of the support of a number of people who have supported, cajoled, criticised (in the best possible way) and helped me on the path from creating those first few paragraphs of an idea, to completing my final draft of *Dear Beneficiary*.

My thanks go to Graham Carlisle, former script writer for such TV classics as Coronation Street and Emmerdale, for getting me back into the creative writing world with his immensely enjoyable courses held in Spain. I was also spurred on by James Essinger of Canterbury Literary Agency who helped shape the style and tone of the story, after a chance phone call put us in touch. His excellent advice and wisdom has been invaluable.

A major player in turning the story into something vaguely professional has been my good friend Susan 'Curly' Matthews, thanks to her sharp eye for detail and ability to deliver tough editorial messages in a palatable manner.

Without my agent, David Headley, whose faith in my writing has been humbling, I wouldn't have the publishing deal with CEP which has been handled so beautifully by Paul Swallow, Martin Hay, Sean Costello, Oliver Keen and Bridget Cassidy. You have honed and tweaked to perfection, for which I am extremely grateful.

Then of course there is my long-suffering husband, Graeme Birch, who has been there to read, re-read, proof check and generally tolerate my moods when things don't go quite right. Not only that, many of the scenes within Dear Beneficiary are based on true tales he has told me about things that happen in his daily work, including the one about the parrot...

But the major influences have been the many people in my life who have been supportive, funny, strong and loyal. While none of the characters in this book represent anyone alive or dead, many of them contain small elements of these interesting people and the stories they have lived.

Thanks again to all of you for helping me make a dream come true.